P9-DCC-728

A Trout in the Sea of Cortez

A Trout
in the
Sea of Cortez

A Novel

JOHN SALTER

COUNTERPOINT
A MEMBER OF THE PERSEUS BOOKS GROUP
NEW YORK

Published by Counterpoint,
A Member of the Perseus Books Group

Counterpoint books are available at special discounts for bulk
purchases in the United States by corporations, institutions, and
other organizations. For more information, please contact the
Special Markets Department at the Perseus Books Group,
11 Cambridge Center, Cambridge MA 02142,
or call (617) 252-5298 or (800) 255-1514, or e-mail
special.markets@perseusbooks.com.

Text design by Cynthia Young
Set in 10.5 point Electra.

Library of Congress Cataloging-in-Publication Data
Salter, John.
A trout in the Sea of Cortez : a novel / John Salter.
         p.   cm.
ISBN-13: 978-1-58243-342-4 (alk. paper)
ISBN-10: 1-58243-342-9 (alk. paper)
1. Middle-aged men—Fiction.   2. Midlife crisis—Fiction.
3. Cabo San Lucas (Baja California Sur, Mexico)—Fiction.
I. Title.
PS3619.A44T76 2006
813'.6—dc22
2006004652

06 07 08 09 / 10 9 8 7 6 5 4 3 2 1

For My Mother and Father

We derive our vitality from our store of madness.
—E. M. CIORAN

Acknowledgments

Thanks to Tina M. Johnson for saving my life, Bill Borden for twenty years of wisdom, Nancy and the kids for cracking the whip, Susan Ramer of Don Congdon Associates for being in my corner, David Shoemaker for the elegant editing, and the Corporation of Yaddo for being there at just the right time.

1

JESUS, he didn't want to go to Mexico. They had the tickets already, in a FedEx envelope on the kitchen counter, sitting there as casually as the unpaid power bill. Pratt hadn't even bothered to take the tickets out and look at them. See if airline tickets had changed in the two years since he'd last flown. That had been when his father had gotten sick and he'd dropped twelve hundred dollars at Lewis and Clark Travel to fly on a day's notice from Fargo to Minneapolis to Salt Lake City to Pocatello, plus another few hundred for a rental car, a Taurus, only to find the old man wasn't really *that* close to death, that the "Code Blue" he'd experienced while in the midst of a colonoscopy wasn't his heart actually *stopping* so much as *racing*, and that he'd even been removed from intensive care by the time Pratt walked into the hospital. Then a bland week at his parents' house while his father, still undiagnosed, watched television in a bathrobe waiting for appointments with various specialists and his mother tried to force-feed Pratt because she was worried at how thin he'd become, when actually Pratt had been steadily gaining weight since turning thirty.

He didn't want to go to Mexico. He confided this to Whitney, his daughter, when he drove up to Grand Forks to bring her a new portable CD player for her dorm room. Her old CD player was "too '80s" and she'd given him specific instructions for the new one, not an old-fashioned black plastic ghetto blaster but an Aiwa with a bass boost. The unit looked like a silver flying saucer from the 1950s. He wondered if designers were stagnant and working backward now, the way Hollywood was simply remaking old films. He parked at Selke Hall and waited for Whitney to emerge at eleven o'clock as they'd discussed but of course she was late. Plus he was a bit early because on the way up he'd been worried about threatening skies to the west, potential wall clouds, and had raced from one infrequent exit to the next, driving insanely to the bridges, the only shelter from tornados in the platter-flat valley between Fargo and Grand Forks. He'd felt exhausted from fear by the time he'd arrived at the campus. He hated the drive, which in the best of conditions was like taking a sedative. He'd wanted her to go to North Dakota State University in Fargo because it was closer to home but she'd claimed a desire to continue the family tradition of attending UND, though Pratt sensed it was less a matter of filial duty than wanting to put some highway between them.

Whitney had also requested a handful of CDs which he'd lazily asked the Target clerk to find for him and purchased without looking at; now out of boredom he took them from the bag and studied the covers. Eminem, Alan Jackson, Tim McGraw, Good Charlotte, Dirty Vegas. Dirty Vegas? It struck him that the country singers were far more bland when it came to naming their bands and he wondered if they simply wanted to make their family name known after generations had been forgotten, reduced to one-inch obituaries, shallowly chiseled tombstones. Then someone was knocking on his window and it was Whitney, a little plumper, he thought, than when he'd last seen her, frumpier also in baggy pants and an oversized Fighting Sioux hockey jersey. Her hair, which he remembered brushing so tenderly when she was six and fresh from the bath, braiding tightly before bed to eliminate morning tangle, was now shorn close to her scalp. She looked, frankly, like a lesbian. These changes had all taken place not over months but in exactly one month since he and Patricia had brought her up to college.

He unlocked the door and she climbed in. No kiss. She grabbed the CDs and flipped through them, leaned around to look at the player in the backseat. "Thanks, Daddy," she said. "I got a god-damned C on my composition and I know it's because the music I was writing to was so shitty."

Pratt had majored in English, had found it easy and hoped she'd follow suit. But he only nodded, not wanting an altercation.

"So do you notice anything different?"

"Your hair."

"Chop chop."

"What prompted this?"

"I've got a class at nine. It was taking me like half an hour to do my hair, and then it hit me, what's hair, you know? I mean, in the caveman days or whatever you needed hair to keep warm but now we have, oh, things like walls and heaters and roofs? Hair is just so fucking obsolete. Like your appendix. Right? I mean, you've got this fucking *organ* in your body that has no purpose. Maybe it had a purpose once but now it's just taking up space. Same with hair. Now I get up at a quarter to nine and take a shower and I don't need a blow-dryer or curling iron. I just get dressed and head out." She reached for Pratt's cigarettes on the dashboard and shook one out, lighted it with her own Bic. Took a terrifyingly deep drag, released the smoke, sucked it up her nostrils. Another new habit. Pratt was starting to feel a bit overstimulated, and driving through campus he was reminded of how he'd felt at the UND Writers' Conference in the late '80s, at parties where as an undergraduate he'd mingled with the likes of James Welch, an early idol, who'd signed Pratt's copy of *Winter in the Blood* with a True Blue dangling from his lip, prompting Pratt to switch to that brand for a while.

Pratt turned west on Columbia Road and they rose over the bridge, crossed the railroad yard, dozens of tracks. He glanced at his daughter, smoking, staring straight ahead, bored, he thought, or sullen. "Where do you want to eat?"

"I don't care."

"Paradiso?"

"That's fine."

"You heard we're going to Mexico in October?"

"Mom only reminds me every time she calls. I swear, it's like she's never been out of North Dakota. It's all Cabo this, Cabo that."

"I know."

"I said, 'Mom, do you even know exactly where Cabo is?'"

"She doesn't."

"Righto. She says it doesn't matter. She has pictures of the villa and the freaking sunset and that's enough."

"It's a nice villa. Right across the street from the beach."

"Do you?"

"What?" Pratt asked. They were nearing Paradiso.

"Do you know where Cabo San Lucas is?"

"One thousand miles south of Tijuana."

"Did you know that before Mom planned the trip?"

"Not really."

"Not really or no?"

"No. I looked it up in the old Rand McNally."

They parked and climbed out. Whitney tossed her cigarette. Pratt watched the wind roll it underneath a yellow Humvee. In the lobby Pratt was assaulted by the usual loud mariachi music and he wondered if that was what Cabo would be like, geared as it was toward tourists, *los turistas*, gringos. Americanos. He had taken two years of Spanish in college as part of his major requirement, thinking it would be more useful than German or Norwegian, but the grammar had thrown him, he'd skipped the helpful tape labs, wound up with straight Cs, and couldn't remember anything remotely useful unless everyone on the trip wanted to go to the *aeropuerto*.

A waitress seated them and brought a bowl of thin salsa and a platter of chips. Pratt scooped some salsa onto a chip and promptly dripped a line down his yellow Polo shirt. "Son of a bitch," he whispered. He started to rub at the stain with a napkin. The waitress came back. She snatched his napkin from his hand and dunked it into Pratt's ice water and dabbed at the stain. He felt the ice water on his chest, looked down at her slender fingers. He felt himself blushing but when he glanced up at Whitney she wasn't even watching, she was looking at her menu. The stain diminished into a generalized wet spot. "Thank you," Pratt mumbled.

"Happens every day."

"I should wear a bib."

"That'll get you by," the waitress told him. Her nametag said *Lisa*. "You'll need to use Spray 'n Wash or Shout or something before you wash it, though."

"I'll try to remember."

She grabbed his glass of ice water. "I'll get you some fresh."

"Jesus Christ," Whitney said.

"What?"

"A few more minutes and I was going to look for a fire hose to spray you guys with."

"Come on."

"You're either real naive or just getting old."

"She was helping me clean my shirt."

"I'm sure *that's* in her job description."

"Maybe she was worried I'd file a claim."

"Maybe she was wishing you'd spilled it on your crotch."

The word coming from his daughter was a little unnerving. Pratt started to dip another chip, thought better of it, ate it dry. Lisa brought his new water and took their order and in spite of himself Pratt glanced up at her to see if any kind of spark would pass between them but she barely met his eyes. Then he wondered if Whitney's presence, her smirk, had some kind of effect on conductivity, like the surge protector his computer was wired to. Then he wondered why he was even wondering this, why he even cared. He was thirty-nine and taking saw palmetto capsules like a dope fiend just to make it through the night without getting up to piss. Still, he snuck a peek at Lisa's rear end as she hustled toward the kitchen. She wore her black restaurant slacks pretty well. For some reason she turned around and smiled before disappearing. He wasn't at all sure he was happy to have seen that.

"What I mean is," he told Whitney, "it isn't like I have anything against Mexico. I've always liked Latin American literature. I took an independent study once on Gabriel García Márquez." He thought for a moment. "Or maybe it was Carlos Fuentes."

"Uh-huh."

"But I always thought if I went to Mexico I'd sort of explore, kind of wander around in a pickup with a camper or something. Or a motorcycle. Hitchhike. See the *real* Mexico."

• • •

Their food arrived. Whitney dove in like a rescued POW. The conversation was suspended. Pratt picked at his lunch, wishing they'd been one of those families that dined together, chatted every evening instead of just grabbing plates and retreating to their separate hideouts. He got up and went into the restroom and in the mirror regarded the stain on his shirt, now fading into nothingness. Looked at his face. Patricia had once said he resembled the actor Patrick Swayze but now he thought his features had homogenized so that he was just another middle-aged dad.

Back at the table, Pratt abandoned his seafood enchilada halfway through, ordered coffee, and watched his daughter eagerly cleaning his plate. He vaguely recalled a phrase describing this ravenous hunger among college girls. *Freshman fifteen?* "Anyway," he said, lighting a cigarette, "I always imagined seeing Mexico like a vagabond."

"But you never did."

"What?"

"You never did that when you had a chance. You got married and did the whole family-guy thing."

Pratt drew on his cigarette. An existentialist coincidence had changed his path. He had a sharp recollection of walking from Merrifield Hall toward the Memorial Union and seeing Patricia on a bench reading Camus's *The Stranger*, which he had read twice, and it was this book in common that had given him, normally too shy to approach girls, the courage to join her and say, "'Maman died today.'" The look she'd given him, a nexus of annoyance and confusion, was exactly the same look she would give him twenty years later when, after she brought up the Cabo trip, he suggested they use the money to waterproof their basement instead.

"You need to lighten up, Dad. It's what, one week out of your life? It's not like you're going in for chemo or something. You can take a book and lie around on the beach and read."

"That's just it," Pratt said. "Your mother has already made it clear that we're not going to just lounge around. Not the whole time."

"Jesus, it's a vacation. What are you supposed to do?"

"These couples we're going with. Well, you know Tim and Kelly. They're adventurous. They have matching Harleys and they've gone to New Zealand. I think they actually met in Belize or something, scuba diving. The other couples, I think we met them at Tim and Kelly's wedding, and they're in that same vein. I think. I don't know. The one guy, Bryce, is a corporate pilot. See? And they're all planning to dive and fish and play golf in Mexico. And your mother thinks we need to be able to join in. At least to some extent. She doesn't want us to be the oddball couple. She doesn't want them to think we're hicks from goddamn Fargo, North Dakota."

"You kind of are."

Pratt laughed. "I know that and you know that and your mother knows that but she doesn't want *them* to know that. She's been tanning and working out. You'd think she was training for a marathon."

Whitney reached across the table for Pratt's cigarettes. Lighted one.

"I wish you wouldn't smoke," he said.

"I wish *you* wouldn't smoke."

"Me too. That proves the point. I can't stop. You probably could."

She rolled her eyes. "I can't remember the last time you and Mom took a vacation."

Pratt shrugged.

"Did you guys even have a honeymoon?"

"Not right away. But later we went to Butte, Montana, and conceived you."

Whitney opened her mouth and stuck her finger inside and pretended to gag. "Dad, please."

"Well, it's the truth.

"Butte?"

"We were going to go up to Glacier National Park but the car broke down near Butte. The transmission went out. We spent all our trip money getting it repaired. We spent two days in a Motel 6. Your mother blamed me because I insisted on taking my car, I had a Camaro back then, a real sweet car, instead of her Chevette. Her Chevette was newer but I didn't think it was a proper car for a honeymoon."

"Chevette?"

"So by the time my car was fixed we both just wanted to get home. We were kind of at each other's throats."

"Not the whole time if you made me."

"It was all downhill after that."

"For eighteen years?"

Pratt wondered how they'd entered this territory. It was like making a wrong turn into a hell of cookie-cutter houses and cul-de-sacs. "Of course not," he said. "I meant the trip."

"Sure you did."

"I did," he said. He thought he did. "Your mother bought me a set of golf clubs."

"Golf clubs?"

"Yes. Full set with a bag. And Nike golf shoes."

"Golf clubs?" Whitney laughed. "I can't see you playing golf."

"It was either that or learn how to scuba dive and you know I can't swim."

"I know. When I was little you used to tell me that if I fell into the water I'd be on my own."

"I never said that."

"You did. You said that. It scared me."

"I don't remember that." But he did remember. When he'd taken Whitney fishing once at the Red River he'd strapped her into a life jacket and tethered her to a dog stake on the bank. They'd enrolled her in swimming lessons when she was three and he recalled the lump in his chest when he'd watched her jump off the diving board, his near panic when she disappeared into the froth before bobbing up to the surface, his relief as she dog-paddled her chubby body to the side of the pool.

Lisa came by, cleared their plates. "Well," Pratt said, when she was gone, "it was either diving or golf so I picked golf."

"That reminds me of those summer camps where you have to pick an activity. Of course I wouldn't know because you never sent me to summer camp."

Pratt squashed his cigarette into the ashtray. "You never asked to go to summer camp."

"I wouldn't have minded."

"We're not that kind of family."

"What kind of family are we?"

"I don't know."

2

PRATT BELONGED TO what he sometimes liked to consider a large and powerful army of overeducated, underemployed men and women, people with BAs and MAs and PhDs manning Mini-Mart counters, sliding underneath automobiles on mechanic's creepers, shoving handfuls of letters into battered country mailboxes, welding huge teeth onto backhoe shovels. He didn't count all the writers and artists and musicians for whom jobs were necessary evils for supporting their artistic selves. He meant people largely without aspirations. When Pratt was at work, processing household hazardous waste for the city of Fargo, emptying mixed flammable liquids, paint thinner and turpentine, thirty-year-old gasoline, automotive lacquer, he sometimes imagined a scenario in which the whole of the U.S. government, as well as academia and pretty much everyone in professional positions, was wiped out, perhaps by some virus attached to stock certificates, and in the midst of the chaos would come forth grocery store clerks and motor-route paperboys, landscape laborers, Wal-Mart stockboys, bearing rumpled diplomas, mostly in the liberal arts, history, or, in Pratt's case, an entirely useless BA in English and theater arts, ready to run the country. With the ability to "think critically" and "communicate orally and in writing," they'd fall into place in empty capitol buildings and soon the country would be running smoothly again. A cranky former customer might recognize the new secretary of defense as the thirty-year-old loser who'd been bagging his groceries a week earlier. Mostly it was the cocktail of fumes that got Pratt tripping on these ideas. He avoided wearing his claustrophobic respirator in spite of gentle warnings by his boss, a kid in his twenties with a biology background who had once gravely held up an anal thermometer and announced that the mercury contained within was enough to contaminate twenty acres of a freshwater lake. Get Pratt away from the fifty-five-gallon barrel into fresh air, watching seagulls circling the nearby landfill, and he saw things more clearly. For what they were. For what he was and was not.

· · ·

"Whitney called," Pratt's wife said when he was sitting on the edge of their bed removing his work boots. He had spilled used motor oil on his right boot and now it was black and he was wondering if it might not be a good idea to pour oil over the left one so they matched. Struck him the oil might also act to preserve the leather.

"She did?"

"Uh-huh."

"Does the CD player work okay?"

"She didn't say so it must. She'd have said otherwise, don't you think?"

"Definitely." Pratt ran his finger over the leather. His finger came back slimy. It was possible the boot was ruined. They were pretty new boots. The oil would probably be there forever. He had once dumped a pan of oil in the backyard by the fence and years later you could still see the dark spot.

"Whitney said the two of you had quite the conversation at lunch yesterday."

"It was a good lunch. We went to Paradiso."

"Did you have the seafood enchilada?"

Pratt pretended to think. Closed his eyes. Much of marriage, he realized, was a game of second-guessing questions, preemptive chess moves, sacrificing bishops to save queens. Et cetera. He glanced at Patricia. She was in the doorway, arms crossed. Her arms were bronze. More brown. What was that crayon color? Burnt sienna? She was getting overly concerned with her tan. She was afraid it was fading even though Pratt reassured her that indeed she was darkening like a Thanksgiving turkey. "Tanorexia," he called it.

"Yes I did have the seafood enchilada."

Silence.

"Why do you ask?"

"It proves a point."

"What point?"

She came into the room and stood before her dresser, studied herself in the mirror. Lifted her blouse and held the hem in her teeth and squeezed her belly. Dropped the shirt and smoothed it down. The glimpse of skin, brief as it was, sparked some arousal in Pratt. He took a softer tone. "What point, honey?"

"I'm talking ruts, routines. The first time we ever ate at Paradiso you ordered the seafood enchilada."

"I can't remember."

"We had our first date there, you bum. You picked me up in that junky old Nova with the broken windshield."

"That was my temporary car. My Camaro was in the shop."

"When you pulled up I told my roommate to say I wasn't home."

"You did not."

"I did. I said, 'There's no way I'm dating a guy who drives a ten-year-old Nova four-door.'"

"You were never that shallow."

"It wasn't a matter of being shallow. It was a matter of wondering about how ambitious you were."

"Maybe it meant I was frugal. On my way to being a millionaire."

"No such luck. Anyway, you ordered the seafood enchilada. And every time we went there after that you ordered the seafood enchilada."

"I like the seafood enchilada."

She held up her hand. "Wait. This is what's always bugged me. You always looked at the menu. You always look at the menu and then in the end you order the seafood enchilada."

Pratt reached under the bed for his sneakers. "So?"

"So why look at the menu when you always order the same thing?"

"I don't know. I have no idea. What did Whitney have to say?"

"She had some interesting things to say, I'll tell you that."

"Like what?"

Patricia turned and examined her profile. Hoisted her rear end and dropped it. "Well, for one thing, she said a waitress was flirting with you."

Pratt shrugged. "Whitney has a flair for the dramatic." He tied his shoes. Time for a bold move. "Did she tell you she lopped off all her goddamn hair?"

"She told me *that* two weeks ago."

"Oh. Well, I don't like it. She looks like a lesbian."

"You're more enlightened than that."

"Than what?"

"Not all lesbians have short hair."

"You know what I mean."

"No I don't."

Silence.

"Do *you* even know what you mean?"

"I need new boots," he said.

3

PRATT THOUGHT it was an odd place for a lemonade stand. Just off the highway, a hundred yards into the long gravel road to the Bonanza Golf Club, where he had decided he liked to play because the trees and curves kept him hidden from more experienced golfers who he feared would laugh at his neophyte efforts. His mind was whirling with the usual anxiety-driven gibberish: chores he had yet to do, taking out the garbage; cleaning the litter box because Patricia claimed she could get a "female disease" if she came into contact with cat feces, which he knew was false except for pregnant women and impossible for her since she'd had her tubes tied but could not convince her otherwise; fear that he'd get to the first tee and a group of roughnecks would appear impatiently behind him as he was about to hit a drive for which there was a fifty-fifty chance the ball would either take off at a ninety-degree angle or simply fall off the tee and roll a few impotent feet. That kind of thing. In the background were more pleasant but equally disturbing thoughts. To wit: Why was he hoping Whitney would call for another CD or a forgotten pair of shoes so he could shoot up to Grand Forks and take her out to lunch again, and why was the Paradiso on his mind, the pale hostess with the improbably round, sad eyes?

So when he saw the girl standing behind the low boulder like it was a table, saw the edge of a cardboard sign, he thought it was a lemonade stand and he thought, What an odd place to sell lemonade. The boulder was on a shallow parking turnout and featured a Plexiglas-covered fact sheet on the tallgrass prairie beyond the boulder, purple and green, wild and even more wild in contrast with the dogleg curve of the first hole at the Bonanza, like one of those crazy haircuts with closely shaved sides and a sloppy top. The girl wasn't more than ten or eleven as far as Pratt could tell. He slowed the car to avoid caking her in dust. What kind of irresponsible parent would allow a child to set up a lemonade stand in what around here would pass as the middle of nowhere? It called to mind the family trip to Flathead Lake in Montana one August when Whitney was ten, a sort of reunion with a handful of Patricia's sisters and aunts at a little resort on the east side of the lake. Driving in they'd stopped at a cherry stand manned by a slow-looking boy with shirt cuffs six inches too short. It had taken the boy way too long to figure change from a twenty for a five-dollar sack of cherries. At the time Pratt had imagined a father and mother dumping the boy off at the stand early in the morning and going home for a day of white-trash television and beer drinking.

Pratt stopped the car. He wasn't especially thirsty. He dug in the center console of his Intrepid for change and found thirty-five cents. Looked out the window for a price on the cardboard sign and saw that it wasn't a lemonade stand after all. The sign was crudely lettered with black spray paint: *Good Golf balls $3.00 perdoz.*

Pratt climbed out and walked over. The girl was smoking a cigarette. She gave him a suspicious eye and then smiled. He hoped she was just young-looking for her age. The golf balls were in an ice-cream bucket. Pratt picked one up, a Titleist. Looked again at the girl. She was gazing serenely at the tallgrass. A smoke ring emerged from her tiny mouth and floated toward the state park, enlarging perfectly. When it was the size of a hamburger patty she reached out and slapped the ring into nothingness.

"You should have let it keep going."

"Now why would I want to do that?" There was a slight twang in her words.

"Maybe it would get as big as the moon."

She placed her hand on her hip like a jaded cocktail waitress and stared at him. This was not a regular child he was dealing with.

"I'll take a dozen."

She nodded and pulled a brittle-looking wrinkled plastic grocery bag from under a stone weighting it against the wind. He began picking through the balls. Grabbed a Titleist, an orange no-name, two Nike balls. She was holding the bag open, watching the balls drop in. He got less picky and just grabbed anything. He spotted a ball he was pretty sure he'd found and played before, a Dunlop with the word *Dad* scrawled across it. "How many so far?" he asked.

"That's ten."

Pratt dropped in two more balls. Laid a five in her hand. She tucked it into her jeans pocket. From the other pocket she drew out two limp singles for him.

"How's business?"

"Not much wind so it should be okay." She turned her back to him and rested her ass on the boulder like a punctuation mark.

4

P RATT topped his ball on the first hole and it went all of ten feet before stopping. He looked around, ran over and grabbed it, replaced it on the tee. Made a couple of practice swings. A cacophony of advice from library golf books splashed around his head like spilled milk: *grip the shaft as if you were holding a small bird keep your left arm straight keep your head down point your left toe at the flag slow down on your takeaway don't think too much.* He brought the club back and swung and the ball flew like a fighter plane low to the ground and then hooked sharply into the swamp. Pratt dropped the club into his bag and began hiking, his steps a little jaunty. A hundred-and-fifty-yard drive, while almost a roller, likely lost forever, was one of his best. This was only his third time on the course and his practice before that had been limited to chipping around the yard and driving plastic balls late at night when the neighbors couldn't watch him, criticize his swing from behind their curtains. Laugh. He saw dust rising from the gravel road and a red pickup roared by. He quickened his pace. He liked having a hole between him and the players behind him and wasn't above skipping a hole to allow this buffer. Intellectually he knew he was a beginner, intellectually he knew people couldn't care less about his ability, intellectually he knew this, but Pratt had always been plagued with irrational concerns.

He reached the swamp, tramped around the edges where he thought his ball had gone in. A frog jumped to safety just before being trampled by Pratt's brand-new Nike golf shoe, another gift from Patricia. She was hell-bent, he thought, suddenly more interested in the frog than in finding his ball, on making a good impression south of the border. She'd lost ninety pounds entirely by riding her as-seen-on-TV Tony

Little Gazelle machine and eating only once a day. Salmon and yogurt. He had to admit she looked good, better, in fact, than the day he'd first seen her. She was for some reason convinced that the other women who would be on the trip were thin. Pratt had been hoping secretly that the other wives would be pale hippos and that Patricia might feel something on the order of reverse pride, maybe some guilt over being the fit and tan member of the party. He wasn't sure why. But Patricia had asked her friend Kelly, who'd organized the trip, for photos, and sure enough the women looked right out of those athletic-shoe advertisements geared toward yuppies. So she'd doubled her time on the Tony Little Gazelle, which was supposed to be a silent machine but whose cables squeaked no matter how much WD-40 Pratt applied, squeaked so much that he spent most of his time at home down in the basement with his putter, trying to send balls into an electric cup or simply smoking and reading and drinking coffee laced heavily with Kahlúa.

He whacked at the reeds with his pitching wedge and was about to take a mulligan when he spotted his Titleist. It was resting in a half inch of brown water. No guts, no glory, he thought. Plus he was hoping to dirty up the shoes a bit so he didn't look like a complete neophyte in Mexico. Pratt stepped closer to the ball. Sank almost to the gunwales. Changed his mind when he imagined slogging the rest of the way with wet socks. He leaned in and took a wild swing, a hopeless swing, sent a cascade of muck into the air. His eyes were closed. When he opened them, the Titleist was gone.

He sighed and backed out. Two men were on the first tee, stretching their muscles with clubs across their backs. Pratt sauntered around the edge of the swamp. He intended to drop a ball on the green when he was out of sight but when he approached the flag a ball was six inches from the hole.

"Impossible," he whispered.

But it was his ball. Still wet. Now he wished he had an audience. He pulled his putter and took a deep breath, released it. Counted to five. Sank the ball. Wrote a bold 3 on the scorecard. A birdie, his first.

• • •

Creedence Clearwater Revival's "Heard It Through the Grapevine," the long version, was on the radio and he listened to it until the end before climbing out. Patricia's car wasn't in the driveway. She hadn't mentioned going anywhere. Something like a broken walnut shell moved in his chest yet wasn't enough to entirely kill his jubilation over the birdie. He took his clubs from the trunk. He felt like a real golfer and wished his neighbors were watching him tote the bag to the garage. Never mind that he had triple-bogeyed the second hole, lost a ball in the pond on the third, sent a drive sideways into the trees on the fourth. Ten-putted the eighth. His score for the nine-hole course was an insane 83, which according to Pratt's math meant an average of nine shots per hole. If Tiger Woods played 83 on *eighteen* holes it would make the news, bring out the would-be sports psychologists. Seventy-three would make most tear up their Bonanza scorecard but when Pratt got inside he set it on the table next to Patricia's ankle weights, folded so the birdie on the first hole faced up. He washed up and poured a cup of that morning's coffee, heated it in the microwave. On the drive from the course he had planned to stop at the girl's golf-ball stand and tell her she'd sold him a lucky ball and maybe buy another dozen but the boulder had been just a boulder again, the sign gone, the girl vanished. Pratt had worried for a moment that some good old boys had abducted her and were now abusing her prior to killing her and dumping her in a gravel pit. This kind of thing occasionally happened in rural Minnesota.

He sat in his easy chair and thumbed through the mail. Bills and catalogs. Victoria's Secret. Pratt gazed at the airbrushed models. He was interested in what they were thinking about as they posed. He had once bought a "couch dance" at the local strip club and behind the curtain felt too awkward to enjoy the girl writhing around on him. Not sure what expression to affix to his face, like when his friend the poet would hand him a typewritten poem and watch intently as Pratt read what usually seemed like a cheap Bukowski knockoff. The girl at the strip club was named Nikki. She had grabbed his knees and smiled up at him as her long hair swayed. He'd been afraid his attempt at a smile looked lecherous, or worse, feral. So he'd wound up trying conversation. "What do you think about when you're on stage?"

"Hmm."

"I've always been curious."

"You don't want to know."

"Yes I do."

"No you don't."

"I won't tell."

"Promise?"

"Scout's honor."

She'd sat next to him on the sofa. Licked her lips. Had come in closer for a whisper. Her first breath in his ear had been like a hot corkscrew entering his brain. "I think about," she'd said, "I think about my parents who live in Iowa. I think about my dog. I think about how I'm going to afford a new alternator for my piece-of-shit car. I think about *ER* because that's my favorite program."

Pratt put the Victoria's Secret catalog on the table. Thought vaguely about masturbating but only because he had the house to himself, more a Pavlovian reaction than anything else. He really felt no drive for it. This was supposedly normal for a man his age. He wasn't about to take Viagra but he was glad it was there for the future, like his Roth IRA.

•   •   •

"That isn't the point," he told his wife later that evening. Fresh from her Gazelle, she was studying his Bonanza scorecard. A drop of sweat from her forehead landed on it.

"I thought the total score was what mattered."

"Well."

"I mean, you could have eight great scores and one bad score and wouldn't that wreck the whole nine holes?"

"Technically. But look at the first hole. Par was four and I got three."

"That's pretty good. But it looks like you still need work if you're going to keep up with the guys in Mexico."

"Of course I need work. Of course I do. But look at that first hole is all I'm saying. A birdie."

"Hmm."

"And it was straight up too. No cheating. You should have seen it. I drove it into the swamp and then I blasted it from the swamp to the green. It was right out of the PGA highlights."

"The swamp?"

"Yes."

She raised her eyebrows.

"What?"

"Nothing."

"No, what?"

"Hitting the ball into the swamp. Isn't that, like, wrong?"

"Of course it's wrong. It's a hazard. The point is that I got out of it and still birdied, see?"

"I think so."

He snatched the card from her. "You always do this," he said.

"Do what?"

"Turn my accomplishments into failures."

"*I* don't do that. I didn't put the ball in the swamp."

"Tiger Woods puts balls into sand traps all the time. The point is getting out of them."

"Honey, you're not Tiger Woods."

Pratt folded the scorecard and tucked it into his pocket. "This marriage is a swamp," he said. Maybe he only imagined saying it because she skipped off to take a shower and in a few moments he heard her singing the Andrews Sisters' "Drinking Rum and Coca-Cola." Anyway there was no indication from her voice that his words had actually emerged from his tight mouth, that she'd heard them. Perhaps she had and didn't care. He wasn't sure what was worse.

5

PRATT DROVE home from work on Seventh Avenue, which ran from the city landfill straight through town to the river that constituted the Minnesota border. Seventh at times reminded him of the narrow nightmare highways in the original *Mad Max*. It wasn't a road for daydreamers. On any given morning or afternoon, driving past an endless string of salvage yards and pallet factories, Pratt found himself dodging lumpy garbage bags, boards that looked like they'd been used for nailing practice, sofa cushions, spilled gravel, daytime alcoholics avoiding the cops, cops in pursuit of daytime alcoholics, tow-chained wrecks being tugged to junkyards, and poorly loaded flatbeds hauling junk to the dump. Pratt liked Seventh, though, because it was a rod through the heart of old Fargo unlike the newer capillaries that were lined with strip malls, boomtown apartment complexes, faux-stucco chain restaurants, BMWs and giant Suburbans, and a general sense of middle-class urgency. Not so on Seventh. Once past Twenty-fifth there was a stretch of ungentrified houses with a few actual minorities sitting on porch rockers and even the occasional old woman pushing a wire grocery cart to the Laundromat. Then it was the hospital and then if you didn't turn, you'd wind up in the Red River, floating north to Canada.

He drove slowly now, more so than usual. He wasn't reluctant to get home. Some days this was the case but not today. For one thing, he was playing golf again and actually looking forward to it. He intended to concentrate and produce a score at least twenty-five percent better than Saturday's, which was entirely possible. He was supposed to play with Carver, the family dentist. Pratt had gone in for a pre-vacation cleaning at Patricia's insistence. His teeth, yellowed from cigarcttcs and coffee, were a perennial focal point in her frequent assessments of his appearance. In Carver's client-friendly waiting room, between the video games and Lego table, under a painting of St. Andrews, he'd discovered a beautiful TaylorMade putter and electric cup and couldn't resist trying it out. When Carver finally came out and caught him, he suggested they play together "sometime," and Pratt had agreed thinking it was the usual obligatory "sometime" but then Carver had insisted they nail down a date.

More to the point, Pratt was driving slowly because his trunk was loaded with five one-gallon pickle jars of mercury. Anyone who looked at his car would see the bumper sagging. He was afraid the jars would tip though they were too heavy for this to be a likely event. It had taken all Pratt's strength to lift the mercury into the car. Ordinarily he would probably not have been able to do it alone, but fueling his muscles had been the knowledge that he was committing a crime. At the very least, it was corruption, the crossing of a line. As corruption went, it was on a level far below what Pratt imagined was happening at that very moment in the dark crusty bowels of "the government," as they called it locally. Maybe a shade above a cop getting a free lunch at Taco Bell. But nothing that could really hurt anybody unless he were to dump the mercury into the river or spread it on the lawn at an elementary school where it would be tracked into the building and evaporate into vapors that would soften young brains and spines. Then again, with the river already polluted and children obese and unable to find Alaska on a map, maybe it didn't matter.

He had been crushing cans of latex paint with the hydraulic press, watching their contents ooze through a grate into a fifty-five-gallon drum, when the man had come in. The paint crusher was loud and his back was to the room when he operated it, so the man was able to walk up to within a few feet of Pratt before he sensed someone behind him and spun around to see a man watching him. The man was frail and his hair was shoulder length and white; he looked a bit like an anemic, emaciated George Custer. Or a ghost. Pratt had turned off the crusher. He was alone at the facility. His boss, Jenson, was on an errand, otherwise he wouldn't have had to deal with customers while bulking the paint.

"Do you have something to drop off?"

"I do," the Ghost Man said. He started off limping toward the open door and Pratt followed, pulling a cart covered with kitty litter to absorb the contents of frequently leaky containers.

The man's limp seemed to come from the hip; he swung his right leg as if it were joined to his body without a ball joint and Pratt had an unpleasant memory of buying Whitney a cheap drugstore doll when she was three, when he and Patricia were in the throes of yet another financial crisis and the Christmas budget was minimal. Pratt had purchased the doll, a knockoff Barbie, and a package of cigarettes with a mountain of change. He recalled how when Whitney, strong for her age, had tried to make her dolly walk the leg had snapped cleanly off. Luckily Patricia had as usual found a way to salvage Christmas by cashing in some of her childhood savings bonds, and there'd been a suitable spread under the tree; the amputee had quietly disappeared. Now Pratt could see the doll's smooth features, her blue eyes as expressionless as a crack whore's.

"I just bought a building downtown," the Ghost Man said. "The old Holloway Building. I'm renovating it for upscale office space. Are you familiar with the Holloway?"

Pratt thought it was an ancient three-story place that had housed a secretarial school. "Isn't it where they used to have a college?"

"I think so."

"Isn't a guy restoring a 1956 Chris-Craft in there?"

The man looked at his watch.

"It was in the newspaper," Pratt said. "Didn't he find it in a farm field or something? And he's got it on the second floor and he's going to cut a hole in the wall and use a crane to bring it down?"

"I believe so."

"Is he done yet?"

"He's dead. Cancer. His kids came and took the boat and they've been parting it out on eBay."

"Man, that's rough."

They were outside then, by the Ghost Man's Lexus. Black and clean, it reminded Pratt of a melted candle. The Ghost Man reached into his pocket and the trunk opened, revealing five jars in a cardboard box. "I was exploring the Holloway after I bought it and found these in the basement, behind an old oil burner."

"What are they?"

"Quicksilver."

"Mercury?"

"I had to hire a high school kid to help me carry them up the stairs."

"Well," Pratt said. He pretended he was playing Jenson in a movie, even leaned on the cart the way Jenson, a farm-raised kid, tended to do when talking with customers, as if it were the cowl of a tractor. "Right now we only take residential hazardous waste. If this is from a business, you'll have to go through a private disposal company."

"Is that right?" The Ghost Man stared at his car. Where was Jenson when you needed him? Pratt wondered. Ordinarily he passed all potential confrontations to Jenson. It was cowardly, he knew, but Jenson was the boss and made three dollars an hour more and in Pratt's estimation that was enough to compensate him for the added stress.

"Yes. That's the policy."

"I'm on my way out of town. I'm on my way to Bismarck. I'm literally on my way as you can see by the suitcase."

A murder of crows blotted out the sun for a moment. Pratt glanced up at the birds, scattering and rejoining over the landfill. He wondered if birds ever collided like air-show jets. He didn't think he'd ever heard of it happening. It wasn't like you saw dead birds on the ground very often.

"And I sure don't want to drive all the way to Bismarck with this in the car."

"That makes sense. That could be dangerous."

"Catastrophic." The Ghost Man held up a waxy finger. "How much do you suppose a private company would charge to take this off my hands?"

"I have no idea. I know they charge five dollars for old air conditioners."

"Do you think it would be, say, more than a hundred dollars?" he asked, reaching for his wallet.

Bats too, Pratt thought. Bats rarely collided with anything. Of course they had radar. Birds had eyes. Pilots had eyes *and* radar and still collided.

"I mean a hundred per jar."

"I don't know. I can give you a phone number."

"Look," the Ghost Man said, "you seem like a reasonable fellow. I have a hard time getting around as you can see. I took a piece of shrapnel the size of a pop-top and it more or less nailed my hip to my pelvis. I'll give you a hundred per jar. You take them in for me. If it's less than a hundred per jar, well, keep the change. If it's more, get rid of what you can and come to the Holloway and I'll give you more. Plus expenses."

"Expenses?"

"Of course."

• • •

He found his wife tanning on the deck. She had applied so much oil to her body that she reminded Pratt of a fish, although he wasn't quite sure what kind of fish. Part of it was in the way she was lying. She was on the chaise, on her stomach, hands outstretched in front of her, ankles together. Patricia's rear end was trussed like a tenderloin in the briefest of yellow bikini bottoms, too small for her frame, she readily admitted, not for public consumption but to allow the greatest possible absorption of sun. The plan was to lose enough weight to look "terrific" in the bikini by the time they boarded their flight.

Her top was untied and the cords hung to the redwood, swaying slightly from her breathing. He studied the cords. There was a definite rhythm happening with them. She was asleep. His fingers were on the sliding-glass-door handle and he removed them and backed away, slowly, as if she might hear his footsteps through the double-insulated glass. He went downstairs and opened his copy of *Salt Water Game Fishes*, part of something called *The Sportsman's Bookshelf*, published in 1951. Pratt had found it at the used bookstore in Fargo. His general tendency when taking on anything new was to read about it first. He had read Harvey Pennick's *Little Red Book* cover to cover before ever striking a ball outdoors. He was halfway through Zane Grey's *Tales of Fishing Virgin Seas*.

He lighted a cigarette and paged through the old green book. He found Patricia on page 64. She was a cobia, similar to a remora, or "sucking fish." The latter was ironic and brought forth a perennially upsetting memory: she had told him that while a young woman, in an attempt—in vain, it turned out—to remain a virgin, she had performed oral sex on her boyfriends.

"To completion?"

"Of course."

"Then why not with me?"

"Because I *married* you."

What fumed him the most was the occasional run-in with one of Patricia's old boyfriends, by and large sort of oafish blue-collar types, working jobs not unlike Pratt's though he liked to believe he was not trapped the way they were, that he was more of a Jack Kerouac type, though his résumé bore no evidence of this. Pratt would stare at these men with a mixture of envy and hatred. Sometimes their return gazes seemed to indicate that they knew he was being deprived of a gift they'd received.

6

CARVER WAS ALREADY at the Bonanza when Pratt arrived, standing beside his car, not a dentist's car at all, a Mercedes or Jaguar, but a battered brown Ford Torino. Pratt assumed that Carver's bag was being a rebel. He smoked, for one thing, and didn't hide the fact like other medical men, even sometimes performed his duties with a half-smoked Kool riding on his ear. Wore cracking alligator boots at the office. Now Carver was performing elaborate stretching moves in a pair of skintight tiger-striped spandex running pants. The Bonanza had no dress code but Pratt suddenly wished it did. It was as if Carver wanted terribly to counter the medical professional cliché by dressing like a freak, maintaining a thick mop of hair in a Beatle cut, sporting an ankh necklace. His shirt rode up and Pratt was disheartened to see the kind of six-pack abs the pursuit of which had become a major industry in America.

"About time," Carver said, looking at his bare wrist.

"Some of us have real jobs," Pratt said, though he worked only three days a week and enjoyed the kind of flexibility in hours meant to make up for low wages.

"Yeah, yeah. Why are we here instead of at the Meadows?"

"Because it only costs nine dollars to play here."

Carver stared blankly at him until Pratt understood that cowboy boots and a primer-covered car couldn't buy you entry into the working class. It was like the so-called nouveaux riches, the accidental Internet millionaires, or rap artists, all of whom seemed to behave in what Grandma would have called an uncouth manner. It was a caste system more or less. Her father, Pratt's great-grandfather, had inherited a family fortune and lost it in 1929 but Grandma could still recall how his *bearing* hadn't changed, how he had walked like a man of means even with his shoe soles torn to pieces. A year later he'd earned another fortune by starting a company that recycled soap from hotels throughout the Midwest by paying off maids for scraps, melting the soap in a contraption of his own design, and forming it into new bars which were stamped with his company name and sold back to the same hotels. Or something like that. Pratt suspected it might be one more family myth contrived to hide an embarrassment, but nothing as glamorous as, say, bootlegging or gambling. There was a rumor that his great-grandfather had made his second fortune by bilking widows. Not that it mattered much; by the time the fortune trickled down through Pratt's grandparents and into the hands of Pratt's father and his two brothers, there wasn't much left and what was left was largely squandered on desperate attempts at recouping the original wealth: Siberian oil schemes, arid Montana land, et cetera.

Pratt felt rich with the Ghost Man's five hundred dollars in his pocket and splurged on a covered cart and fairly moist cigar. He allowed Carver to go first on the tee, mainly to size him up. The dentist owned an enormous custom-made driver with a head the size of a Pomeranian. His swing was rubbery but the ball went straight and high. Pratt lost sight of it. Carver held his follow-through for an eternity, as if he was posing for a wristwatch ad. "See it?"

"Sorry," Pratt said.

"We'll find it," Carver said, still holding the pose. His biceps were rippling.

Pratt set his cigar on the ground and pushed his tee into the earth. His hands were clammy. This was the first time he'd played with anybody. He didn't feel ready for it. He addressed the ball, went through his internal dialogue. His positive visualization. He could sense Carver behind him, watching. His own cheap equipment, a complete set Patricia had found at Wal-Mart for a hundred dollars, seemed to shout something tawdry. Pratt brought his club back, resisted the urge to shut his eyes, and hit the ball. Heard a fairly satisfactory, almost metallic collision. On follow-through he saw the ball, plenty of loft, going straight, high, before something as forceful as the hand of God itself pushed it to the right, into the swamp. Deeper this time.

"Bummer," Carver said. He hopped into the cart, behind the wheel. Pratt climbed in and they raced down the fairway. Carver dumped him off at the swamp and went on to find his own ball.

Pratt and Carver had a history. That is, their paths had crossed before. Or more accurately, they'd met on the path, like Oedipus and Laius, back in the mid-'80s, when both had been in a course called Analysis of Literature. Their professor was a statuesque Lauren Hutton type who carried herself like a New Yorker and littered her lectures with French phrases that were like coins flying from her mouth for Pratt and Carver and a dozen other young men and women to catch and treasure. Kathleen Lambert wore fur, real fur, and made no bones about it. She smoked long cigarettes, Canadian Players, and talked frankly about cocks and orgasms. They'd been reading Balzac as interpreted by Roland Barthes, heady stuff that Pratt couldn't wrap his mind around. Back then Carver was just another student Pratt chatted with in the hallways but one day, after watching Dr. Lambert move down the hall, Carver confided in Pratt that he'd give "his left ball" to sleep with her. Pratt said he knew the feeling even though he was recently engaged and Dr. Lambert, in her early forties, seemed rather ancient to a twenty-year-old. But at the end of the semester Lambert invited the class to her home by the Red River for a party. Patricia was not interested in attending and Pratt didn't push too hard, not wanting his worlds to mix. Not many students showed up but Carver was there, soaked in cologne and smoking what looked suspiciously like Lambert's brand. Quite a bit of wine was consumed. Lambert regaled them with tales of nude beaches and Manhattan parties. By one o'clock everyone was gone except Pratt and Carver; Pratt mainly because he'd discovered Lambert's reel-to-reel tape player and was in the corner with headphones on listening to some incredible Andre Gagnon. With this fascinating music as a soundtrack he watched Carver's advances, first marked by smooth body language, sliding closer to Lambert on the sofa, turning to face her, placing his left hand on her thigh. When she did not respond and in fact brushed his hand from her leg as if it were some cigarette ash, Carver's face began to fall and rendered itself not unlike an Iroquois false-face mask but with the lips moving rapidly; Pratt found the visual more interesting than hearing any words would have been and kept the headphones on. After a bit he tired of the scene and closed his eyes, letting the music and wine drive him into a swaying sort of high, and then when he opened his eyes Dr. Lambert was standing before him in a silk kimono, no doubt an authentic one from Japan, and led him not to the bedroom but to the kitchen where she had a sleeping bag laid out and on which she proceeded to do things to him, with him, so purely animal in nature that twenty years later he still reddened a bit thinking about it. The worst part aside from a sense of guilt—rationalized away by thinking of it as a seduction verging on rape—was that when he finally left Lambert's house, spent, bewildered, he saw Carver's 450 SL convertible lurking under a great elm, with a cigarette cherry that told him Carver had been watching the entire time, not at an angle to see anything remotely sordid but the possibly far worse turning on and off of lights. Perhaps he'd heard Dr. Lambert moaning in French since it was a warm May night and the windows were open.

He hadn't really seen much of Carver after that, not until Whitney was ten and their regular dentist had died and Patricia's sister had recommended Carver, who'd returned from dental school and various adventures to partner with his father. Pratt's relationship with Carver had been so inconsequential that he had not made the connection even after meeting him; it wasn't until later that Pratt matched the face with the name and the past. He hadn't ever mentioned to Patricia that he and Carver were fellow alumni. The event with Dr. Lambert was not something he wanted to dredge up, as surreal and short-lived as it had been. This was in part because he'd read somewhere that she'd been found dead in her apartment in Manhattan, where she'd gone a few years after her tryst with Pratt, and he did not like thinking about people he knew who were dead.

He pushed through the reeds and studied the watery muck. He'd been told that deer sometimes hid in the swamp and would break free and run across the green doing incalculable damage. Course etiquette called for entering the swamp from the green side to push deer the other way, down the more durable fairway on the first. He wondered why they didn't just dry the swamp and replace it with a sand trap but it was possible the clump of weeds was a designated wetland and subject to federal regulation.

He couldn't find his ball. He used his pitching wedge as a machete to part the reeds and brush. Through a gap he spotted Carver taking a ball from his pocket and tossing it toward the flag. Carver hadn't tried very hard to find his ball either, though it was undoubtedly in a better position than Pratt's, maybe even in a great position. You had to wonder about someone like that. Pratt imagined him now, cheating on his dental exams, writing answers to questions in the bill of his baseball cap, a favorite method in farm country where every lecture hall was a sea of John Deere and Chevrolet and Minnesota Vikings colors. The technique called for casually pulling off the cap to rub your head while glancing at formulas and notes on the fabric. Maybe Carver was a fraud. Pratt made a mental note to ask his daughter how her teeth were holding up.

Pratt emerged from the swamp. "I've got to take a drop," he said.

Carver pointed to his phony lie. "I really lucked out."

"Nice," Pratt said. He dug a fresh ball from his bag, went back to where his ball had gone in, dropped it according to PGA rules which he'd tried to memorize. Gave it a distracted whack with his pitching wedge. The ball nearly took off Carver's head, hit a tree, landed in a muddy ditch.

"Ouch," Carver shouted just before sinking his putt.

They caught up with a foursome teeing off on the fourth hole, a long par five that crossed the Buffalo River. Most players tried to lay up before the water but there was always a traffic jam as balls went over the bank and people spent time looking for them. People from the northland were known for their frugality and this extended to spending a half hour wading for a cheap ball. Pratt relighted his dead cigar and they sat in the cart. Carver had birdied on the first, bogeyed the second where he couldn't cheat, and made par on the third. Pratt's scorecard was his worst ever, though he'd made a pretty fairway shot that thumped the green. But even that was followed by an insane round of putting. He felt dejected. One of his golf books had suggested playing with a better partner as a way to improve your skills. It wasn't really working, unless you counted learning how to cheat. After the first hole, he had feebly tried to tell Carver about his successful up-and-down from the swamp a few days before but Carver had launched into a strange monologue about a new fabric that contained a kind of sunscreen allowing the wearer to limit application of lotion to the face and hands.

They watched the foursome finish teeing off. They were old men and taking their time. They hadn't offered to let Pratt and Carver play through. Carver didn't seem to mind waiting. He tapped a Kool against the steering wheel and fired it up. "I saw your wife the other day."

"Patricia?"

"I didn't recognize her."

"She's reduced a little."

"That's an understatement. She looks fucking fantastic."

"I'll pass that along."

"I told her already."

"Oh?"

Carver inhaled deeply on his cigarette. "She didn't tell you?"

No, the cobia had not told him anything. Pratt shifted in his seat. Reached into his shirt pocket for a cigarette and realized he was already holding a lit Macanudo. "I haven't seen much of her lately, we've been so busy."

"I saw her in the mall. I was looking in Victoria's Secret for a little something for a lady friend and Patty came up to me and said hello. I drew a blank. What's it been, anyway, a year since her last appointment?"

"That sounds about right."

"Goddamn, that's a big change in one year. She looked like she had bypass surgery."

"She didn't. It was all through her own efforts."

He patted Pratt's knee. "You're a lucky man."

"I know."

"I mean, it's like you've gotten a brand-new woman. Like you get another one."

"Kind of like that."

"I told her that at lunch."

"Lunch?"

"I said, 'He gets a new woman, what do *you* get?'"

Pratt's mind turned into a Rube Goldberg machine consisting of screaming monkeys with ball-peen hammers. He tried to sound casual but was aware that his voice was a chirping bird. "What did she say?"

Carver laughed. Aimed his Kool at the green, where the old men were finishing up. "Our turn," he said.

7

AHEAD OF PRATT, Carver was pushing his Torino sixty miles an hour down the narrow gravel road, fishtailing on the soft spots, leaving behind a plume of dust that envied Breedlove's run at Bonneville. Pratt crept along, worried that his sagging bumper would bash the ground at every rut, shattering the jars in the trunk. When Pratt slowed by the rock, the girl and her golf balls were caked in fresh dust. She was rubbing her eyes. Pratt stopped the car. Patricia kept a box of Wet Wipes in the glove box and he jerked one from the container, climbed out, and offered it to the girl. She didn't wipe her eyes. She began cleaning the top layer of golf balls in the bucket, folding the wipe as each portion of it became tainted, getting the absolute most from it. She said, "That guy was going too darn fast if you ask me."

"That's an understatement."

"What?"

"You're right. He was going way too fast."

"You know him?"

"He's my dentist."

"He's a dentist?"

"Yes."

"He drives too fast."

"Well, he cheats at golf too."

She anchored the wipe to the rock with her bucket. "That figures. My daddy says all doctors are liars."

"Well."

"They lie about what's hurting you and then they call the cops." She stared at his shirt. "Can I have one of your cigarettes?"

"Aren't you a little young to be smoking?"

The look she gave him indicated that he was violating something though Pratt wasn't sure whether it was trust or something else. He shook a cigarette from the package and handed it to her. She snatched it from him with a tiny hand and poked it into her mouth, dug into her jeans for a blue-tip match, struck it on the rock, lighted the cigarette, whipped the match dead. Pratt lighted his own cigarette and began picking through the balls. He didn't need any more but he felt obligated. He glanced up at the girl; she was smoking the cigarette in the manner that reminded him of a factory worker more than a prepubescent nicotine adventurer.

"Do you live around here?" he asked, setting a Dunlop and a Topflite aside.

"That's a lady ball."

"Excuse me?"

"That pink one is for ladies. It says so right on there."

Pratt felt his face reddening a bit. He dropped the Dunlop back into the bucket. He dug back in and quickly set eleven more aside. She bagged them and he paid her. Again she folded the bill into a tiny square.

"Okay," he said. "Thanks." He headed for the car.

"Thanks for the smoke," she said.

8

PRATT MOVED THE mercury from the trunk to the garage at two in the morning. He draped a green tarp over the jars. Stepped back to look at his handiwork. It was way too obvious that he had hidden something under the tarp. Patricia, taking out the garbage, would see the tarp and lift up the edge. He imagined this very clearly, saw the black plastic kitchen garbage bag slipping from her slender fingers into the can, saw her eyes locking on the tarp, saw her standing before it, hands on her hips, brow raised in curiosity. She wouldn't necessarily open one of the jars because they were tightly sealed and dirty, but she might.

He removed the tarp. The jars looked innocuous, reminded him of his mother's single attempt at canning and pickling. This was when they lived in Iowa, when Pratt's father taught at the university and they rented a college-owned house with a backyard that, while narrow, went on forever. Idyllic, in hindsight. There were grapevines, mulberry trees, and plenty of space for Mother's garden, a sprawl of weeds concealing beans and carrots, lettuce. Rabbits had soon overtaken the property. Nobody in the family had wanted to eat the lettuce because worms occasionally fell from the leaves and his mother had turned to yogurt making and, later, weaving.

Pratt sat on the step and lighted a smoke and stared at the mercury. He didn't know much about it. At work it showed up mainly in the form of thermometers brought in by concerned citizens or the occasional jelly jar containing a teaspoonful that someone had discovered in a shed, waiting out eternity on a windowsill. Jenson had told him that in certain cultures, in Latin America and also Appalachia, people still used mercury as a folk remedy, sprinkling it in a room or some other form of what Jenson called "mumbo jumbo." Jenson said it was the equivalent of forcing infants to chain-smoke Camels. Mercury evaporated but fumes tended to remain close to the ground where toddlers breathed them. It was Jenson's theory that people in the South were stupid because of mercury. Jenson had never been farther south than Omaha but claimed to have read some in-depth scientific studies backing up his claims. It could be true, Pratt thought, recalling other forms of home-grown lunacy even within his own family: the way his father, well educated at Arizona State University, once chewed Red Man tobacco, pressed the slimy lump against a boil on Pratt's hip, and wrapped the entire mess in a strip torn from a white sheet. Pratt was forced to wear the tobacco for twenty-four hours, including at school. When his father cut the bandage with his Bowie knife, the entire family watching what was supposed to be a dramatic unveiling, the boil was not only still there but larger and more menacing than before. Rather than admit defeat, the old man blamed chemical additives in the Red Man that had not been present when he was a child and the poultice was used.

Pratt ground his cigarette against the garage floor and began loading the mercury back into his trunk, this time in sturdy cardboard grocery boxes to minimize the risk of having a jar tip and break. He regretted having taken the bribe. It was a problem of conscience. Free-floating conscience, like mercury itself trapped in a thermometer, constantly rising and falling. His conscientiousness was low when he took the money but rose too high for him to do something as simple as find a dumpster and bury the jars under bags of normal household garbage. Besides, he thought, shutting the trunk, there were cameras all over the place these days. He could see the mercury leaking from a garbage truck, the cops reviewing a security tape, enlarging it to reveal his car and license-plate number. Jenson sadly shaking his head. Free-floating conscience, free-floating fear.

9

"WHAT do you have in your trunk that's so heavy?" Jenson asked. They were standing outside.

Pratt looked at his car, the lowered rear bumper. He pretended to think. "Sand."

"Sand? What, are you afraid there won't be enough in Mexico?"

"They're for our horseshoe pits. Patricia wants me to fix them up for when her relatives come over. Her nephews. They get bored."

"Ah."

Pratt pushed his cigarette into the butt can, a vintage galvanized-metal pail filled with kitty litter. "Women, you know?"

"No."

Jenson was single at thirty. He had high standards, evidently. And the kind of romantic patience that Pratt envied. He sometimes wondered what might have happened if he'd hung by the wall a little longer at the proverbial dance instead of marrying the first girl who scratched "I love you" on his frosty windshield while he was fast asleep in the house. You come out shivering on a twenty-below morning and find something like that staring back at you, it's hard to imagine that anyone better might come along. Less than a week later, while studying with Patricia at the Village Inn, a local pancake place, feet locked under the table, Pratt had blurted out his proposal. He'd been too broke to afford a ring but presented Patricia with a 1939 silver dollar as a symbolic clincher. She'd said yes and they'd celebrated by sharing a banana split, feeding each other across the table, ignoring the ice cream dripping onto their textbooks as well as the annoyed glances of other patrons. He hadn't thought about that for a long time and wondered now where the silver dollar was.

. . .

He was in the office, drinking a cup of coffee and paging through the Merck chemical manual, when Patricia called. "I bought you some Hawaiian shirts," she said. "Try them on when you get home but don't take the tags off yet."

"Where will you be?"

"I'm going biking with Bruce."

"Bruce?"

"Carver."

"*Dr.* Carver?"

"He's got this killer route on the trails along the river he's going to show me. I had to buy a rack for the car, by the way. A bike rack. The guy at the bike shop put it on for me."

Pratt felt a little overwhelmed. Information overload. He was still waiting for her to mention lunch with Carver and now *this?* "Killer route"? She never talked like that. His head swooned.

"Are you there?"

"I'm there. Will you be home for dinner?"

"We'll probably just grab something on the go. What are you going to do?"

He came up with what he hoped was an offensive contrivance. "Jenson and I might hit the strip club tonight right after work."

"Really?"

"We're thinking about it. They have a buffet. The roast beef girl is topless. If you tip her she makes a nipple print in your mashed potatoes."

"Well, have fun."

It wasn't the response Pratt expected. It was as if she wasn't listening. "I will," he said. "You too."

. . .

Barring other options, Pratt sat in the empty house with the cat on his lap and dialed Whitney. The phone was answered by a hostile-sounding girl who responded by demanding to know who was calling.

"Her father."

He heard a sigh, then unintelligible mumbling. Then Whitney came on the line. "Daddy?"

"How's it going?"

"Fine."

"Good."

"Is something wrong?"

"No. Who answered your phone?"

"Carrie."

"She sounded kind of cranky."

Whitney laughed. "That's how lesbians sound on the phone."

"She's a lesbian?"

More laughter, from Carrie also. It went on for quite some time. Too long? Pratt petted the cat. "What's up with you?" his daughter asked him.

"Oh, nothing. Just sitting here alone."

"Uh-huh."

Pause.

"Yep. Your mother is on a bike ride with Dr. Carver."

"That loser?"

"Why do you say he's a loser?"

"He's just kind of creepy."

"I played golf with him yesterday. He cheats."

"Everybody cheats a little, don't they?"

"What do you mean by that?"

"Daddy, are you okay?"

"I'm fine." Pratt's cat jumped from his lap and moved to the sofa. Glared at him before curling into a tight ball. "I'm fine," he said again. "Fine and dandy. Dandy and fine. And you?"

"Are you mad about something?"

"Not a thing."

"Well, you sound a little icky."

"How's the CD player working out?"

"I said you sound a little icky."

"Icky picky, Ricki."

"Daddy."

"I'm fine. Thinking about going out to the Bonanza to play nine holes."

"So are you getting into it? The golf?"

"You sound disappointed."

"Surprised."

"Why?"

"You don't seem the type."

"What type am I?"

"I don't know. I'll have to get back to you on that."

• • •

He pretty much had the course to himself but in spite of the freedom to take his time and play without fear of even the most benign scrutiny, Pratt played a lousy five holes, racking up such a high score that he stopped recording his strokes and simply folded the card into his pocket. On the sixth hole he lost three balls in a row from the tee and didn't have the heart to look for them. He felt a new appreciation for Tiger Woods, playing with a parade following him, or that time Woods had food poisoning but kept going and even winning. What made a person good or great at something? Pratt wondered, taking a smoke break on the bench at the seventh hole. To his recollection Pratt had never been the best at anything in his life. In second grade he'd won an award for best spelling but he'd lost the title in the third grade. And he wasn't the best speller on the planet like Tiger Woods was the best golfer on earth. He was only the best in a class of, what— twenty students? And a handful of them were recent Vietnamese immigrants so they didn't really count. Patricia used to say he was the best lover in the world but how could she know? He thought of her biking the trails with Carver. Working up a sweat. Carver lived in a funky house by the river; during the last flood he'd made news by saving his place when his neighbors had given up hope and loaded their heirlooms and photographs into cars to head for high ground. Pratt recalled a photograph of Carver in the *Fargo Forum*, standing atop a mountain of sandbags like the captain of a listing vessel. Carver had set up generators and thirty pumps to keep his place dry. Pratt imagined Carver inviting Patricia over to shower and have a glass of chardonnay et cetera. He'd never worried about Patricia cheating on him. To be frank she'd been overweight since he'd known her and had let herself go a bit after they married, wearing what she called her "fat clothes," stretch pants with elastic waistbands and oversized sweatshirts. She'd always been pretty in his eyes but she liked to point out, perhaps rightfully, that "pretty" was usually a euphemism for having potential if enough weight was lost. Pratt had never really been bothered by the excess weight. He rather liked being smothered between her heavy breasts, found something comforting about her bulk pressing him to the mattress when she rode him. And it was just about all he'd ever known. Now she was slim, not rail thin but slim and getting slimmer every day. People didn't always recognize her at first, like Carver had said. Pratt had noticed that she actually turned heads when wearing snug-fitting jeans. This was all new territory for him. He was happy for her and thought they made a sharp-looking couple but at times he secretly wished she would fail, maybe fail just a little, make things closer to the way they used to be. Not entirely but a little closer. His life wasn't terribly exciting and when it came right down to it, he wasn't sure he wanted it to be. He was doing what millions of Americans did: go to work, keep the house up, fool around with his wife now and then, watch a little television. Worry about his daughter. He hoped Whitney wasn't a lesbian but if she was he hoped she'd try to look normal, attractive. What was the term? *Pass.* He hoped she would pass, unlike the throng of leather-jacketed women he and Patricia had found themselves squeezed among when attending a Wynonna Judd concert at the Fargo Dome a few years back. Pratt had been a little intimidated, sort of the way he often felt in taverns populated by brutish laborers. Places like that had him on edge from the moment he walked in, afraid a stray and drunkenly misinterpreted glance might lead to the kind of altercation he wasn't at all mentally prepared for. He had studied tae kwon do and could take a kick in the guts, take the pain, but was terrified of getting into a fight. It didn't help that Patricia when buzzed had a way of speaking her mind. One particularly harrowing night at Chumley's in Moorhead, she'd had the gall to tell a bikerish dude to quit making his wife run to the pull-tab counter and popcorn machine for him. "You look like you could use the exercise," Pratt's wife had shouted. "Get off your fat ass and buy your own goddamn pull-tabs." Pratt's heart had almost stopped but then through some sort of divine intervention, the biker had torn open one of the pull-tabs and won a hundred dollars and the comment was lost in the bliss of new wealth.

Pratt ground his cigarette into the dirt, a violation of club rules, and brushed dirt over the butt to hide the evidence. The course was so cheap to play on that it tended to draw undesirables, and to keep order it employed a ranger, an ex–railroad cop named Tripp. He was an asshole and was rumored to have lost a testicle in whatever event had caused his early retirement. The old men who gathered in the clubhouse every morning drinking bitter coffee from Styrofoam cups liked to speculate. The most popular theory was that Tripp had been practicing quick-draw moves when the grisly accident had happened. Either way, he'd been forced out and now drove around in his own spotless cart with a flashing red light and a .410 shotgun mounted between the seats. The shotgun was supposedly for eliminating beavers and other vermin but Pratt thought it was nothing less than an intimidation tool. And too, there was something phallic going on. Tripp was often seen parked in the shade, running a black-gloved hand up and

down the .410's slender barrel while observing the course from behind huge mirrored shades. Tripp wasn't stupid, though. Earlier that
summer someone had driven a cart over three putting greens, leaving
deep ruts by the flags. Tripp rushed to town for plaster to make cast-
ings of the tracks and isolated the fifteen carts used that day by locking them in a steel Quonset, into which he disappeared with a lunch
bucket. Twenty-four hours later he emerged with a match; the two
men who'd rented cart number 7 were called to the Bonanza on the
pretense of having won a free round and cart rental. When the two arrived, they were met at the door by Tripp and the Bonanza manager
and presented with a bill for the repair of the green as well as Tripp's
overtime pay. Further, they were banished from the course, and a
poster bearing their photographs was tacked to the pro shop bulletin
board: *If you see these varmints, contact the ranger immediately.*

Pratt sighed and readied himself to tee off on the fifth. This time
his drive defied physics by going almost straight up and arcing back
toward him. The ball hung in the air above Pratt like a small dimpled
planet for a little eternity before landing three feet behind the tee.
Pratt swore and stormed the ball, brought back the driver, and gave
the ball a whack that sent it on a beautifully straight and rising path
over the trees, over the Burlington Northern tracks, possibly all the
way to the highway. One for the books, but the wrong book.

10

HE EXAMINED HIS wife's panties on the laundry room floor. Held the white satin in his hands, flipping the panties back and forth, as he had held a dead white rabbit—Whitney's beloved Doodle, who in the manner of rabbits inexplicably just died one day when she was six.

"*Doodle won't wake up.*"

"*He won't?*"

"*I keep poking him with a stick and he won't wake up.*"

"*He must be tired.*"

"*Will you wake him up?*"

"*I'll try, baby.*"

The panties were slightly damp from sweat even hours after she'd arrived home. They were new but then again all her panties were new. She'd lost weight so steadily and quickly that rumors had flown, bits and pieces of which he'd caught like dirty grocery bags trapped with a rake as they skipped across the lawn. Patricia was bulimic, Patricia had cancer, Patricia had gone to Sioux Falls for stomach stapling. His favorite was that Patricia was taking cocaine, the further evidence of which seemed to be her brisk and cheerful early-morning walks with her dog, Fancy. The dog had a way of appearing to be smiling also, so maybe she was doing a line with Patricia in the garage before they struck out.

Pratt understood that what he did with the panties in the next few seconds could become a watershed moment in the marriage. In nineteen, almost twenty, years he'd never had occasion to think about sniffing his wife's underwear. Men with a penchant for that kind of thing had always struck him as pathetic; he'd seen, on the Internet, sites where people traded used underwear like baseball cards. *Sealed in a Ziploc the moment she took it off, this fishy thong will provide you with hours of nut-busting pleasure.* How pathetic was that? But how pathetic was it to be on your knees on a hard concrete basement floor looking for evidence that probably didn't exist anyway since without a crime how could there be evidence? He had scrutinized her carefully from the living room window upon her return, watched her expertly unhook her bicycle from the new rack on her Mazda, bounce the bike on its tires to shake dirt from the frame—that was a new move, probably learned from watching Carver—observed her pushing the bike into the garage, coming back around to the front of the house, pausing to inspect a flower bed—was she stalling?—before bending low and rubbing her calf as if it were sore. Then she was inside and gave him a peck on the cheek before hitting the shower. He had tried to take a whiff of her as she passed, caught nothing but the faint aroma of the litter box, which he'd neglected to clean and whose scent tended to travel up the laundry chute and infiltrate the upstairs.

The panties. When she was overweight Patricia had worn matronly white cotton underwear, so worn that fissures appeared around the band, no longer white and so much resembling worn dish towels that Pratt had once begun wiping glasses with panties he had inadvertently shoved into the narrow drawer next to the sink while putting away the laundry. He had made the mistake of shouting toward the living room to tell Patricia about it, thinking she'd find it as funny as he did, and she'd responded by jerking the panties from his hand and disappearing into their bedroom, slamming the door, which wasn't as dramatic an act as she'd perhaps hoped because it was a hollow-core door, light as a feather.

He wanted to sniff the panties yet he didn't want to. He held them.
"How come Doodle won't wake up?"
"I don't know, honey."
"Ohh. Ick."
"What?"
"Doodle has magnets coming out of his butt."

"Magnets?"

"Look."

"Fuck!"

"Daddy!"

"Maggots, honey. Not magnets."

In the end the decision was made for him. The phone rang. Pratt was startled and threw the panties across the laundry room; they hooked on the fluorescent fixture. In a moment Patricia came downstairs, in a long t-shirt, holding the cordless. She didn't ask why he was on the floor and if she saw her panties hanging from the light she didn't let on. She cupped her hand over the receiver. "It's for you. It's some old man."

"Old man?"

She shrugged. He took the phone and watched her not so much walk as scamper up the stairs.

"Hello?"

"Son?"

"Dad?"

Coughing. Pratt could almost feel the moisture coming through the line.

"Dad?"

"Hang on." His father didn't sound like his father. His father sounded like an old man, a wheezing octogenarian instead of someone who'd been hiking on BLM land earlier in the summer, who sported a rattlesnake bite on his boot. Pratt's father was sixty-seven and could beat both his sons at arm wrestling up until he'd fallen ill. Pratt listened, heard water running, his mother's quiet voice. Then his father again. "Well, they finally figured out what the hell's wrong with me."

"Cancer."

"Guess again."

Pratt couldn't think of anything worse. "West Nile?" he asked, only because it had been in the news so much lately.

"Lupus."

"Lupus?"

"I went to that specialist." Coughing. Pratt took the panties from the light and dropped them onto the heap of dirty laundry on the floor.

Pratt's mother came on the line. "Your father is not doing too well."

•   •   •

"That's a bummer," Patricia said. She was wearing only panties, sitting on the edge of the bed, applying lotion to her tan, smooth legs.

"What do you know about lupus?"

"Lupus means *wolf* in Latin."

"Well. That really helps."

"What I mean is, that's about all I know about lupus. Doesn't it have something to do with skin? Like skin cancer?"

"This is a different lupus. This is systemic. It's affecting his whole system. All his organs."

"It must be kind of a relief, though."

"How so?"

"To finally have a diagnosis. Now they can treat him."

"That's true. I guess that's a silver lining."

She turned halfway and began rubbing lotion on her upper thighs and rear end. She wasn't happy with the loose skin that hung from her legs and stomach. Someone had told her that no amount of exercise would tighten these areas. Of late she'd been hinting about plastic surgery. Pratt had made the near fatal mistake of wondering aloud what the point would be if there was a chance she might regain the weight. Now he found himself aroused watching her kneading herself with lotion. It seemed antithetical, given his suspicions, given the news of his father's illness. And he thought, If I get a boner looking at my wife after getting bad news, what does Carver think when he looks at my wife? The primal nature of the human male wasn't very comforting at a time like this.

"Do you want me to rub that in for you?"

"No."

"How come?"

"Because you'll use it to try and get me horny and I'm so sore and tired that's the last thing I want and then you'll get frustrated and we'll fight and the night will be shot."

"That isn't what I want."

"That *is* what you want."

"I just found out my dad has a terminal illness and you think I want *sex?*"

"Lupus is terminal?"

"Well, it can be. It's like AIDS. It fucks up your immune system. He gets a cold and it can rub him out." Pratt drew a finger across his throat.

"I'm sorry about your father, honey."

"Can I do the lotion?"

"No."

11

THERE was still the problem of the mercury, of course. Pratt found himself checking the trunk every morning to make sure the jars weren't leaking, that they weren't rolling around in the trunk like triggered hand grenades. At work on Monday morning he probed Jenson mildly about mercury, trying to speak in general terms. As in how fast it evaporated into the air, how quickly it would simply disappear if left to its own devices in an open container. Jenson was horrified at the very idea. "It gets into the atmosphere and becomes rain and poisons the lakes. Last year I caught a trout in Canada and it was popping while I fried it. Pop pop pop."

"Was that from mercury?"

"Well, I don't know. Phosphates maybe. But the point is, that kind of stuff never goes away. I mean never."

"Was it a big fish?" Pratt asked, wanting to shift gears.

"Heck yes it was." Jenson slipped into the kind of reverie Pratt had seen with ex–high school athletes or middle-aged men around these parts who "used to" own something, a GTO or an especially reliable snowblower, or who had "almost" become a firefighter, or who had "come close" to moving to Oregon once. As if existing in the Northern Plains was so bland that all they had to work with were missed opportunities and lost objects.

Pratt and Jenson were working a meth lab, dropped off by a deputy in a series of ominous black garbage bags. Most of the lab was junk, throwaway stuff, coffee filters and plastic tubing, but there were lithium battery strips that had to be taken care of by embedding them in a coffee can filled with ready-mixed concrete. Jenson liked to involve Pratt in new projects so Pratt's role was to hold the Folgers can steady while Jenson used tweezers to poke the lithium strips onto a bed of fresh mix before dumping the rest over the top. Now they were using taxpayers' money to watch cement dry.

"Canadians have terrible environmental laws," Jenson said. "That fish sounded like a string of ladyfingers."

"Did you eat it?"

"Yeah."

"Was it good?"

"I couldn't taste anything but fish if that's what you're asking. Poke your finger in there."

Pratt complied. The cement was still muddy.

"I was sort of drunk, though. And I was starving."

"Did I tell you I'll be fishing in Mexico?"

"I thought you didn't want to."

"I wasn't sure but Patricia's friend called last night and they have the boat booked already."

"So you're going."

"I have no choice."

Jenson pretended to crack a whip.

"Laugh all you want but someday you'll be married. You'll see what it's like."

"I doubt it."

"Anyway we'll be fishing. Maybe I'll catch a marlin."

"You better start working out, then."

"What?"

"A marlin is not a trout. Trout don't fight. They give up right away. It can take hours to reel in a marlin. Days."

"No way."

"Haven't you ever read *The Old Man and the Sea?*"

"Of course."

"Well, you should read it again. They're huge and they'll fight you. They'll fight like heck. You hook one and it'll be *work*."

"The crew will help. They're supposed to."

Jenson shook his head almost sadly. It was hard to tell because he was wearing goggles and a mask. "Do you want to say you caught it or do you want to say some Mexican did all the work?"

Pratt considered this. He poked his gloved finger into the can. Harder now. "I don't know if it would matter to me."

"It should."

12

CARVER had left a message saying he wanted to play golf at the Bonanza again. Pratt listened to the message three times and decided there was an absolute pause at the beginning that indicated the golf story was a device of some sort. It was likely that Carver wanted to leave a message for Patricia but thought better of it after beginning to speak and the golf idea was the first thing that popped into his head. Carver was, as Whitney would say, "creepy," but he wasn't stupid. He was doing pretty well as a dentist, with a fancy new log-sided office resembling a northland hunting lodge. Inside it was like a giant rec room with a cooler full of juice boxes for the kids and gourmet coffee for adults. He'd built the place after his father had died in his ice-fishing shack one December on Pelican Lake. Carbon monoxide had gotten him. He'd been running a propane heater without enough ventilation. Flash forward and now the younger Carver was who most people thought of when they thought of Carver Dentistry. He wasn't visibly ambitious but his father had been and the son had inherited clients and then the sons and daughters of clients. Pratt wasn't sure how much dough Carver had but he lived in a nice house and had no children to support, having gotten a vasectomy at twenty-five after deciding population was the world's number-one problem and that he would not contribute to it. Or so he'd said after their first golf game when from the parking lot they'd observed a father with his three young children at the driving range. Pratt was beginning to doubt the veracity of anything Carver told him.

He deleted the message in case there was some code involved, key words contrived to cover what seemed to Pratt as more and more an obvious or at least probable affair, whether it had moved into the physical realm or not. Patricia was still at work. She was putting in some overtime at the title company, this being the season for hurried closings as people rushed to move into new homes before winter. *Supposedly* putting in some overtime. Pratt walked through the kitchen opening and shutting cupboard doors. The refrigerator was a vast wasteland. He wasn't hungry but he was bothered nonetheless by the lack of food. Patricia had been slacking. Grocery shopping was supposed to be her job. She didn't like the way he shopped. Minimalist shopping, she called it, because he tended to buy only what was required for their typical meals, Italian sausage and pasta, chicken breasts and parmesan cheese. Patricia, at least before she'd lost weight, before she'd "reduced," as the old ladies called it, liked to load the cart with seemingly disparate ingredients that she could pull together into something interesting by strumming through her cookbooks as fluidly as Chet Atkins on his twelve-string. And the snacks! Before she'd rendered her body a vault for salmon and yogurt, Patricia had liked her snacks: ice cream with dry-roasted nuts and hot butterscotch topping, or white-corn tortilla chips covered with melted cheese and peach salsa. Pratt had tended to overlook those options while pushing a cart up and down the bright aisles unless specifically told to find them. He thought it was the difference, simply, between men and women, and regardless of the reason, Patricia had taken over the shopping long ago. But now it was a moot point because she had lost interest in food except as a means of survival and boosting her energy so that she could exercise more. It was like a junkie fixing and then stealing so he could fix some more. The tables had turned and if he wanted food he had to give her a list or go himself. And why should he have to? He felt cheated. He still had to clean the litter box, do the laundry, take her car to Jiffy Lube every three months.

He stepped into the garage, hit the button to open the door. It was like a curtain rising on a version of suburbia as seen by Fellini. Both his neighbors across the street were mowing their postage-stamp lawns on their tiny John Deere tractors while their wives stood on their respective porches holding their respective tiny babies. The houses were identical, joined at the driveways. Pratt remembered when there had been no houses across the street, just endless farm fields. Now even Fargo, small as it was, was getting too crowded and people were fleeing across the river to once-dying Minnesota farm-elevator towns like Pratt's, within commuting distance. Cookie-cutter houses were spreading across the fields like creeping Charlie. Summer evenings the streets were filled with young couples pushing strollers and walking Labrador retrievers that Pratt observed locked in narrow chain-link kennels while their owners clocked in the hours at jobs in Fargo, the babies in the charge of what seemed to be a cabal of Bible-thumping day care centers with names like *His Little Lambs* and *Son-Shine Child Care*. He sometimes wished he worked regular full-time hours so he wouldn't have to witness this insanity. When had things gotten so, so, what was the word? he wondered. Banal? Bourgeois? He lighted a cigarette and stood in the garage watching the post-work crowd doing its thing. Same thing every night. When it was dark you could see the blue glow of television sets in every living room window. He and Patricia kept their television in the bedroom. When people came over, though that had become rare, when they were seated on the sofa holding drinks in their laps, they always glanced around as if something wasn't quite right, perhaps like the first ripple of an oncoming stroke, a tremor. Invariably the recognition that the Pratts's living room was without a television and sometimes but not often a polite, "Where's the television?" as if something essential, a ceiling or load-bearing wall, had vanished. Pratt liked to think of the missing television as a statement: *We are not slaves to the box. The box will not dominate our lives. We are not barbarians.* Closer to the truth was a trip Patricia had taken to see Kelly in Oklahoma, the same trip on which the idea of the Mexican trip had originated; upon her return she'd declared a TV in the living room "white-trashy." Oh, and it was no longer the living room

but the "sitting room." Patricia had also affected a slight but noticeable and fairly irritating Southern accent and for at least a week had
set the table each night with cloth napkins and finger bowls for the
salt, using china that had been boxed, in one basement or another,
since their wedding day.

•   •   •

At the Bonanza Pratt was standing by his car, putting on his golf
shoes, when Tripp rolled up in his cart. He aimed his shades at Pratt
and said nothing for what had to be a full minute. This was unnerving
but Pratt was getting used to it. He suspected it was either an old cop
habit or a cinematic affectation. Either way, he caught a glimpse of
himself in the twin mirrors and didn't care for what he saw. It might
have been an effect of the lenses but Pratt thought he looked kind of
old, especially with the bifocals he'd begun wearing. Reading had
started giving him headaches. And he looked gaunt. He couldn't recall his last meal. It might have been a bag of potato chips at work.
And that might have been yesterday. Or even the day before.

"Listen," Tripp said, "did you buy some golf balls from that little
gal by the entrance?"

"I might have."

"I know you did."

"Then why did you ask?"

The long stare. Pratt averted his eyes. He fixed on his golf shoes.
They were still too white, too new, and he recalled being nine and
purposefully scuffing his shoes on the way to school to avoid calling
attention to them. We are all just children, he thought, nobody ever
really grows up, and this epiphany seemed capable of going somewhere. It had legs, but Tripp ruined it by clearing what sounded like a
throat crowded with wet, fat polyps. "We don't like it."

"We?"

"The board."

Pratt hadn't known there was a board.

"See, we sell balls here. Right here."

"I know that."

"And we suspect that little girl has been stealing balls from the water hazards and the trees and selling them. We almost have the proof."

"Proof?"

Tripp reached into his pocket and produced a yellow ball. He handed it to Pratt. Pratt turned it in his hand. Nothing unusual jumped out at him. He wondered if his wife and Carver were together at that very moment. His hand shook.

"Are you an alcoholic, Pratt?"

"No I'm not. Why?"

"You've got the tremors."

"I was using a hammer at work all day. My hand is fucked up."

Tripp sighed.

"What?"

"Try to keep the profanity to a minimum out here, okay?"

Pratt nodded and handed back the ball. "I don't get it."

"I put special ink on this ball. You hold it under a black light and it says 'Bonanza' on it."

"That's, um, cool."

"And we need your help. You seem to have gained her trust."

"What do you mean?"

"We've seen you talking to her. Saw you give her a cigarette."

"What are you, spying on me? Her?"

"This is only a nine-hole course, Pratt. It's not hard to keep tabs."

"Well."

"What we're saying is this. Next time you buy balls from her grab all the yellow ones and give them to me."

"I've got plenty of balls now. I'm not losing as many."

"Your game is improving. Good for you."

"Thanks."

"I've been authorized to reimburse you."

"Well."

"It's a crime to sneak onto the course and steal balls. Plus there's a liability issue. Doc Carver says if she gets hurt or drowned our goose is cooked."

"Carver?"

"Bruce Carver. He's the chairman of the board."

"Carver is on your board?"

"Since day one. Well, his father first and then him when his father died. Gosh darn he was a good golfer. I mean Bruce the elder. He used pretty much only a seven iron for everything. Carried a driver and a putter and his seven. Chip shots, hundred-yard shots, you name it. Seven iron. But do you think his bag was light?"

"What?"

"You'd think so but it wasn't. He kept all his booze in there. Must have had three or four quarts of Old Crow in his bag."

"Really."

"Because he wasn't supposed to be drinking. Had to hide his booze from his old lady. This is common knowledge by the way or I wouldn't be talking to you about it."

"Right."

"The last thing we need is some kid drowning or getting hurt after hours here."

"I understand."

"Carver said that could flat shut us down."

"I worry more about a young girl like that working by herself in the middle of nowhere."

"Huh?"

"Well, you know how it is these days. Someone could abduct her."

"Say again?"

"Kidnap her, rape her, kill her."

"That's a hell of a thing to say."

"It happens."

Tripp pulled off his glasses. Pratt couldn't recall ever having seen his uncovered eyes. They were pale blue, like a sun-faded dinner plate. Watery. Pratt decided the glasses were an improvement. Tripp looked down at Pratt's feet. "Nice shoes."

13

THE CASTLE ROCK restaurant in Hawley, Minnesota. The old-time supper club was red-carpeted and filled with nooks and crannies, its walls frosted with rusting tin oil signs, small farm implements, dried berry wreaths. There was something both tacky and quaint about the decor but the decor was secondary to the food, especially the steaks, known widely as being of superior quality. Castle Rock had its doppelgängers, Smokey's of West Fargo, the Bronze Boot in Grand Forks, all holdouts in a way to an earlier time or maybe just hostages to the demands of regular clientele who saw even a laminated menu as a dangerous step closer to the day when meals might arrive on a plate as a simple pill à la *The Jetsons*. Castle Rock was where Pratt and Patricia went for celebratory dinners, anniversaries, Pratt's birthday, the occasional night out when Fargo seemed too congested and hurried, when the idea of sharing a restaurant with a gazillion yuppies in black leather and expensive haircuts seemed too much to bear, and more than once, winding through a parking lot crowded with gleaming SUVs and sporty PT Cruisers, the Pratts had been known to shoot over to the interstate, zoom east to Highway 9 at Barnesville, haul ass north a few miles, and climb the rim of ancient Lake Agassiz to Hawley and Castle Rock. They didn't go there often enough to be considered regulars, to be recognized by the management or staff, but it always felt like home and Pratt thought that was important.

So when Pratt returned home at six-thirty and Patricia suggested he clean up and they go to Castle Rock, Pratt was interested but mildly suspicious. He didn't shower but he dampened his hair and rubbed an egg-sized glob of mousse into it, brushed it back. He needed a haircut.

"Are you ready?"

Patricia was in the doorway. She was wearing a summer dress, cut above the knee, hung from her shoulders by narrow ribbons of fabric. This was new. Not just the dress but *wearing* a dress. He left his gaze on her too long and her eyebrows rose.

"What."

"What what?"

"You're thinking something."

"Of course I am."

She looked down at herself, smoothed the dress over her hips. Tugged the hem a bit lower. There was something vulnerable in the way she did this that was not entirely lost on Pratt, but suspicion bulldozed empathy over the edge of the cliff. "What made you decide to buy a dress?"

"I don't have any dresses. Well, just my fat dress, the one I wore at Brenda's wedding. And that's not even a summer dress."

"Is this the first time you've worn it?"

"Yes. Well, I tried it on. What are you getting at, anyway?"

"I'm not getting at anything."

"You sound like you are."

"I was just wondering, that's all."

"Don't you like it?"

"You look awesome."

"It was only fourteen dollars at Wal-Mart."

"It doesn't look like a Wal-Mart dress."

"That's what I thought too."

.   .   .

"Can we take your car?" Pratt asked, finishing his cigarette in the yard while Patricia knelt by her magnolias, pulling a few ambitious tiny weeds. Her knees were showing. They'd gone from softballs to tennis balls.

"I guess so. Why?"

"There's something wrong with my rear end. Maybe the suspension."

She straightened up. Looked at his car. "The back end is all low."

"That's what I mean."

They drove east in Patricia's Mazda, Pratt behind the wheel. He wanted to open the sunroof but she stopped him. "It's warm out," he said.

"My hair."

He nodded. Watched her fingers punching the buttons on the stereo. She was an impatient listener. She had eclectic tastes like Whitney but if the next song wasn't one she liked, Patricia would hit the presets until she found something tolerable. Pratt on the other hand didn't mind waiting. He sometimes wondered if it was the difference in their intellects, if he had the ability to withdraw into his thoughts while something he hated, the Doobie Brothers, perhaps, came on, while Patricia could only go so far inside. There was no way to test this theory, though, without insulting her.

The passed the entrance to the Bonanza. Pratt thought that Patricia's eyes seemed to linger on the sign. "Did you know Carver is on the Bonanza board of directors?" he asked.

"Really?"

"I just found that out. He's been a member for years, evidently."

"Hmm." She held up her hands, examined her nails. "Do you think this color is too bright?"

"The orange? No. Not for summer."

"It's fall."

"Indian summer."

"I like it. I get tired of the same old thing."

"In every respect?"

"What?"

"Are you bored with me?"

She turned to face him. "What kind of question is that?"

A deer ran across the road. The deer was a good hundred yards away and well toward the median but Pratt swerved, went onto the shoulder, overcorrected. The car fishtailed.

"Jesus, are you trying to kill us?"

Pratt was silent.

"That deer was like a million miles away, honey."

"I saw another one."

"There was only one deer."

"I know what I saw."

"Do you want me to drive?"

"I'm not stupid, you know."

"I never said that."

"Just remember that. I'm not stupid."

"I know you aren't."

"And I'm not blind either."

She sighed. "Are you trying to get at something?"

"Should I be?"

"What you should be doing is concentrating on driving."

•   •   •

The dinner was neither a feast nor a famine in terms of anything. Pratt ordered his usual, the Babylonian steak, a huge butterflied hunk of beef marinated in garlic and covered with mushrooms. Patricia used to be able to match Pratt on the full-sized Babylonian, bite for bite, but this time ordered a swordfish steak and left a good quarter of it on her plate. Pratt finished it for her and wondered what the human body thought of the mixture of beef and fish when for millions of years it had been used to one or the other. When he brought up the notion to Patricia she rolled her eyes. They were seated behind a family who seemed fresh from performing some kind of agricultural chore; the smell of wet earth wafted over the booth and seemed to hang above Pratt's head. Moreover, the father of the group wore a dirty baseball cap. This was one of Pratt's pet peeves. He refused to go to Red Lobster anymore because the place had seemed to skid down-hill from moderately upscale to fast food in a matter of several years. The last time he and Patricia had gone to Red Lobster, they had dressed up, not to the nines but in slacks and nice shirts, only to find the place heavy with rowdy softball players fresh from a tournament, running the waiters ragged with their heroic attempts to outdo each other in the all-you-can-eat shrimp special.

But the family behind them now was the kind of boisterous unit he had always wanted his family to be. Why hadn't they had more children?

"Why didn't we have more kids?"

Patricia set her fork down. "Is there something wrong?"

"What do you mean?"

"I mean you're acting all, I don't know, crazy lately. All these questions."

"It's called communication."

"Whatever."

Pratt rendered his fingers into quotation marks. "'Whatever.' That's great."

Pratt's wife leaned forward. He could see flecks of gray in her hair. "The reason we didn't have any more children," she said, "is because you didn't want any more."

"That's not true."

She leaned back and crossed her arms. "Oh yes it is. Whitney was three and we were at Detroit Lakes and you were a nervous wreck about her playing in the water. You'd think she was in the ocean or something. It was awful. And you said, you said, 'I couldn't handle keeping track of more than one kid.' You said that. You said you didn't have the energy to be a guardian angel for more than one child."

"I don't remember that."

"I know you don't. But I do. See, you have like this selective memory thing going on. I started on the pill right after that. You probably don't even remember that."

He didn't. He lighted a cigarette and took great interest in a tin sign nailed to the wall above the booth. The sign said,

NORWEGIAN PARKING ONLY

"See, you don't remember that."

"Maybe it isn't too late."

"For a baby?"

"Why not? We could adopt one of those cute little Chinese babies."

She shook her head. "I'm not even going to answer that."

"Why break your streak?"

"What?"

"You haven't answered any of my questions tonight."

"What questions?"

"I think you're the one with a selective memory."

The waitress appeared. "Are you interested in dessert?"

"No."

"No thank you," Pratt said. "Maybe a cup of coffee."

But Patricia was already gathering up her purse and jacket.

"Maybe not," he said.

14

JENSON dug a can of Copenhagen from his back pocket, fished a dip from the bottom, and stuffed it into his mouth. He stared at the mess of dozens of four-foot fluorescent bulbs strewn by harsh winds across the parking lot. Many of them were broken. Someone had dumped a load overnight. He took off his hat, revealing a balding head, tinted pink, the only evidence of his ire. "People," he said.

Pratt surveyed the bulbs, like Q-tips spilled on a bathroom floor. "Be nice to catch one of these bastards."

"Hmm."

"I mean, it says right there on the building there's a five-hundred-dollar fine for illegal dumping. Don't we ever try to enforce that?"

Jenson spat. "I wish. I've been asking for surveillance cameras."

Pratt started picking up the broken bulbs and putting them into a plastic garbage can. They were trash now, their diabolical gases on their way up to scratch away at the atmosphere. "What if someone dumped something really nasty?"

"Like?"

"I don't know. Well, say, mercury."

"They do it all the time. Remember that box of smoke detectors?"

"I mean like a large quantity. Gallons."

"We don't see large quantities of mercury."

"Just suppose, you know?"

"Nobody would have that much mercury. Not even in Alabama."

"You wouldn't try to go after them?"

"For something like that, the city might do *something* because it would cost us so much to get rid of. You hit City Hall in the pocketbook and they'll investigate."

"What would *you* do?"

"I'd be on my knees asking God for the person or people responsible to get a conscience." Jenson was a Lutheran but a beer drinker, had not been to church in years, and attempted to stay in God's good graces by listening to Christian pop music during his breaks though he admitted he couldn't stand it. The rest of the time the radio was set to hard rock oldies. He carefully lifted an intact bulb and slid it into a cardboard box. "Yep, this has all the earmarks of a commercial enterprise trying to subvert the normal channels to save a few bucks."

Pratt nodded. "Nice vocabulary."

"I've got those tapes. I'm gunning for a promotion. I want to be head of recycling."

"Cool."

"And if I move up, buddy, you move up."

Pratt nodded.

"Remember that."

"Will do."

Jenson waved his arm theatrically, sweeping across the pallets of ancient oil paint, UN-banned pesticides, domestic Agent Orange, photographic chemicals, carbon tetrachloride, hydrochloric acid, cracked and leaking batteries, unknown substances in milk bottles, mountains of rusty cans of oil paint, motor oil. "Someday all this will be yours."

Pratt looked, and looked hard, but could not find a trace of sarcasm in Jenson's quiet voice.

"God willing," Pratt said.

• • •

The Holloway Building, downtown Fargo, had the air of condemnation about it, with brittle-looking brickwork, soapy windows, a few sheets of plywood here and there where vandals or age had dissolved the ancient glass. It was too plain a building to be nominated for any sort of historical register, local or otherwise. Sitting across the street in his car, smoking a cigarette, listening to some John Hiatt, Pratt found himself mourning the loss of old architecture. Never mind that nobody had mentioned anything publicly that Pratt was aware of concerning the Holloway. And if the Ghost Man was turning it into upscale offices, it would buy the old building a few more years, though anything referred to as *upscale,* even informally, seemed doomed in Fargo. This was a town where the most popular joints were all-you-can-eat buffets, especially one that specialized in cheap steaks and sour-cream-laden hash browns. Before she had lost weight, Patricia had liked going to the steak place and Pratt's gut still hurt whenever he recalled the time he had eaten four steaks and four heaping piles of hash browns, washing it down with glass after glass of raspberry iced tea. They'd gotten their money's worth that day, as the locals would proudly announce.

Pratt craned his neck to look up at the Holloway, three stories of history. Even the old gray grain elevators across the river in Moorhead were doomed as commerce closed in around them. Everything that had once seemed durable now seemed to be made of rice paper. At work they were constantly taking in electronic waste, televisions and computer monitors, as disposable now as Bic lighters or baby diapers. Pratt was old enough to remember the television repairman arriving at the house with a black bag, his asthmatic humming as he knelt behind the RCA console and unscrewed the back, revealing a mysterious network of banded wires and missile-like tubes. Now when televisions went bonkers people just bought new ones.

He threw his cigarette out the window and stepped from the car. Crossed the street. The entrance to the Holloway was up four steps and as he approached the door, Pratt wondered how the Ghost Man planned to make the place ADA compliant. You'd need a ground-level entrance, more fire exits. The potential for failure seemed to increase. Pratt climbed the steps and peered through the glass door. He could see a light burning in the hallway. He knocked but the pane was so heavy he sensed that the report never made it through to the

other side. He tried the door. Unlocked. Stepped inside a cool lobby
wrapped in dark woodwork. There was no evidence of any renova-
tion. He sniffed the air and his nostrils filled with the scent of ancient
dust. There was something else. Faint but it was there, something rec-
ognizable, though he couldn't put his finger on it. He thought he remembered an article about olfactory memories, how strong they
were, how they were the strongest memories you could have, and it
was true that sometimes, especially in summer, he'd catch a whiff of
freshly cut grass and be thrown back to childhood and the undistilled
joy of riding his Schwinn Stingray bicycle after dinner with no homework or bedtime imminent. The recollection immediately unveiled
the source of the odor. It was turpentine. He closed his eyes and clari-
fied it among the musty odors, separated it like some element being
spun against the wall of a centrifuge. Turpentine and old wood. That
was what it was. His grandfather had been a landscape artist of some
renown in Arizona and Pratt recalled his front-room studio in
Flagstaff, the scent of turpentine, the worn oak floor. He felt a bit
dizzy from the accompanying, unexpected emotion. He rested his
palm on the banister for a moment and then began ascending the old
stairs, built so solidly when quality mattered that he didn't hear a single creak under his feet. He rounded a landing and went up to the
second floor, a cavernous room that he recognized as the great classroom where a hundred young men and women had sat at typewriters
while bespectacled teachers in vests patrolled the aisles holding stop-
watches. Pratt was able to visualize this because he'd seen a photograph of just such a scene in the newspaper when they'd run a story
on the man restoring the vintage Chris-Craft and as he popped up to
the room, there was the man himself, in a recliner. Pratt recognized
him because he'd thought at the time that the man was identical to
the poet Thomas McGrath, whom Pratt had heard read at Moorhead
State years earlier. If he was dead, as the Ghost Man had claimed, nobody had bothered to remove the body. And if the boat had been
parted out by ungrateful heirs, the planks and fittings had somehow

flown back to the Northern Plains like homing pigeons and reattached themselves in perfect order. Beyond the boat was a wall with chalked-out markings for when the boat would be lowered to the ground. The *Forum* article had mentioned something about a champagne christening in the Red River with, perhaps, Angie Dickinson, a North Dakota native, doing the honors, or at least the wife of the mayor. Yes, it was all coming back to Pratt now.

"Can I help you?"

Pratt spun. A woman was sitting on a stool behind an easel near the window. She was holding a brush. He closed the distance between them but noticed that she leaned into her easel as if to hide it. He stopped.

"Uh. Well."

"If you're here to look at Jim's boat, go ahead. Try not to wake him up. He's almost deaf and he sleeps hard but he'll know if you're touching the boat and he'll wake up to talk about it. I swear he spends more time showing it to people than actually working on it."

"How is, um, Jim doing, anyway?"

"Just fine." Her brow furrowed. She was about Pratt's age, give or take a few years. High cheekbones and blond hair. She was a big-boned girl.

"I heard he was ill."

"Not that I'm aware of."

"Actually someone told me that he had, well. Passed on?"

She laughed. Jim stirred on the recliner. She brought her hand to her mouth. "Who told you that?"

"The owner of this building told me that."

"Really. What did this person look like?"

"I'd say late fifties. Gray ponytail."

She pointed to her head. "No gray. And you're off by about ten years."

"I'm off by more than that. It was a man."

"I've been mistaken for many things but never a man," she said.

Pratt blushed. "You own this building?"

"I'm Martha Holloway Olson."

The words were like pistol shots, fired right into his guts. Well, he'd been taken. Again. "Ah."

"And you?"

"Dennis Pratt."

She leaned from the stool and shook his hand. "So what brings you here, Dennis Pratt? Are you an aficionado?"

He went blank. His face must have said so.

"Boats," she said. "Are you into vintage boats?"

"Nope." He turned to look at the boat, up on a rack, a gleaming thing of beauty against a background of aged and cobwebbed timbers. "I mean, it's a nice boat. Hard to believe he found it in a field."

"Someone offered him seventy-five thousand dollars for it the other day."

"I believe it."

"So you're not here for the boat?"

"I'm looking for the owner of this building. Not the real owner. Not you but the guy who said he was the owner."

"Was he trying to sell the building to you? Was it some sort of a scam? I love mysteries. Can I have one of your cigarettes?"

"Sure," Pratt said, reaching into his jacket pocket. How did she know he smoked? He worried that his breath stank and was reaching out to her. He shook out a Marlboro and handed it to her. Flicked his lighter. She steadied his hand with hers. He lighted his own cigarette. "How did you know I had cigarettes?"

"I saw you in your car. You smoked three cigarettes one right after another and stared at my building. It was like one of those 1970s private-eye shows. Maybe like *The Rockford Files*."

"I was thinking about how sad it is that buildings like this are a thing of the past. Now it's all one-story fake adobe strip malls."

"And cul-de-sacs."

"And those steel buildings."

"Yes. Yes. I *despise* steel buildings." She stood and went to the window and tried to push it open. The window was sticky and he came over to help her. Together they managed to get the window open a few inches. Cool air rushed in. The air bore a faint trace of autumn that Pratt hadn't noticed before; he wondered if being on the second floor versus wandering about at ground level with its ambient aromas made a difference. He was aware that Martha was staring at him. He felt himself reddening and the more he tried to ignore her by staring out the window at the light traffic, the worse it got.

"You're a painter?" he asked.

She sighed.

He waited but the sigh seemed to be a statement in itself rather than an introduction to something else. He drew on his cigarette and tapped the ash on the sill, watched the ashes swirl into the air and disappear.

"I'm a painter in the way that women my age take up painting as an entrée into a world that has eluded them, a world they might have been able to be a part of if in their early twenties they'd had what you men refer to as the *balls* to go their own way instead of marrying the quote unquote right man. I applied secretly and was accepted into the San Francisco Art Academy but I went to NDSU instead like my father and grandfather, and I majored in psychology and *minored* in art blah blah blah and met a nice man who became a pharmacist and was indicted ten years ago for fraud and shot himself in the left eye up on the roof of our house. So now I paint and go to local arts events and why am I telling you all this?"

Pratt shrugged. Her eyes met his and remained there. Ordinarily this would make him blush again, look down, but there was something about her eyes, not something mesmerizing but something else. He hadn't felt this way since he was nine and looked across the classroom to see lovely Hope Nelson staring at him. For weeks they'd had a passionate eyes-only romance though both were too shy to ever speak to each other.

"Anyway I own this building, for better or for worse. It is my inheritance. I have no desire to do anything with it except paint here and let Jim work on his boat. Jim is my father-in-law. Was my father-in-law? I have no interest in turning this into an office building, or apartments, or a farm-toy museum, or an abortion clinic, which was the latest offer. I intend to let this building die slowly and naturally, let the wood dry and crack, let the bricks become dust, et cetera. But who knows? It may outlast me. Does any of this make sense or do I sound like an utter crank?"

"It makes perfect sense. Don't you have kids who'll want it?"

"No."

Jim coughed and they both turned to look at him. Pratt was glad when the old man turned and resumed his snoring. He wasn't sure why he was glad.

"Do you?"

"Excuse me?"

"We were talking about children."

"I have a daughter. Whitney. She's a freshman at UND."

"Does she have a major?"

"Lesbianism."

Martha laughed. "*Lesbianism?*"

Pratt laughed too. "I think so."

"And how do you feel about that?"

"I'm not sure. In theory I'm all for it."

"But when it's your little girl?"

"Right." Pratt looked around. "Do you have an ashtray?"

"God, no. I don't smoke."

"Okay."

"I'm one of *those* people."

"That's okay."

"And anyway I can't leave any evidence. My insurance agent would have a cow if he thought I was smoking in here."

"Could be dangerous."

"Actually sometimes I wouldn't mind if the place went up in a great blaze and send cinders blowing all over those godawful subdivisions on the south end. But I'd hate to see Jim's boat get destroyed."

"A moral dilemma, then."

"Is there any other kind?"

•   •   •

Pratt did what he often did when faced with insurmountable brainwork: he slept. Went home and took off his shoes and dragged a blanket from the bedroom to the living room, stretched out, removed his glasses and set them on the coffee table, tried in vain to get Patricia's dog to join him. The dog was loyal to Patricia and hid under the buffet. Pratt pulled the blanket over his head and closed his eyes. He had intended to give the Ghost Man back his five hundred bucks and his mercury. Now another mystery had unveiled itself before him. He and Martha had crept past Jim and gone downstairs to investigate the possibility that the mercury had in fact come from the Holloway. In the dim basement stairwell at one point when something scurried by she'd grabbed his arm. Grabbed his arm and he realized now he could not recall any woman ever having used him for support. And then rather than finding a dank network of catacombs, nooks and crannies, cobwebs, and dusty vats, they'd been greeted when he'd hit the light switch by a bright, fluorescent-lit white-tiled cellar with a suspended ceiling and no junk around other than a broken drafting table and a disassembled fabric-covered cubicle. She'd claimed to have never been down there and he had believed her, just as he had believed her about not knowing about the mercury. He'd told her he must sound crazy but she'd said no, looked him in the eye again, said humans since day one had been dumping baggage, literal and figurative, on each other. Anyway, they'd been unable to find anything to connect the Ghost Man and his jars of mercury to the Holloway. Pratt had been disappointed when the expedition was over, less for the lack of answers than for it simply being over. He'd been enjoying it, or feeling something close to enjoyment anyway. At the very least it had been a distraction. They'd lingered by the front door and he'd even tried to buy more time by offering her another cigarette, which she'd refused, saying the light upstairs would only last another hour and she had painting to do. But he *had* pried from her the name of a local coffeehouse where some of her work was hanging. Was it Nuclear Coffee or was it Coffee Power? He couldn't remember now.

It had been asking too much, he realized, for things to resolve themselves in a tidy way, the way the last two minutes of *The Rockford Files*, for example, made sense of so many disparate facts with the cops rolling up to reluctantly save Jim Garner's ass and admit that he'd been right all along. Who knew what was going on? Pratt certainly didn't. He felt ignorant and helpless. He imagined a list entitled "What I have." On it the first item would be "Inconsistencies." Then "Suspicions" as his thoughts roamed toward Patricia.

"Fears," he whispered. "Fears too."

15

THE GIRL was back at her rock, peddling balls. Pratt rummaged through her bag but couldn't find any yellow ones. He was hoping to buy them and make them disappear to derail Tripp's investigation. He glanced toward the course, wondering if Tripp had him framed in binoculars at that very moment. "No yellow balls?"

She shook her head.

"Because I was kind of hoping for some yellow balls."

"You'll have to ask that guy with the sunglasses."

"Who?"

"And the gun."

"Oh. Him."

"Him."

"How come?"

"Because he hid a bunch of them all over the golf course."

"Ah."

"My daddy says it was like the Easter bunny, sort of."

Pratt laughed; she started to but drew her usual deadpan expression across her face.

"Do you still want a dozen?"

"Why not?"

• • •

Pratt was at the eighth tee, atop what in western Minnesota would pass as quite a hill. Climbing it on foot with his golf bag had left him winded. He'd been smoking at twice his usual rate. Despite the wheezing he lighted a cigarette while waiting for a pair of couples to finish the hole. They were hitting pretty poorly and then one of the women swung from the rough and fell on her back. Her companions tried to help her up but she launched into loud peals of laughter. She was not a small woman and outsized her two male companions by quite a bit. One of the men gave up, wandered over to the cart, and mixed what looked like a whiskey Coke. The other man and the ambulatory woman gave up on their fallen comrade and joined their friend for a drink. One of them saw Pratt up on the hill and waved cheerfully but nobody seemed in a hurry to get out of his way. The woman on the ground sat up and motioned for a drink.

"This wouldn't happen at Augusta," Pratt said aloud. Then it occurred to him how ridiculous that sounded, given the fact that this was only his ninth time playing golf in almost forty years, that he was using hundred-dollar Wal-Mart clubs, that more than half his drives if traced would look like a geometry textbook page on angles. He drew on his cigarette and made a few practice swings. What he had discovered about golf was one simple truth: each time he played, he discovered more problems with his game. His first time on the course there'd been a certain amount of fun involved, a feeling of accomplishment in just getting the ball to the green and into the hole no matter how convoluted the route. Now he imagined himself in Mexico, the other members of his party whispering among themselves while he made stroke after stroke to get to the hole. And he had nobody to blame but himself. Patricia would have gotten over it if he'd refused to take up the sport. She would have made some mildly insulting comment and that would have been that. He would have made up for it by buying everyone dinner. Or something. In fact, he'd almost gotten out of the golfing entirely when one of the other fellows had e-mailed and said he wasn't sure about playing after all, about lugging his clubs from Michigan to Mexico. Then another of the group had expressed some uneasiness as well. Pratt had boldly announced in his reply that although he was new to the sport and not an expert, he intended to play at Cabo even if alone. This was more for Patricia's sake but then the other fellows had seemed bolstered by

Pratt's commitment and said they'd be bringing their clubs as well. A backfire.

Down on the green the foursome was still drinking. Pratt snuffed out his cigarette and shoved the butt into his pocket. He was no longer sure that Tripp wasn't in the forest, watching him, though he couldn't see Tripp allowing the obvious breach of rules playing out with the foursome. Unless the foursome had some kind of power over Tripp. Pratt wasn't up to snuff on the club politics. He hadn't even known there was a board. The thought tumbled over to thoughts of Carver lying about being affiliated with the Bonanza. Well, he hadn't lied, but he'd committed lies of omission. You'd think it would be something to mention. Now Pratt wasn't sure whether Carver had actually said he'd never played the Bonanza or just intimated the fact. Inferred it. Implied? Pratt walked to the trees, took a leak, zipped up. The foursome was finally whacking away at their balls again, hitting one-handed with drinks in their free hands. They were doing better one-handed than before with two. It was possible there was something Zen-like going on, with their minds on not spilling their drinks rather than on the golf. Pratt thought maybe he should give it a try. His head felt like a railroad roundhouse at full operation. Way too much going on. He addressed his ball with his driver and sent one into the trees by way of practice. He heard a resounding crack as the ball hit a tree. He set another one on a tee and drove again. This time he heard nothing. There was something liberating about simply hitting into the woods without worrying about where the ball would land. He had plenty of balls thanks to the girl. He drove another one, trying to get some loft, watched it clear the trees before ripping through the foliage like a saw. He glanced back at the foursome. They were on the green. One of the men was using the flag as an air guitar.

16

WHITNEY reminded him. They were at the truck stop at Hillsboro, roughly halfway between Fargo and Grand Forks. Pratt had agreed to meet her there with a basket full of "female necessities" Patricia had picked up for her. Pratt had no idea what was in the basket. He didn't want to know.

They sat at a hard plastic booth with a

NO SMOKING

sign screwed to the wall nearby. Pratt was relieved. He didn't want to light up and have Whitney ask for a cigarette. It bothered him that she'd taken up the habit and he preferred that if she smoked he didn't have to be reminded of it. He looked at his daughter, who was sipping carefully at a too-hot cup of black coffee. Her hair, short as it was, was askew. She looked hungover and it was only Wednesday. Back in his day, they'd tried, albeit sometimes unsuccessfully, to limit their bacchanalian outings to the weekends. He felt tears welling behind his eyes. This was the girl whose name was still on the high school gymnasium wall for holding the school's 440 record. Whitney had never been lithe like those African marathon runners whose legs moved like smooth hydraulics, but she was fast and more than that, she was motivated. She wasn't very tall either, but she'd excelled in basketball. And the last time they'd arm-wrestled, Pratt had faced the distinct impression that his daughter had let him win.

"You look all bummed out," she said.

"I miss my little girl."

"Christ."

"I want you to be five again."

"Can't happen."

"I wish it could."

"Like Grandpa says, 'Wish in one hand, shit in the other, see which one fills up faster.'"

"I hate that saying."

"I know you do."

"When you were five you used to sit on my head and rub my hair." She nodded. "I remember that."

He wiped at his eyes.

"Would you please quit staring at me?" she said.

Pratt reached across the table and squeezed her hand. "I'm sorry."

"I'm sort of worried about you, Daddy."

"I'm okay. Just a little stressed out."

"How's Grandpa Pratt doing?"

"Fuck if—I mean the heck if I know. I told him to go to a real city. Denver or Salt Lake City. But he won't. Mother has him on garlic and vinegar."

"Yuck."

"It's more than *yuck*," Pratt said. He patted his shirt pocket for his cigarettes, remembered the sign, drummed his fingers on the orange Formica instead. "It's crazy, if you ask me. It's like Appalachia out there. Vinegar and garlic. Next thing you know they'll be handling snakes."

"They will not."

"And these are people, these are educated people. My mother graduated summa cum laude from Augsburg. Dad has a goddamn MA in anthropology."

"I thought it was sociology."

"What? Maybe. Well, it's driving me crazy but if they won't listen there's not much I can do about it. Let your Aunt Marcia deal with it. She lives near them, she can deal with it." He held up his hands. "If they won't take my advice I'm not going to try."

"You will."

"Probably." Pratt looked through the window. "Only because I don't want *you* to stop trying if I'm ever in the same boat."

"You want good karma."

"Something like that."

"So. What did you get Mom for your anniversary?"

"Christ." Pratt's face heated up; he felt like he was going to slide like oil to the floor. Had he missed it? "What's the date today?"

"Daddy, it's the fifth."

"Okay. Good."

"It's your twentieth, so you better get her something good."

"What is the gift for the twentieth? Is it paper?"

Whitney dug into her purse. It wasn't a regular purse. It was a Josie and the Pussycats metal lunch box. Antique or reproduction, he couldn't be sure. He wasn't sure she was even old enough to recall watching the cartoon, unless it had been in reruns when she was small. She pulled out a small square calendar book. Opened it and ran her finger down a page. "Twenty years. Platinum."

"I'll be damned. Platinum?"

"Any ideas?"

"Yes. No."

"You better do right by her."

"I will."

"I mean, it's your twentieth."

He nodded. Something within his field of vision was disturbing him. It was like a hair in his mouth, a tiny hair but irritating nonetheless. He stared at his daughter's face, saw in her high cheekbones and full lips a little more of himself than Patricia. Her eyes were his eyes. He had always thought he was a bit homely and regretted that his genes had flooded her tiny DNA. But this wasn't the hair in his mouth. It was something else. He looked down. She shut the book and there was the Carver Dental logo.

"Where did you get that calendar book?" He tried to sound upbeat, unsuccessfully.

"This? Mom gave it to me. Why?"

"Nothing."

"Did you want it or something?"

"No."

"Because it's no big deal, Daddy, you can have it if you want."

"Keep it."

17

AT IRON GATE COFFEE, Pratt ordered a cup of Sumatra, paid for it, dropped his change in the tip jar. The kid behind the counter didn't acknowledge the gratuity. Pratt decided he was conflicted, with an eyebrow piercing and Che Guevara shirt on the one hand but needing some extra coin on the other, probably for video games or music CDs and not rifles and ammunition or even novels, since Pratt noticed that after serving the coffee, the kid sat on his stool and stared morosely at the stereo behind the counter, set to the alternative music station.

Pratt strolled between two rows of tables littered with newspapers and the debris of what seemed to have been a brisk morning crowd, scone crumbs and liquid rings, empty paper cups, the odd tall glass latte mug, a chess board abandoned midmatch. The clerk didn't seem in much of a hurry to clean things up. Pratt wondered if this was some kind of Marxist reaction or just sloth. Either way it was the sort of place that would drive Patricia crazy. It wouldn't matter anyway as she didn't drink coffee. It was a little ironic because on their first date, after seeing a movie—what was the movie? *American Gigolo?*—Pratt had taken her to Jeannie's, a Grand Forks twenty-four-hour restaurant habituated by chain-smoking AA types but with an interesting decorative scheme that consisted of animal heads, Cape buffalo, elk, bighorn sheep, killed by the owner. These unfortunate beasts all bore a yellowish tint from years of cigarette smoke and grease. Anyway, that night Patricia had poured cup after cup of plain black coffee from the so-called bottomless pot placed on their table by a tired waitress, talking with Pratt, no she didn't mind if he smoked, yes she'd liked the movie but thought it was *different*. It was only much later that Patricia admitted she hated coffee, had only drunk it to be polite, that she'd gone back to her dormitory and lain awake all night, at first happily falling in love but growing more and more irritable and annoyed with Pratt as light began to break in the east, briefly rendering the English coulee that curled through the heart of campus worthy of an Ansel Adams photograph before the sounds of traffic ruined any chance she might have had of getting a good night's sleep. She had, she confessed, considered not seeing him again when noon came and she was still wired. But then she'd crashed and dreamed about him and when he'd called, that evening, she had been refreshed and in love again.

Pratt surveyed the walls, covered with paintings, mixed-media works, black-and-white photographs. There was something, well, cool about the place. No coffeehouses had existed when he'd gone to college. Like new fashions or dances, methamphetamine, these things took a while to move into the heartland from the coasts. The closest thing to coffeehouses back then had been places like Jeannie's, Perkins, the Village Inn, where students gathered at night to study and take advantage of cheap coffee and snacks. Pratt felt a bit jealous of young people now with their laptops and Internet and gourmet coffee. Then again, they couldn't smoke anywhere these days. So it was a trade-off.

He moved between chairs to study a photograph of a dead horse half buried under snow. He liked it. He was pretty sure Patricia wouldn't like it. He turned and studied the opposite wall. When Martha Holloway Olson had said she was showing her work here, Pratt had imagined a more elegant venue, white walls and track lighting, maybe some New Age flute music in the background. He was a little disappointed. And for all he knew this was top billing. He scanned the wall. There were three paintings in a row hung above a rack of backgammon cases and checkerboards and magazines. The paintings were definitely by the same artist. They were all abstracts featuring *eyeballs*, distorted, manic, fearful, bloody. One of them had realistic-looking silver cartridges floating about like small planets orbiting the eye. Pratt moved closer. He looked at the signature, a typically illegible smear of paint. But it didn't matter. He knew it was hers. He lifted the painting from the wall. The clerk was watching him through heavy-lidded eyes.

"I'll take this," Pratt said.

18

Two buses were parked in the Bonanza lot when Pratt arrived. He had forgotten there was a tournament scheduled. He put his car into reverse and started to leave. Someone knocked on his window. Tripp.

Pratt hit the button and lowered the glass exactly three inches. Tripp was dressed spiffily in a khaki shirt with epaulets and large chest pockets, dark-green slacks, a Sam Browne belt for his two-way radio, and what looked like either a can of pepper spray or an asthma inhaler. He seemed to be waiting for Pratt to lower the window before speaking. Pratt wanted to win this one but Tripp's mirrored glasses unnerved him and he pushed the button and held it until the window was all the way open. Now Tripp leaned into the car like a highway patrolman. He looked around before speaking. "You try to get those yellow balls for me?"

"I did. She didn't have any."

"I know. They're still out there."

"Well."

"I think they're on to me is what I think. I think *someone* tipped her off."

"Maybe she didn't find them."

"They weren't hid all that good."

"Well," Pratt said, lighting a cigarette, hoping the cloud of smoke would push Tripp away. It didn't. He seemed impervious to everything, hints and fumes, gestures and body language. He was like a galvanized roofing nail. "Maybe she isn't getting them here after all. Maybe she has another source."

"I don't think so. They live right over yonder at the campground in a piece-of-crap camper looks like something even a Mexican would be too proud to call home. Where else is she getting her balls? They don't grow on trees."

"Good point."

"You know what I'm saying, Pratt? They don't grow on trees."

"I dig it."

Tripp's face twisted. "You *dig* it?"

Pratt nodded.

"You have a thing for that little girl, Pratt?"

"A thing?"

"This course will be here long after her and her father have moved on to the next stop on the scofflaw trail. If you're conspiring with her in some way, your membership here could be in jeopardy."

"I'm not a member."

"You're not?"

"I pay by the game."

"You could get banned for conspiracy, you know."

"I'm not conspiring with anyone. I bought some balls from her. That's all."

"Just letting you know."

"I hear you."

Tripp patted him on the shoulder. Pratt didn't like it. He imagined rolling up the window and dragging Tripp around the parking lot until his khaki was flayed. Tripp seemed to read his mind and yanked his arm back.

"We like you, Pratt. You're careful around the greens. We'd hate to lose you."

"Thanks."

"Your game is improving, by the way."

"Really?"

"We've all noticed."

"That's good to hear."

"Look into a membership. It hurts for a second to write that big a check but you'll save money in the long run."

• • •

Patricia seemed a little flustered, a little flushed, avoided looking into his eyes when she got home. "I thought you were golfing," she said on her way to the bathroom.

"There's a tournament going on."

"Bummer," she called out from the bathroom. Then she shut the door and he heard, was pretty sure he heard, the click of the lock. Pratt was stretched out on the bed and had found his golf for the day: Tiger Woods taking the others to the woodshed once again. He was trying to watch "critically," the way he'd been told to read as an English major, not just absorbing words and story but taking mental notes, reading in a way that was completely unnatural. Trying to decipher Tiger's swing was as difficult as trying to "decode" Balzac via Barthes. Pratt had escaped with a B in that class, probably, he thought, as a form of hush money for sleeping with the teacher, who'd been part of a movement to push out a male professor for doing essentially the same thing, though in a much more public and crude and ultimately unsuccessful manner. Anyway he'd found a happier home the next semester in the classroom of an old codger, Ben Collins, who'd encouraged smoking as they sat around a conference table discussing novels of World War II—*From Here to Eternity*, *The Tin Drum*, *Tales of the South Pacific*—discussions that primarily involved Collins telling war stories of his own which all seemed to feature a lot of debauchery.

Pratt heard the shower starting. He imagined her process. When he figured she was rinsing her hair, the spray against her ears, he got up and went to the bathroom. His hand lingered near the knob. She would have no logical reason to lock the door after twenty years of not locking the door, not always shutting it for that matter, to the point where Pratt sometimes found it annoying to walk down the hall and glance over to see his bride grunting on the pot. He turned and went outside, peeked through her car windows. Saw her water bottle on the passenger seat. Went around and opened the door. The passenger seat was pushed back quite a bit. This was odd since whenever he and Patricia went anywhere in her car, Pratt always drove. He climbed in. The seat was all the way back and tilted quite a bit. He leaned forward and looked at the floor. There was gravel on the floor mat though none on the driver's side. He opened the glove box. A plastic container of baby wipes sat atop the owner's manual. He pushed the trunk button and climbed out, walked to the rear of the car. Patricia kept a neat trunk, to the point of vacuuming it when she cleaned the car. No mercury for Patty. She had the usual milk crate in there with extra wiper fluid and oil, a pair of new work gloves. A blanket for winter breakdowns. He pulled back the blanket and looked underneath it.

"What are you doing?"

His wife was on the front step, in her bathrobe, holding a hairbrush. She did not look happy.

"What?"

"What are you *doing?*"

"Looking for something."

"For what?"

Pratt grabbed the oil. Held it up victoriously. "Can I borrow this? My oil light came on."

"Why didn't you stop at the Exxon?"

"I had to pee."

"You couldn't pee at the Exxon?"

Pratt felt like he was in quicksand up to his waist. He wished for an asteroid collision or a stray 30-30 slug, at least a ringing telephone. He stared at the oil bottle intently.

"Whatever," Patricia said. "Just make sure you replace it."

"I will."

"I thought you were going to get your shocks looked at. Your car is still all tilted."

"It's on my agenda."

"Yeah. Sure it is."

"How did you get gravel all over your floor?"

"Gravel?"

"On the passenger side."

"Dennis, I have no idea what you're talking about."

He started to explain but she went back into the house, shaking her head. He dropped the oil bottle back into her car and slammed the trunk. Went inside. She was back in the bathroom, brushing her hair. "I'm just curious about who was in your car."

"Nobody was in my car."

"It's not a big deal. I'm just curious."

She shook her head. They were entering dangerous territory, standing at the edge of the canyon. Another step or two and things could get pretty ugly, silent treatment or perhaps even screaming and horrible insults, honed like fine steel after twenty years, designed to slip between the ribs into the heart with ease, serrated to cause the most possible damage. One part of him recognized this and told him to back off but something else, like a car with bad alignment, pushed him closer to the rim. "Are you having an affair?"

She slammed the brush down against the sink hard enough that Pratt was surprised it didn't shatter. "Am I *what?*"

"Are you cheating on me?"

"Get out."

"Answer me."

"Get out."

"I deserve the truth."

She pushed the door shut. He blocked it with his foot. She stomped his toes with her heel and that was that. She locked herself in. He heard the same click as before. He went to the kitchen and lighted a cigarette, poured a few fingers of Karkov into a rocks glass, started for the freezer and ice but in the end drained the vodka straight and warm. Paced around the tiles smoking. His hands were shaking. He went to their bedroom and opened her dresser drawers, rummaged for evidence, found nothing out of the ordinary but a brassiere that may or may not have been new. She had so many of them it was hard to tell. And it wasn't particularly sexy. He went back to the bathroom door and knocked. She didn't respond. "Come on," he said. "Open the door."

"Leave me alone."

"Don't you think we should talk?"

"Talking is the last thing I want to do."

"Why are you being so goddamn stubborn?"

"Why are you being such an asshole?"

"Open the door."

She turned on her blow dryer, jacked it up to the highest setting.

• • •

There was only so much a person could do when it came to aimless driving in western Minnesota. Jenson had worked in Montana one summer and liked to reminisce about cruising mountain roads for hours at a time, unpaved roads with steep drop-offs, spectacular views, heartbreaking erosion, dense trees. Best of all he said it was easy to get not so much lost as happily, temporarily disoriented, and it was rare to come across anyone else. Pratt thought about this as he drove on what must have looked from the air like a piece of graph paper colored on by a child with only a green and a brown crayon. Up a few miles, right turn, a few more miles, left turn. He had booze with him, not vodka but a few tallboy cans of Miller Light left over from a night many weeks earlier when they'd had the neighbors over for a game of Trivial Pursuit. You shouldn't have opened your big mouth, the endless fields seemed to be screaming. Maybe so but after an hour of driving and two beers he felt oddly relieved that she'd gotten so angry. If she was guilty of something, would she not have been reassuring and had an explanation ready? The proof was in the pudding of silence and his still-sore toes. He turned and headed north on gravel.

Unless the anger was a *cover*.

He cracked another beer.

•   •   •

He bought a single-day pass to the Buffalo State Park. He couldn't recall how many years had passed since he'd been beyond the guardhouse. When Whitney was small the three of them liked to load the
car with a cooler and snacks, inflatable toys, sometimes a portable
grill. The park featured a picnic area whose central attraction was a
swimming area created by diverting water from the Buffalo River
through a weak filtering system into a man-made pond. The water always looked a bit murky and ominous. Every few summers a child
drowned while surrounded by other children, usually in full view of
parents. But the pond was bordered by a nice sandy beach and a band
of shade trees, as well as a sturdy WPA-built stone bathroom and
changing house which Pratt had always found reassuring, since it was
obviously stout enough to serve as a tornado shelter. Bad weather was
one of his heavy phobias. As was water, not generally, not water from
the shower or sink like the stinky crazies with water fears, but water
deep enough to drown in. Bridges, docks, small boats, riverbanks,
anywhere the potential to drown existed, Pratt was nervous.

He parked among the trees and wandered over to the beach area.
This late in the season there weren't many people around, not on a
weekday evening, but there were a few families wrapping up their pic-
nics, gathering things. Pratt ran his hand along the big stones of the
building. His father-in-law had helped construct the building but had
mentioned this only in passing during a Fourth of July gathering,
while waiting for brats to finish cooking. Jerome had talked about laying the stones one by one. More: he and his little brother had skied
eleven miles to work and home every day. Still more: they had made
the skis themselves with drawknives. During the Great Depression. Et
cetera. Jerome had not been bragging but simply killing time while
staring at the little black Weber, and had seemed almost relieved

when the sound of bursting sausage meant it was time to eat and he could stop talking. Now it struck Pratt that if he himself had done something like that, built something so durable, endured times so harsh, he'd be unable to stop telling everybody about it. It wasn't generational, he didn't think, because his own father, who'd been at various points in his life a forest-fire fighter, trapper, soldier, journalist, civil rights activist, and finally professor, was known to regale all comers with sections of his biography to the point that people were encouraging him to write a memoir, with the mixed intentions of thinking it would be a good read on the one hand and to quiet him down for a while on the other.

Pratt leaned on the building and smoked a cigarette, watching the last swimmer leave the water, shivering. If it wasn't generational, then what was it? He thought of Hemingway, whose exploits seemed superhuman, though doubtless there were a million other people on the planet who'd experienced plane crashes and affairs and war and didn't talk about it. Ego, then? Pratt had no such stories himself, having always been too cautious to come close to getting killed. He'd scarcely been in any fights, finding it easier as a child to befriend the playground bullies than to antagonize anybody. Once on the way home from school a bigger kid with a mean streak jerked Pratt's arm behind his back and marched him through town, occasionally pushing Pratt's arm higher to remind him that a little more pressure would result in breaking the bone, one of Pratt's great fears as he'd heard from the school nurse that no pain other than childbirth could rival the pain of a broken bone. It wasn't clear where Cooper, the bully, was taking Pratt, but he could only imagine it would be some secluded area where Cooper could beat the snot out of him. The incident had its origin, as far as ten-year-old Pratt could tell, in a classroom word game which Pratt's team had won easily, garnering him a hug from Susie Hoffey, the obvious object of Cooper's clumsy affection. It eventually became plain they were headed toward the river—secluded enough—and as they drew closer, Pratt concocted a lie about his father being the vice president of Mid-States Tractor, where he deduced Cooper's father worked by the number of company hats and t-shirts in Cooper's wardrobe. He knew he'd struck a nerve because Cooper's grip on his elbow loosened a bit. By the time they hit the bridge Cooper had let go entirely and was trying awfully hard to pass the abduction off as a joke, and would not let Pratt leave until he'd accepted Cooper's Barlow knife as a gift. Pratt hadn't told his father about the event, afraid to admit himself a coward. Pratt's father had been a big guy until he'd gotten sick and had probably never known the sensation of having his legs turn into overcooked spaghetti in the face of a conflict.

The water smoothed out in the absence of wind and swimmers. Pratt lighted another cigarette from the butt of the first one. For a moment he held the two cigarettes, one in each hand, and for a moment he forgot which one he was supposed to be smoking. He had to consciously think about it before dropping the shorter butt to the ground. He wondered if this slip was a precursor to Alzheimer's. He wondered the same thing when he forgot certain phone numbers. Alzheimer's or else the first press of a brain tumor against important tissue. Here he had been smoking for twenty years, twenty-two years, always with his left hand, always, yet he was capable of forgetting. Was that a good sign or a bad sign? Was it good the way it was possibly good to laugh at a cartoon you'd laughed at as a child and then thought banal in your twenties, ignored in your thirties because you were preoccupied, and then turned the channel and saw when you were almost forty and laughed? Which definitely seemed like a good thing, a return to something.

He saw her then, carrying a bulging plastic bag in one hand and a stick in the other. She opened a garbage can by the picnic tables and reached in, tossed one two three Schmidt cans onto the grass. Jabbed the stick into the garbage can and stirred it with both hands like a witch muscling over some heavy brew, reached in again and pulled out a crumpled Pepsi can. More stirring and she found three more cans. Put the lid back on the garbage can and lifted the cans from the grass, shaking each one dry before dropping it into her bag. The bag was so full that Pratt could see the form of the cans testing the integrity of the plastic, turning it pearly white in spots. She pulled the bag over her shoulder and marched toward the building, toward Pratt. His first instinct was to turn and go back to the car, to put the squat building between them. He was not sure he had not been hoping to see her but anymore he was uncertain of his motives in all areas. To wit: Had he come to the park because he was a little buzzed and didn't want to be on the road at risk of a DWI yet didn't want to go home yet? To wit: Part of him hoped Patricia would confess to fucking Bruce Carver. It would be a confirmation of his worst fears but in a way it would be a relief to know he wasn't crazy. To wit: A small and secret part of him wished his father would die rather than continue to waste away, to erode like a desert wash, to mistake—as his brother had reported after his family had gone for a visit—the television remote for a telephone, picking it up when the real phone rang and saying, *Hello hello hello* hoarsely into it, then pretending it was a joke later when the clouds in his mind thinned enough to allow some sky through.

He didn't turn and run. He watched her approach. So far he had only seen her across a boulder and he was surprised at how small she really was, though it may have been an illusion of contrast, her form under the huge bag. He was taken aback by how spindly her legs were. Her knees were dirty. She looked younger than he'd thought, not an adolescent but ten, maybe eleven. Then she spotted him, squinted, and came closer. "Hey, you're the golf guy."

"Sometimes."

"Bum a smoke off you?"

"I'm out."

She jabbed a thin finger at his shirt pocket, the bulging package of Marlboros.

"What I mean is," Pratt said, "you shouldn't be smoking at your age."

"But it's okay at your age?"

"You've got your whole life ahead of you."

She set the bag down. "I'll quit tomorrow."

He shook one loose for her, glanced around for witnesses. There weren't any unless Tripp's binoculars could see through stone. She lighted the cigarette with her own lighter and smoked greedily for a few moments, eyes closed. "Thanks."

"Lot of cans you got there."

"They're not paying shit for aluminum these days. When we were in Omaha you could do okay but then the prices went way way down. Daddy says you can blame the fucking Japs."

Pratt winced; she caught it. "I mean *freaking* Japs."

"I wouldn't know."

"Bet you recycle."

"No," Pratt said. It was a lie. Well, partly a lie. They had the bins in the garage but usually when Patricia wasn't home he threw his empties into the garbage, especially those she'd insist he wash: cans of re-fried beans, pickle jars, beer cans if he didn't want her knowing how much he'd drunk on a given day.

"Yeah, right."

"I've got a bunch of cans in the car if you want them."

"Hell yes."

They started for the parking lot. Pratt took the bag from her. It was heavier than he would have thought. "Are all these from the park?"

"I start at the campground after dinner when everyone is done cleaning up and then I come down here and then sometimes I walk the hiking trails. Kids will leave cans on the trails. Grownups won't."

"How do you tell?"

"Pop versus beer."

"I see."

"I saw a moose in there two days ago."

"A moose?"

"Not a deer either. Daddy said it must have been a deer but it was a moose. Any retard can tell a moose from a deer."

"That's pretty neat."

"It scared the shit out of me. Scared the heck out of me, I mean. I looked up and he was right there looking at me. Had those big-ass Bullwinkle horns and all that."

"What did you do?"

"Closed my eyes and went to Greenland."

"Greenland?"

"You never heard of the country of Greenland?"

"Of course."

She stopped and inhaled deeply on her cigarette. "Don't you have a place you go to when the shit hits the fan?"

"Sleep."

"Sometimes you can't though. What do you then?"

"Vodka."

She spat. "I hate booze. I even hate the smell."

"Good."

"Greenland is all green like the golf course except there aren't any people or golf carts or sand. Just green as far as you can see, and rabbits, and flowers, not stupid old-lady flowers like roses and tulips but tiny flowers, these little flowers that make the hills all different colors. And the water there is like well not like that crappy brown water back there. It's more clear and if you stand still you can see fish and they aren't ugly carp or catfish like we caught in Mississippi. These fish are all the colors of the rainbow. All of them. I mean every fish has every color. That's Greenland."

"That sounds nice."

"That's where I go."

"I can see why."

"I thought everybody went somewhere when they didn't like what was happening to them."

Pratt didn't know what to say. They had reached his car. He dug into his jacket pocket and felt for his keys. He tried to press the door unlock button but pressed the trunk button instead. It popped open.

"How did you do that?"

"What? Open the trunk?"

"Yeah."

"Magic."

"Come on."

Pratt shut the trunk, stepped back. She was watching him intently though not especially happily. Not the way a child might watch a birthday-party magician but the way a pit boss would watch a black-jack player who'd won a bit too much. Pratt waved his left hand theatrically. "Abracadabra," he said, wiggling his fingers at the car. With his right hand he dipped into the pocket. She caught him. He laughed and pulled out the keys, showed her the button pad with the picture of the trunk. "Push it."

She did. The trunk sprang open. Too late he remembered the mercury and she saw it, the big jars bundled in the center with Pratt's complicated network of bungee cords running through the box handles. "What's that?"

"That? Just some stuff. Nothing."

"I bet it's something bad."

"Not really. Well. It could be bad or good. Depending on how it's used."

"Like a pistol."

"Well. Yes."

"My dad has a pistol. He has a .44 magnum. He lets me clean it for him. Not the inside where the bullets go but the outside part."

"That's something else." Pratt slammed the trunk lid. Opened the passenger door and pulled out three empty Miller Lite cans. "Here you go."

"Big ones."

"Big ones, that's right."

"All you have is the three?"

"Sorry."

She stuffed them into her bag. They stood in the dusty parking lot. "Good luck in the can hunt," Pratt said.

"I'm all done now. This is enough cans."

"Do you want a lift?"

She gazed in the direction of the campground. It was a good quarter mile. "These won't fit into your car."

"We'll put them on the roof."

"That's nuts. They'll blow off."

"I'll drive slow."

She seemed to be contemplating it. Weighing the risk against the benefit. Risk-benefit analysis, Pratt thought. He mentally skirted an epiphany that perhaps he should have majored in business, settled in after college to a career where terms like "risk-benefit analysis" would be thrown about very seriously rather than at his present job, where Pratt had once been about to open a bulging drum of unknown liquid when Jenson had halted him.

Before you do that we need to perform a risk-benefit analysis.

Meaning?

The risk is that you'll catch a blast of something that'll melt your face like Jack Nicholson in Batman.

The benefit?

I'll get overtime until we replace you.

The girl nodded. "Okay but drive real slow."

Pratt reopened the trunk and unhooked one of the longer bungee cords from his mercury. Set the bag of cans on the roof and folded the top underneath. Started the car, rolled down the windows, hooked the bungee to the window frame, threw the bungee over the bag. The girl stood on her tiptoes and grabbed the end, pulled it taut. Hooked it on her side. Then they both realized at the same time they'd essentially wired the doors shut.

"Through the window," Pratt said. He climbed in a bit clumsily and she was already in the passenger seat. She reached out and turned on the radio, changed the station from talk AM to country FM. George Strait was on. George Strait was always on.

"Do you like country music?" she asked.

"Lately I do," Pratt said. "It all sounds like the truth."

• • •

Somehow Pratt had envisioned her father, her *daddy*, as one of those overweight, hairy men you see frequenting small-town taverns all over the northland, with fat asses swallowing barstools, faces dull as fish until the subject of the Vikings or Green Bay Packers or auto mechanics came up, a sure reanimation potion. Instead the man on the aluminum lawn chair looked like a kid himself, in his twenties, lean and muscular with a face either clean shaven or naturally hairless. He seemed to be petting a cat perched near his feet but hurried to cover it with a piece of cardboard, the golf-ball sign, when Pratt stopped the car. The cat didn't move. Pratt reached up and unhooked the bungee; it went flying. When he climbed out the girl's father was standing in front of the cardboard, arms crossed. When he saw his daughter get out he came over. Glared at her. "Did you get in trouble?" He looked at Pratt. "Is she in trouble?"

Pratt shook his head. "Just helping her bring her cans home."

"This isn't our home, sir. We're camping here is all."

Pratt lifted the bag from the roof and set it down. The girl's father studied the bag for a moment. Then he shifted gears again. Grabbed his daughter by the collar and brought his hand to within inches of her face. His hand was shaking. She went deadpan. Off to Greenland. For a moment Pratt thought he was going to slap her. "What have I told you about riding with strangers?"

"He's not a stranger, Daddy. He buys golf balls all the darn time."

The father looked confused as if normally simple circuits had crossed, sparked, burned up. His grip on her relaxed. He let go and slowly turned to face Pratt. Stepped closer. Pratt wasn't at all sure what was about to happen. He thought that anything could happen. The man's arms were cordy and the veins on his neck were like earthworms trying to escape from his pale skin.

"I'm sorry if she's been pestering you."

"No biggie. It was my idea. I saw her with that big bag of cans. I was going this way anyway."

"You sure?"

"I'm sure."

"You want a beer? Candy, run in and get us two beers."

"I should get moving."

"Hell, you can have a beer."

"Maybe one."

They shook hands. His hand was rough and his grip was too hard. "My name is Marty Cole."

"Dennis Pratt."

Cole went back to his chair. Kicked the cardboard from the cat and it wasn't a cat but a dead beaver. "Look at this son of a bitch. Must weigh in at forty pounds."

"Well."

"I found him this morning down to the river. Someone gut-shot him upstream. See?" Cole parted the beaver fur to reveal a dark spot. "Gut-shot him and then he must have floated. He's been in the water, anyhow, otherwise he'd be all buggy by now."

"Interesting," Pratt said. His great-grandfather had owned a beaver coat, made from prime fur back in the '20s, and the one time Pratt had tried it on, the weight had been too much for his knees and he'd collapsed to the floor. "What are you doing with him?"

"Skinning him first of all. Might tan him. Make me a hat. I don't know. He was too good to pass up."

Candy came out with the beer, two cans of Budweiser. Tripp had been right about their home, a tiny lima bean–shaped camper. Several of the windows were covered in plywood. Someone, Candy maybe, had painted frames on the plywood to make them look like windows, complete with tied-back curtains, just like Whitney had drawn on her simple rectangular houses with their triangle roofs, like Pratt had too, for that matter. He wasn't sure about Patricia. She claimed to have never drawn as a child, something he found impossible to fathom. She had colored but never drawn. Pratt cracked open the Budweiser. It wasn't very cold but he didn't like them very cold. Cole held up the beaver as if the disheveled creature was on its hind legs and pretended it was drinking beer. Cole laughed. Candy walked over to Pratt's car; he saw her reach in for the keys. He wasn't sure what she was up to but then she saw him watching, brought her finger to her lips, held her hand with the keys behind her back. "Daddy, watch this."

"Look at these fucking teeth," Cole was saying. "Chop down a goddamn *tree*."

"Daddy, check this out."

"Check what out?"

"Abracadabra," she said. She waggled her fingers at the car. The trunk opened.

She had his attention. Pratt watched his face. He wanted to see something good there. He wanted to see a skeleton of paternal grace under the yellow skin that was now drawn taut in concentration. He didn't see it. "How the fuck did you do that?"

"Magic."

"Magic my ass. You tell me or you'll get an ass thumping right here in front of this gentleman."

She held up the keys. He snatched them from her. "Let me try that."

Candy went to the car again, pushed the trunk lid shut. Pratt sipped his beer. Guzzled it, actually. He wanted out. Cole aimed the key pad like a Star Trek phaser and pushed the button. When the trunk opened again he walked over to it. Pratt tried to beat him but Cole saw the mercury. "What do you got there?"

"Some stuff from work."

"Work?"

Pratt started to shut the trunk but Cole's head was in the way. He reached in and grabbed one of the jars and pushed it back and forth. "Is this what I think it is?"

"What do you think it is?"

"Quicksilver."

"Yes."

"That's more than I've ever seen at once."

"Well."

"I've only ever seen little bits of quicksilver." He held his fingers together. "Enough to roll around on your palm. We used to play with it. My little brother ate some and it didn't even hurt him none."

Candy was at the bumper now. "He said it can be bad or good like a gun."

Cole cocked his head. "Like a *gun?*"

"Something like that," Pratt said. "I meant—"

"What do you have it for?"

"I'm just storing it. Until I can dispose of it."

"You know you can cut it with a knife and put it back together again?"

"I know."

"It's heavier than shit. No wonder your car is all low and all."

Maybe it was the beer, three tallboy Miller Lites plus the Budweiser, maybe it was the stress of the day, perhaps even a loose camaraderie he felt with Marty Cole in the September twilight, but a notion formed in Pratt's head and, very much like mercury, rolled like a heavy ball right through the doorway of reason and into the communication center of his brain. "Say. How'd you like to make, say, a hundred dollars?"

Cole straightened up. Looked at his daughter for a few unnervingly long moments. "Just what exactly do you have in mind, Mr. Pratt?"

"I need to store this somewhere safe for a while."

"Is it hot?"

"No, no, nothing like that. But I need the trunk space and my wife doesn't want it around the house."

"Women."

"That's right."

"Store it until when?"

"Couple weeks. Maybe less. Are you going to be around that long?"

"We can be, for a hundred bucks."

19

PATRICIA was on the sofa when Pratt walked through the door. She had been crying and turned to face the wall behind the sofa when he entered. Pratt felt liberated without the mercury weighing him down, at least for the time being. He had thought briefly about dumping it off at work after hours but realized he had blown this option by posing his hypothetical question to Jenson. Jenson's mind, unoccupied by marital issues, hobbies, or interests, was intensely focused on work and he would remember. Once again Pratt's big mouth had complicated things. Now he intended to do the right thing and get on the Internet to research recyclers and pay whatever it took to properly ship it to a disposal outfit. Doubtless it would be more than he had left over from the Ghost Man's cash and Patricia would question the expense but he'd just have to cross that rickety bridge when he came to it.

"What's going on?" Pratt asked his wife. He sat on the sofa but allowed a full cushion between them.

"What's going *on?* What's going *on?* What, did you forget what an asshole you were?"

"No." He recognized too late that it was a loaded question. "I mean, I just asked you a question. I didn't think that was being an asshole."

"Of course you wouldn't. That's the problem."

"I'm sorry if it came out wrong."

"You asked me if I was cheating on you. How is there a right way to ask that?"

"I was just wondering."

"Why?"

"Because you've been acting funny lately."

"Funny?"

"Like today. When you locked the bathroom door."

"So I locked the bathroom door. So what?" Her eyes were watery but sharp, not blurry, like acid, Pratt thought.

"You never lock the door."

"So because I locked the door I've been cheating on you."

"It's not just that."

She shook her head and stared at the wall again.

"Like," Pratt said. But he could think of nothing else tangible. He shut his mouth and regarded his wife. She was still in her white bathrobe, still bore the aroma of shampoo. He looked at her breastbone, defined now after the weight loss. She had bones now, angles, that had been buried for more than twenty years.

"You know what?"

"What?" she said, not looking at him.

"You remind me of a sculpture."

"Dennis, stop it."

"No." He rested his palm on her calf. She didn't push his hand away. "I mean it. It's like when Michelangelo would take this big goddamn block of marble or whatever and start hammering away and reveal something utterly beautiful. Something timeless."

"Get real."

"I'm serious." Pratt ran his hand farther up her leg, jumped over to her thigh. Her skin seemed softer than ever. He wondered if it was a result of losing the weight or the subsequent attention she'd been giving to herself in the form of lotions and creams, expensive treatments. "You made yourself into something beautiful."

"I've got all this flabby skin on my thighs. What did you call them? Saddlebags?"

"That'll go away."

"Can I get a tummy tuck and a thigh tuck?"

"Of course."

She placed her hand over his.

"I'm sorry if I was an asshole," he said. "But you're such a knockout I can't help being jealous."

"Jealous of who?"

"Everyone. Bruce Carver."

"Bruce? Bruce is my bike buddy. If I was going to have an affair it wouldn't be with Bruce Carver."

"Would it be with some young stud?"

She smiled. "Younger than you."

"Younger isn't always better."

"Prove it," she said.

∙   ∙   ∙

In the midst of it, though, her bathrobe still on but splayed open like terrycloth angel's wings, Pratt's enjoyment was slowly overtaken by a complex of thoughts as precarious as any tropical ecosystem or Jenga tower. Patricia's eyes were closed and he wondered if she was imagining another lover, bearing his own thrusts and nibbles only by rendering him someone else, not a celebrity like Brad Pitt or Tom Cruise, which would be a blow though understandable, but a *real* person, Bruce Carver or someone else. She seemed to be enjoying herself quite a bit but she often did. And when he thought of this for some reason he grew more aroused but also went too close to the edge and had to imagine her and the someone else laughing at him to cut the arousal. Like chasing bourbon with beer. And he was relieved that she was making love with him but also wondering if she was trying to throw him off the scent. And when they rolled so that she could be on top, when he reached up and held her shoulders, his eyes scanned her for hickeys, whisker burns. So in that sense it was good and not so good, soft butter on burned toast, prime rib left under the broiler a bit too long, more of what seemed to have become his theme song.

20

THERE WOULD NOT be many warm and sunny days left, that was for sure. In the morning there was a thin layer of frost on the windshield and while he scraped it, Pratt watched no less than fifty geese booking south, flying low, honking crazily. He had taught Whitney how to count birds in a flock, the way he had learned, not from his father as might have been poetic but from a sidebar in some magazine, *Field and Stream,* maybe, or *Outdoor Life*. You were supposed to isolate five or ten birds in a group and then estimate the total number. Since learning that at the age of ten or eleven, Pratt had ever after been unable to see a flock of birds without counting them. It was a habit, the way at every red light he would close his eyes and think, *If the light is green when I open my eyes everything will be okay*. Same with time; Pratt would think, *If it's nine-thirty I'm going to die* and he'd look at the clock and be grateful that it was nine-twenty-eight. If it was nine-thirty his day would not be ruined but for a moment he'd be seized by fear. He watched the geese disappear over the roof peak. Their two young maples had started to turn. Pratt hadn't noticed it happening until now.

He let the car warm up, listening to morning talk on the local AM channel. The big issue in Fargo was still mosquitoes, the danger of West Nile, which had killed a few people in North Dakota, and how poorly the local government was handling the problem. Jenson had warned him that people were showing up asking for leftover insecticides long since banned. There was a can of DDT missing, Jenson said. "Black Flag. I might have hidden it somewhere but I think someone saw it and took it. That shit will be in your yard for *years* after you lay it down."

"Not good."

"Not good at all."

Pratt himself had snuck home a brown bottle of rank Malathion, some Tempo, a bit of 2,4-D, mixed them all together, and coated the yard with a one-gallon pump sprayer from Sears. That had seemed to do the trick. Patricia liked to work in the yard in the early evening and said the bugs weren't too bad anyway. She wasn't a hard-core gardener but she had flower beds in front of the house and talked every fall about getting tulip bulbs. They had a list of projects for what they both called "the future," as if "the future" would arrive all at once. Pratt wanted to tear out the crumbling asphalt driveway and replace it with bricks. They both wanted to shit-can the 1970s faux-redwood deck in back and build a new one, two levels with built-in planters. Patricia mentioned the crappy gutters every time it rained and she stood by the picture window watching water pouring from all the joints. And so on. It struck him that most of their conversations over the last twenty years had revolved around either Whitney or material items or home improvement. When was the last time they'd discussed a movie? Beyond saying *I liked it I didn't like it I hated the ending I didn't like seeing Denzel as a bad guy*. He put the car into reverse and backed away from his house.

· · ·

"Qué pasa?" Jenson said. He was standing in the parking lot lighting a firecracker and throwing it into a fifty-five-gallon barrel. Pratt waited for the report, not very impressive, more like the sound of a hammer striking a nail than anything else.

"Uh," Pratt said. "Oh. De nada."

"Sí."

"Amigo."

"La cucaracha."

"I'm out," Pratt said. "Wait. Quién es la biblioteca?"

"What what biblio what?"

"Where is the library?"

"I'm sure that one will come in handy." Jenson handed Pratt a handful of firecrackers. They looked ancient. "Some old lady brought them in. We don't technically take fireworks but she was freaking about them. I called the bomb squad and they basically laughed in my face. I could soak them in water but this is more fun."

Pratt lighted a cigarette, touched the cherry to a fuse, threw the firecracker into the barrel. Nothing happened.

"Dud," Jenson said.

"Tell me about it."

The next one Pratt lighted burned too fast and exploded just as it left his hand; the impact was as if he'd slapped a brick wall and his palm went black. Jenson was trained in first aid but responded by bursting into laughter.

Pratt examined his hand, both relieved and disappointed that he had not lost a finger as his mother had warned him about. Independence Day when Pratt was growing up was a dismal scene of watching ashen black snakes emerge from pellets on the sidewalk and holding sparklers at arm's length while the rest of the neighbors were reenacting World War II with Roman candles, M-80s, bottle rockets, and the occasional 12-gauge shotgun fired into the air.

"Does it hurt?"

"It hurts."

Jenson looked around. "We better just soak them."

"That's okay. You can blow them off."

"It's only fun until someone gets hurt."

"My mother used to say that."

"Every mother says that."

Inside, while Jenson searched for an appropriate vessel, Pratt went to the bathroom and vomited. He would blame the pain in his hand but knew it was something else, the accumulation of stress over his marriage, the notion of his wife's eyes shut tightly as an orgasm rippled through her and pressed against the skin of another man; a tongue free of nicotine exploring her sweet lips. He puked into the toilet, grateful to the Americans with Disabilities Act for the stainless-steel handrail because he needed that handrail. He puked coffee and when that was gone he puked bile until his stomach shrank, until it was like a rag squeezed and wrung into something shapeless and damp. He flushed the toilet and washed his face, ran a brown paper towel over his teeth. Tried to regain his composure. When he opened the door, Jenson was standing in the hall, looking concerned.

"I puked," Pratt said.

"I know."

Pratt made a show of examining his hand. The black was wearing off already. It didn't really hurt that much.

"Maybe you better have that looked at," Jenson said.

"I'll be okay."

"I should write this up."

"Don't."

"If I don't write it up and something happens and you file for workman's comp I'll get my butt fired."

"If you write it up that we were blowing off Black Cats you'll get your ass fired."

"Good point."

"I'll be fine."

"Maybe you should call it a day, then. Go home and ice it. "

"Maybe."

"In fact, that's an order. Go home."

"Do I get paid?'

"Of course not. You know better than that."

• • •

There were three messages on the voice mail when Pratt got home. The first was from his brother in Nebraska, sounding more than a little frantic. "Dad's in the hospital again. I might go out there. I was thinking you could swing down here and we could go out together, drive straight through. Call me."

The second was from Pratt's mother. Her voice was a cobweb. "Did Steven get in touch with you? Your father is in the hospital. Again. I have to go. Call your brother. Well, he's supposed to be calling you." There was a long pause. "Maybe you better go ahead and call him."

The last message was from Jenson. "Uh. Let me know how the, uh, situation. How the situation is going."

Pratt erased everything. Went to the fridge. Found a Tupperware containing a remnant of salmon and picked at it with his fingers. It struck him it was probably the only thing he'd eaten in days. In fact he couldn't recall the last time he'd actually eaten a full meal. Patricia was on her own strict diet and didn't pay attention to what he ate because they didn't eat together unless they went out somewhere. The salmon tasted and smelled a little bit too fishy and he wondered how old it was. He closed the Tupperware and went to the liquor cabinet. For a time, he and Patricia had been into stocking the cabinet with an eye on doing more entertaining, especially with Whitney away at college and the evenings free of her bass-heavy music and black-cloaked friends. So far nobody had come over and the booze was largely untapped. Pratt ran his fingers across the wall of unopened bottles: Tanqueray, Absolut, Crown Royal, J & B, a squat bottle of Knob Creek. But he settled on the usual plastic jug of Karkov vodka and poured three or six fingers into a plastic cup and drank some down, fast, to chase the possibly tainted salmon and kill any bacteria before it could spread. He felt a little wobbly within seconds. Felt like he might puke again. Fresh air. He lighted a smoke and went outside to the deck and leaned against the rail. His hand was still sore. There was a familiarity to the pain but he couldn't pin it down. It was like trying to remember what you'd been sent to the store for without benefit of a list. He stared at his palm. Then it came to him, a memory of slapping Whitney one night when she was raging about her homework and Pratt was stressed out trying to help her. She had said something, lipped off, and he'd slapped her so hard his hand ached. Her cheek had turned red immediately and the rest of the night Pratt had worked to reduce the swelling, terrified that snoopy teachers would call the cops. Ice and heat and first aid cream over and over. He'd felt terrible but Whitney had seemed to almost appreciate the act and resulting tenderness Pratt had displayed. By midnight her face had looked almost normal and in the morning there were only a few red bumps behind her ear. They had not told Patricia. His hand had ached like it ached now. That was how hard he'd struck her, stuck his nine-year-old daughter. So hard his hand ached all night as a reminder of his sins. And Whitney bless her heart had smartly suggested that if her teacher asked about the injury she'd simply say she'd gotten hit with a football. Always trying to protect her daddy. Was she protecting him now? Did she know about Carver and was trying to spare him? He drained the Karkov and went back in. He picked up the phone and dialed his daughter. The phone rang, rang, rang, and finally not a person but her voice mail kicked in. His eyes were filled with tears by the time the robotic instructions were over and he could leave a message. But then he had no idea what to say. How could a taped apology make up for something so terrible? For all he knew she'd forgotten it. Or for all he knew it was the reason she was down on men, if she were in fact down on men. He listened to the cave-like silence. "Uh," he said, and hung up.

He poured more Karkov. Almost a half glass this time and he allowed the vodka into his mouth all at once and held it there like Listerine and for some reason, he had no idea why, he recalled reading "Hills Like White Elephants" in college, and the character, he couldn't recall if it was the woman or the man, saying something was "like absinthe." "Absinthe," Pratt said, aloud after he swallowed. He couldn't remember much more than that and went downstairs to look through his books. For a time, after college, he'd kept on amassing books, finding the rare treasure, a Camus or McGuane, perhaps, at a rummage sale, putting them on the shelf. He'd always intended to read more but like everyone else found himself sapped by his days and staring at a television. And when he did try to read he had great trouble keeping his mind on it. He ran his finger over the spines, the colorful Vintage Contemporaries he'd been so fond of in college, his Raymond Carvers and Denis Johnsons, an Exley, the Cormac McCarthys. *Suttree*. He had hoped to become a writer but in his senior year had read a story his father had published in *Argosy* back in the 1950s and found it so fucking *good* compared to his own minimalist efforts in which the characters were chain-smoking alcoholic caricatures of Raymond Carver's people that he'd hung up his typewriter, so to speak. His father's story, about an old trapper and his friendship of sorts with a mountain lion, had had an air of true talent; what was more, Pratt's father had been only twenty when it had come out in the magazine, and getting in *Argosy* back then was akin to getting published in *Esquire* now. Pratt's surrender was not a huge loss to the literary world, he figured. When push came to shove, he'd been more intrigued with the notion of being a writer than with actually writing, a notion made exponentially stronger when at one of the UND Writers' Conferences he'd shared a booth at Whitey's Wonderbar with Jay McInerny, who'd had to bat off pretty girls like they were mosquitoes. Instead of going to graduate school, Pratt had taken his English major and split without even a public school credential to fall back on. Thus no career but a string of *jobs:* grant writer for a failed early-education center project, tutor for Native American Upward Bound students, relief postmaster, interlibrary loan clerk. Et cetera. To Pratt they were all tin charms on a bracelet. He didn't mind working but once he mastered a job he grew bored and looked elsewhere. Patricia's more Protestant work ethic provided them with health insurance and a retirement plan.

"Absinthe. Absinthe," he said. No, the Hemingway book was gone. He could see it, fat and tattered, even see himself buying it used at the UND bookstore, choosing it over a less battered version at the same price because he thought it would make him look as if he had perhaps already owned and read it.

Now he remembered. His brother had the Hemingway. Steven had borrowed it when he had stopped by on his way to Michigan with his brood to stay at a cabin owned by his employer, a regional newspaper chain. That was a few years back but Pratt plucked the phone from the wall and dialed Lincoln. One ring and his brother answered. "Talk to me."

"Hey, do you still have my Hemingway?"

"Your what?"

"You borrowed it when you were going to the UP."

Silence.

"What?" asked Pratt.

"You're a real prick, you know that?"

"What?"

"Our father is fucking *dying* right now and you're looking for a book."

"Oh Jesus."

"I mean, I'm packing my bag and trying to get the credit limit on my card upped and you're worried about a goddamn book."

"You called today."

"Hell yes. Why didn't you call me back?"

Pratt fished a cigarette from his shirt pocket. Lighted it. "When are you leaving?"

"Didn't you listen to my message?"

"Yes I did."

"So can you?"

"Can I what?"

"Can you swing down here on your way? Distance-wise it's a little more but time-wise we'll save because we can both drive. Terri did the math. It's six of one, a half-dozen of the other."

Pratt eyeballed the laundry heap. Walked over, stretching the phone cord taut, knelt to pick up a pair of Patricia's panties. A thong. He wasn't sure if you'd call it a pair of panties if it was a thong. He squeezed it into his fist until it all but disappeared, that was how small the thong was. He couldn't recall seeing her wearing a thong. She had once said, while browsing through a Bon Prix catalog, that nothing looked more uncomfortable than having a string buried in your ass, but then again, that was before she'd lost weight.

"Are you there?"

"I'm here."

"So what's the plan?"

Pratt dropped the thong. "I'm not sure if I can get away right now."

"What the fuck are you talking about?"

"Work. You know."

His brother hung up on him. Pratt stood by the telephone, smoking. This had happened before. He was quite sure his brother was doing the same thing, puffing on a Marlboro, waiting for his phone to ring. Seething. This could go on for hours. Pratt didn't have the energy. He went upstairs and left the house.

21

GRIPPING his driver made his hand hurt so he put the clubs away and drove down to the park. At the campground the little trailer was there but the chairs were folded and leaning against a tree. The old Ford pickup was gone. Pratt took two empty cans from his trunk and lined them up on the steps. It seemed a meager offering, almost patronizing, so he opened his cooler and cracked a fresh beer. Stared at his eyeball painting, in the backseat, where he'd left it after buying it at the coffee shop. How would he react if his wife shot herself in the eyeball? Or not necessarily *his* wife but *a* wife, in one of those near-perfect television marriages. Mike and Carol Brady. After things had calmed down, then what? He couldn't paint it but maybe he could write it, a poem or a short story. That was the essence of being an artist, he decided. That ability to turn pain into something else. Regular folks just cried or drank too much or took some therapy. Well, they planted flowers on graves and tended the graves. That was something. When he'd bought the painting the kid at the coffee shop had offered to wrap it in brown paper but then couldn't find the brown paper and some joker had come in with an order for a single cappuccino that sounded like a recited poem, a complicated poem with more than a single stanza, that called to mind having to memorize "To His Coy Mistress" in oral interpretation class, so Pratt had grabbed the painting and left, shoving it behind the mercury. The mercury the mercury. He was suddenly worried about his mercury. He walked up to the trailer and knocked on the door though he expected no answer; it was a precursor to peeking through one of the actual versus plywood windows, and he was shocked when a towel-curtain was pulled up and Candy's face appeared in the narrow pane. "Hey."

"Hey."

"What do you want?"

"Uh. That stuff I left with your father. Just making sure he still has it."

"You want to see it?"

"Kind of."

The curtain fell. He waited for her to open the door but she didn't. Then he saw the hasp, mounted on the outside, and the heavy combination lock.

She returned. "I can't lift them."

"That's okay. Don't try. What's with the lock?"

"That keeps the kidnappers out."

"You don't have a lock on the inside?'

"It's broke. Most everything in here is broke. That's why we're getting a house in Florida."

"Florida."

"Next door to Disney World. As soon as we get enough coin together."

"I brought you some cans."

"How many pounds?"

"I don't know. Two cans. Three in a second here."

She laughed. Pressed her face hard against the glass so her nose flattened.

"Where's your dad?"

"Out."

"Well," Pratt said, "will he be back soon?"

Her brow furrowed. "He'll be back when he's back."

"Okay."

• • •

Driving away, he thought briefly about, as they said in the old movies, "dropping a dime," calling Patricia's friend in Social Services and reporting the apparent neglect with a sock over his mouth. But then they'd find the mercury and he would be involved. And he did remember a time when Whitney was four, only four, and it was ten below zero outside and he needed cigarettes and left her alone rather than bundle her up and risk having her tiny fingers freeze and snap off like twigs. The store was only a quarter mile away after all. He took the phone off the hook in case Patricia called, set Whitney down by the television, promised to be home within a few minutes. Promised a treat if she would in turn promise to stay on the couch, not answer the door, not play with the stove. And he made it to the store, bought his cigarettes, bought her a bottle of Orange Crush, rushed home and there was a train on the tracks, not hurtling through town as usual, shaking the ground so that when he was in bed at night two blocks away Pratt could feel the bed trembling, not a graffiti-spotted ribbon heading west but a long train just sitting there, blocking his path home. To go around it would have meant going back to the highway and driving several miles, maybe more depending on how far the train had gotten before stopping. And so Pratt had waited. And waited, smoking and staring at the dead train's wheels, that oddly poetic three-bolt combination, waiting, waiting, afraid to look at the dashboard clock. And of course just as he was going to put the car in reverse and go around the train, a car pulled up behind him, effectively blocking him in. Not that much time, maybe ten minutes, passed before the train shuddered and began moving, and maybe another five minutes, tops, went by before he pulled into the driveway, half expecting to see the house on fire, or a patrol car. Whitney was fine, though she'd wet her pants because he had said not to move. As he cleaned her up in the bathroom, they agreed to keep the event a secret. Another secret. She'd left a small stain on the couch and although you couldn't really see it unless you tried, for several years it was like a blaze-orange marker reminding him of his neglect. All for a package of cigarettes. At least Cole had had the foresight to lock his daughter in so she could not be removed by molesters. Who was to say that Cole hadn't simply made a run for cigarettes, beer, a phone call?

. . .

"It's nothing," Pratt said, pulling back the ice pack to reveal his blackened hand. Not so much black now as gray, in the heel.

She touched his hand and he winced. It was a fake wince, more or less. His hand no longer hurt. But if she wanted to care for him he would wince for her. The ice bag was merely a prop. Actually, he had been stretched out on the sofa with the ice on his forehead to cool what felt like the screaming, smoking workings of a machine whose gears were running without lubrication. He had imagined being able to attach a hose to a steel Zerc on his skull and pump in some lithium grease to make everything run smoothly and silently.

On his chest was a library copy of Hemingway's stories he'd picked up on the way home. He'd suffered an odd event leaving the stacks. A crazy woman, a bag lady, had pointed at him as he walked by the study carrel she was using as a temporary spot for her belongings. Pointed at him and said, "You did it," loud enough to gather looks from staff and patrons alike. His face had reddened and he'd been unable to swallow and stumbled a bit so that he must have looked like a drunk, though a fairly well-dressed drunk with most of his teeth intact, thanks, he reminded himself, not to Bruce Carver but to good genes. Then he'd discovered he owed thirty dollars in overdue fines and there was some reluctance on the part of the clerk to take his check. They'd made him show his driver's license for the first time.

He had found the reference to absinthe in "Hills Like White Elephants" but couldn't remember what had sparked his curiosity in the first place. Patricia lifted the book and stared at it. "I thought you said Hemingway gave you a headache."

"I'm trying to get in the mood for Mexico. The sporting mood."

"Finally."

"What do you mean by that?"

"Well, you know. You've seemed kind of, what's the word?"

"Ambivalent?"

"Probably. Ambivalent about the whole thing. Like it's a chore, like shoveling snow. Except you don't even shovel snow."

What was there to say? Pratt closed his eyes.

She patted him on the forehead like he was a child. "Anyway, I'm glad you're getting into it."

"What do you want to do for dinner?"

"I'm just having some tuna."

"Tuna salad?"

"Nope. Straight tuna. Out of the can. You want some?"

Pratt shook his head. "I've got an errand to run."

"An errand?"

Her voice contained a thin wire twang of concern. He rather liked it. "Yes," he said. He tried to sound grave.

"What kind of an errand?"

"Just an errand." He opened his eyes and sat up. His head felt like a collapsing barn, timbers creaking and snapping, ancient square nails squeaking loose. It was hard to maintain an air of Bogart-like coolness with all of this going on.

She stared at him. "Well, I won't pry."

"Pry all you want."

"If I'm gone when you get back I'm out riding my bike."

"Alone?"

He immediately regretted the question. He had gone from Bogart to Woody Allen in less than a second.

"What do you mean, alone?"

"I don't know."

"Are you talking about Bruce? Is that what you're driving at?"

"No."

"Then who were you getting at?"

"Nobody. I just worry about you riding alone after dark."

"So I should call Bruce and see if he wants to ride with me, then?"

More beams twisted and fell. A cloud of dust rose. Escaping pigeons blotted out the sun. Pratt shrugged. "Do what you want."

She was up now, no longer beside him, no longer a nurse unless a nurse like Nurse Ratched in *One Flew over the Cuckoo's Nest*, her words coming out slowly, coolly. "Maybe I will, then. Maybe Bruce and I will go for a romantic sunset ride."

"I'm sorry," Pratt said.

"'I'm sorry' just isn't cutting it anymore, Dennis. Not when I hear it a hundred times a day."

"I know."

"I know you don't trust me and I think it's insane. Twenty years together and all of a sudden you don't trust me."

"I do trust you."

"Were you in my purse yesterday?"

"What?"

"My purse. I always put my calendar in with the spine down so my stamps don't fall out. And yesterday when I went to pull it out, it was in there with the spine up."

"I needed a stamp."

"We have stamps in the desk."

"I couldn't find them."

She rolled her eyes and shook her head at the same time, a feat that seemed like an accomplishment. "Forget it. But don't say you trust me."

"I really do."

But she was already walking off, giving him the palm of her hand.

22

PRATT wasn't much in the mood for aimless driving so he went to the Holloway Building. What he wanted was the title of the painting. There was nothing on the reverse of the canvas. He did not want to present his wife with a painting on their twentieth anniversary and have absolutely nothing to say about it, which might lead her to believe that he'd picked it up at the Dakota Boys' Ranch thrift store, which for him, he knew, would not be totally out of character. He wanted to make it clear that it was actual art, worth the seventy-five dollars he'd paid for it, that it was a gift more unique, more valuable, than the leather jacket he'd given her for their tenth and which was now too big for her. He wanted her to understand the painting and needed to understand it himself first.

It was a crapshoot of course whether Martha would even be there. But he parked in the same spot as last time and looked up at the window. He couldn't tell if there were any lights on. He wondered again why the Ghost Man had concocted such a complex lie, but then again, they said the best lies were filled with details. Lately Patricia had been awfully specific about her whereabouts, now that he thought of it. *I went to Kohl's to look for sandals for Mexico and then I blah blah blah.* He couldn't tell if she was trying to assuage his fears or cover her tracks. His head started to hurt again. He lighted a cigarette and stared through the windshield at the steady flow of cars oozing through downtown Fargo. Mostly just passing through on their way to Minnesota and home. Downtown had all but been declared officially dead after the arrival of West Acres Mall and the subsequent bloom field of chain restaurants, strip malls, and outlet stores. What was left: a collection of ill-managed knickknack shops and college

bars, deep doorways for homeless Indians to lurk in, the odd pawn-
shop and overcrowded book swamp. The whole thing made Pratt feel
suddenly inconsolable. He looked up toward the window again. He
wasn't sure but he thought the window was open a crack now. He
squinted but squinting made his head hurt. He wondered if he
needed a stronger prescription for his glasses. Maybe. Maybe he was
like certain cars that held together well for years and then began to
disintegrate all at once. There was definitely more hair in the bathtub
lately after he finished showering. Lately Pratt had been checking out
men around his age to see who was losing the hair-loss race. As far as
he could tell, he was in the middle of the pack, not in the pole position but not dragging a bumper either. He wasn't at the point of mea-
suring his thin spot but he was aware of it, spreading. He was behind
Carver in that particular contest. He lighted another cigarette. He regretted the comment to Patricia about riding alone. He regretted it
but at the time he'd felt no control over the words rising from his gut.
He wondered if he was channeling someone, getting taken over now
and then by some mischievous spirit. Who? It wouldn't be anyone interesting, nobody famous, not Steve McQueen or Jim Morrison,
Hemingway or Faulkner, but some moron whirling about looking for
open soul doorways the way meth fiends roamed the mall parking lot
searching for unlocked cars in which they might find a package of
cigarettes, a few CDs to pawn, the occasional gold mine of a purse. If
he owned a hole how would he close it, though? That was the question. A couple days earlier Patricia had left to pick up some yogurt
and Pratt had found himself watching the clock from his easy chair,
okay, ten minutes and now she's pulling into the parking lot, okay, fifteen and she has the yogurt, twenty and she's at the checkout, give
her an extra five for other stuff she decides to pick up, twenty-five and
she's on the way home, thirty-five where is she? Forty minutes and
Pratt was standing by the window, forty-five and his hands were shaking as he imagined a quick assignation being performed in the car in
a park, images of Kleenex and quick sharp moans permeating his

mind, fifty minutes and he was sobbing, an hour and he was pouring vodka into a tall cup and wondering how she'd feel upon walking into the house if he was dangling from a rope or more likely a red bungee cord since they didn't have any rope. Then she'd cheerfully walked in and he'd been upon her like a raging tiger, wanting to know where the hell she'd been before she had a chance to pull out the new sandals she'd bought for him at Target after leaving the supermarket. Tears and apologies, hours of her deadly silent treatment during which he realized how impossibly foolish he'd been, how ridiculous it was to think that in the space of a half hour she'd have been able to pull off an affair, even a quickie. But later, after she'd gone to bed, he'd dug through her purse for the sandal receipt when it had occurred to him that she might have had them in the trunk as cover for just such an occasion. And of course the time on the receipt offered her an airtight alibi. If there was someone, some poltergeist or evil spirit inhabiting him occasionally, it was getting pretty old. He looked up at Martha's window again. If she was up there she'd have seen him and if she wanted company, she'd wave. Or something. He certainly didn't want to intrude. He did not want to be not wanted. He started the car and drove home. He took the long way.

• • •

Guilt finally drove Pratt to call his brother back. Steven was gone, his wife said, her voice a bit cold. Terri had never forgiven Pratt for getting drunk at their rehearsal dinner and making a crude joke about priests while at the altar, not just in earshot of Father George but rather directed at Father George.

"When will he be back?"

"He went to Idaho? To see your dad? In the intensive care unit?"

"He was going to wait for me."

"Dennis, that was two days ago."

"Are you sure?"

• • •

Patricia came home while he was packing. He had not taken a trip on his own in a while and the task seemed insurmountable. In his suitcase were four polo shirts and a thick wad of underwear. That was as far as he'd gotten.

His wife sighed and took over. He sat on the edge of the bed and watched her folding his jeans, counting socks. She took the polo shirts out and refolded them, added a sweatshirt, slipped in dress slacks and a dress shirt and his brown loafers. Just in case, she said. "How long do you think you'll be gone?"

"I don't know. Why?"

"Why?"

"Why do you ask?"

"Dennis, you're *packing*. It helps to know how long a trip is going to last."

"Sorry. I'm just a little off-kilter over this."

"I know."

"Will you come with me?"

"You know I can't."

"Why not?"

"I can't get the time off. Not if we're taking a week off for Mexico."

"Fuck Mexico."

"I'm just being realistic."

"This is my father we're talking about. I only have one father."

"Stacy is on vacation and Simmons has surgery in two days and we've got closings up the yin-yang this week. You know that fall is our busy time. And the economy, you know. The better the housing market is, the busier I am. You know that."

"I know. I just wish you'd be there with me."

She reached up and placed her palm against his cheek. He tried to cry but nothing came forth. He wanted her hand to become wet with his tears, for his tears to be an elixir, to change her heart, like holy water thrown on a vampire. But there was a wall between his wishes and his tear ducts and she pulled her hand away dry.

• • •

On the road. I-94 West. Eight P.M. Pratt sipped foul coffee from a truck stop in Jamestown and smoked one cigarette after another, listening to talk radio. He'd thought he would have no trouble staying awake but by the time he was leaving Bismarck, four hours from home, eighteen to go, his eyes were heavy and he was resorting to chewing his lip in between drags to stay awake. Just across the Missouri River in Mandan he stopped for more coffee, splashed cold water on his face in the bathroom. He looked like a meth addict, sunken cheeks, wild eyes, hair forced up in a near Mohawk, rather like the kid behind the counter. He bought a prepaid calling card and dialed home but Patricia didn't answer. He got the machine and hung up. He wanted to remind her to call Jenson early in the morning and let him know the scoop. That was his story anyway. He tried again. And again. She was a sound sleeper but how could anybody sleep through a barrage of four-ring bursts? Maybe he'd dialed wrong. He tried again. He did this fifteen times. Fifteen times four rings was sixty rings. Sixty rings when the full REM sleep hadn't yet kicked in. He pocketed the card and washed his windows, got back onto the interstate, brought the car up to seventy-five, set the cruise, worried about hitting deer, slowed to sixty-five. Pretty soon he was in that radio no-man's-land between Bismarck and Billings with nothing to listen to but preachers. They were doing a call-in show and most of the callers seemed to be women fretting over husbands who were losing interest in them now that they'd "borned children." The host of the program had a voice like lightweight motor oil and urged the women to try harder to do *something* but Pratt's mind slipped away before he heard the solution. He had the highway to himself, not unusual in the Northern Plains. He met only an occasional fellow traveler. Dimmed the headlights. He was no longer sleepy. His mind was back east. Patricia had kissed him good-bye but had there been something forced and had she glanced at the clock as they embraced in the living room? He was a good hour from the nearest telephone now and sped up. She had seemed to be undergoing the beginnings of her nightly routine when he left; she'd changed from her work clothes into shorts and a t-shirt, put on her fuzzy slippers. Of course she could have run out, could have gotten a craving for popcorn, maybe she'd been watching a movie and found the cupboard devoid of microwave popcorn and slipped out to get some as she was unable to watch a movie without popcorn. He threw his cigarette butt out the window and watched the comet of red ashes spray across the road in his rearview mirror. Lighted another one. He was in Teddy Roosevelt country now, the badlands. Getting closer to Montana. If the next mile marker is *even* she's cheating on me, he thought, and it *was* even, eighteen, but he decided he might have unconsciously seen the previous marker and his mind was fucking with him again. His mind. Things fall apart. The center cannot hold. He looked at the glowing numbers on the clock. Two-fifteen. He closed his eyes. If it's two-sixteen when I open my eyes everything is okay. He kept his eyes closed until he imagined the car crossing the median and rolling. Two-sixteen. At Glendive he fueled the car and bought coffee. Paced around the parking lot under the big Montana sky. He went to the phone booth but the receiver was missing from the steel cord, which swayed in the breeze like a snakeskin hooked to a branch. He imagined an angry cowboy husband ripping it away after getting sordid news from home. The notion saddened him. He got into the car. Closed his eyes. Opened them abruptly. She'd mentioned that Simmons, her boss, was having surgery in two days. But two days was Sunday. Since when were surgeries scheduled on Sundays? When he lighted a cigarette his hand was trembling. He pulled away but instead of getting back onto the interstate he drove down a dark narrow road. He had to urinate now, again, and wasn't about to go back inside the store and have to ask again for the restroom key attached to part of a broken broomstick. He pulled off and took a leak over sagebrush along the shoulder. Patricia had not suggested he fly even though they could afford it.

"Stay as long as you need to," she'd said. He zipped up and stared hard in the direction of Minnesota as if he might see something telling. He turned and looked to the west. Steven was out there now, and his sister, Marcia, and her son, a premed student. Things were well in hand. He wasn't sure what awaited him. Hostility, that was for sure. Steven was moody in general and Marcia was an emotional wreck. She had described having to clean their father when he'd fallen in the bathroom. It was the single worst twenty minutes of her life, she'd told them in one of her long, self-pitying (justifiably, Pratt and Patricia had agreed) e-mails. Not something a child ever dreamed of having to do. There wasn't any dementia to deal with but it struck Pratt that it might be worse having to butt-wipe a *lucid* adult than a baby-like adult. Both Marcia and Steven would jump him for his neglect the moment he walked through the door. He didn't need that. To be frank, he decided, climbing back into the car, there really wasn't much point in going. If Dad was dead by the time he got there, well, he'd be as useless as a screen door on a submarine. Pratt's father had always been adamant about wanting no service other than to have his ashes dumped in the Tetons. And if he wasn't dead, it would probably be like last time. Dad would come home from the hospital and sit in his chair and watch the American Movie Classics channel while the rest of them sat around the dining room table bickering and drinking Jim Beam under a haze of cigarette smoke. No thanks. Pratt turned around, drove past the gas station, up to the exit, past the westbound and onto the eastbound. He calculated, his mind turning numbers like the reels of a slot machine. If he hauled ass he'd be home before nine. Her car would either be in the driveway or it wouldn't be. If it was and she was home, well. But if it wasn't? He looked down at the speedometer and realized he was going ninety-five miles an hour. He lowered the speed to ninety and set the cruise. If the car wasn't there at least he'd know for sure. He'd know for sure. His heart was pounding. He pictured her at this very moment, her tanned back straight as a fencepost as she rode somebody else, saw her tempo pick up and her eyes close and her right hand, always her right hand, move up to her right breast and caress it as she bounced away and he was shocked to be getting a hard-on thinking about it. He wanted a drink. She could have come with him and now she'd be sleeping against the window, her mouth slightly open, her pillow damp from drool, and they'd be cooking through Montana. Steven's wife couldn't go because they had three boys in elementary school but Pratt also couldn't imagine Terri ever cheating on Steven. Ten years of marriage and they were like two college students holding hands in poli-sci. The last time Pratt had gone down to Lincoln he'd been embarrassed to see Steven rubbing Terri's feet with lotion while the three of them watched the evening news. He had actually sung to her while doing this, "Unchained Melody," or something like that. "Jesus," Pratt said now, lighting yet another Marlboro. He saw Patricia's slim ankles wildly kicking the air while Carver pumped away at her like he was riding a bicycle uphill. He wished to God he had lung cancer and could just die. A moment later he felt a pain in his chest and worried that he had lung cancer and was going to die. He sped up again to ninety-five and set the cruise. The white lines blurred. He crossed back into North Dakota. Before leaving home, during his usual evidence hunt, he'd both found a new brassiere and noted that she had three douches remaining in the Massengill box in the bathroom cabinet. He'd also found a tube of an antifungal cream and was horrified to think she'd contracted some sort of VD but after calming down he'd remembered that it was his cream, prescribed when he'd gotten a sort of crust in the corners of his mouth and she'd insisted he go in to have it checked out. "It's just the way your mouth is formed," the doctor at the walk-in clinic had told him, "you have a kind of frown that makes creases. Nasty things like to grow in creases." Patricia had thought it hilarious that his lack of smiling, which she always ribbed him about, had led to a rash. Later he'd worried that it wasn't what the doctor—he was awfully young—had thought and was in fact something she'd passed to him. Some research had led him to think it might be candida but a call to Dial-a-Nurse had ruled that out. He'd tried to smile more to help the healing but it had felt as unnatural as writing with his left hand. And why had she been so adamant about him going to the doctor anyway? It was possible she'd worried that it was something that she might give to someone else. He passed Dickinson. Came to Mandan. Crossed the river. Rolled up and down smooth hills and saw the faintest of light forming in the east. Fueled in Jamestown and wanted to scream at the pump, which seemed to be dispensing molasses and not midgrade unleaded. Thought about calling her but thought it better to surprise her. Someone could be at the house for all he knew and they'd have plenty of time to sanitize the scene. He bought another coffee and two packs of cigarettes and finished everything by the time he was in the Fargo metro area. Having to slow down to sixty-five after cruising over ninety was like going backward. It was eight-fifty when he pulled into the driveway. Her car was there. He felt the hood but it was cool. Unlocked the door and went inside. Went straight to the bathroom and looked in the Massengill box. Two left, not three. He got the shakes again. Smoked a cigarette in the kitchen and gulped Karkov from the bottle. Instead of calming him he felt a great knot tightening in his stomach and barely made it back into the bathroom before everything came up. He was not a quiet puker and Patricia came to the doorway, face pale, in her t-shirt and sweats. "You scared me half to death. What the heck are you doing here?"

He rested his forehead on the padded toilet seat. Started to try to say something but felt more vomit coming for which he was, above all else, thankful.

23

"DO YOU want some advice?" Carver said.

Pratt had just driven the ball from the fourth; it rolled five feet and stopped. He was beyond embarrassment after watching Carver's drive arc through the air and plug itself neatly to the green, only a few feet from the hole.

"Sure."

"Slow down."

"Slow what down?"

"Everything. And don't try so fucking hard."

Pratt stared at Carver but no elaboration followed. In fact, Carver was already heading for the cart, leaving Pratt to wonder: Was this a philosophical comment? Some kind of warning about his marriage? Did it mean back off a bit from Patricia and allow her some "space"? He wondered what they talked about and how often they talked. Were there daily updates? Carver's gravelly voice reassuring Patricia? This time it had been Pratt's idea to play golf with Carver. After their last blowout he had insisted to Patricia that he had no problem with Carver. "Hey, I like the guy," he'd said.

"No you don't. You don't like him."

"I do. He's a good guy. I can see why you'd want to be his pal."

"I wish I could believe you but I know the next time Bruce comes up you'll be freaking out again."

And so Pratt had called the dental office. Carver had not seemed surprised to hear from him, as if he'd been warned. Who knew anymore?

Pratt walked up to his ball and with his five iron gave it a thrashing that sent it another ten or fifteen feet. He marched up to it, shaking his head. Tried again. Well, he slowed down. Brought his backswing up in slow motion, slowed down his swing, watched the club head connect with the ball and on follow-through saw it beeline for the flag. The trajectory was too flat and the ball was going too fast. But it was going for the flag. It landed somewhere beyond the green but not *that* far beyond the green

In the cart, Carver slapped Pratt's knee. "See?"

•   •   •

Three times on Sunday he picked up the telephone to call Whitney and tell her his suspicions. He needed an ally but felt an awful lot like Harrison Ford in *The Fugitive*, alone and pursued, unable to trust anyone. If his father were in better shape he could talk to him about it. No he couldn't. They'd never talked about such things.

But each time he picked up the phone and began to dial, his chest tightened. Whitney would not, he thought, lie to him if asked a direct question. But he didn't even know what to ask. He doubted if Patricia would confide something as seamy as an affair to her daughter. But then again, she might need to confide in somebody. He poured a glass of vodka and sat out on the deck with the cordless. He didn't really expect her to be home anyway. But she was.

He made pleasantries, spoke of a forthcoming check. Then: "You once said Dr. Carver was quote 'creepy' unquote."

"So?"

"What did you mean by that?"

"I didn't mean anything except he's weird."

"Weird how?"

"Daddy, you seem to be getting kind of obsessed with Dr. Carver."

"You're my baby girl. I'm just looking out for you."

He heard mumbling. Then a giggle. Giggles.

"What?"

"Carrie says you need to get laid so you won't be so uptight."

"It's not up to me."

"What?"

"Nothing."

"You know, Daddy, I'm not blind and deaf."

"Meaning?"

"I don't know what's going on between you two but it sounds like you have some issues."

His heart started pounding. This was it. She was going to spill the beans. He tried to sound calm. Like the kind of man who could handle anything, a bespotted lung X-ray, a pink slip. "What kind of issues are you talking about?"

"Oh, let's see. Have you ever heard of a little thing called, uh, *communication?*"

"Communication?"

"Maybe instead of talking to me, you should be talking to her."

"About what?"

"About anything. You call me up and all you want to talk about is Mom going biking with Dr. Carver or Dr. Carver being weird. You didn't ask me how I did on my trigonometry test I was freaking out about."

"I didn't know about it."

"I rest my case."

24

THERE were only a few hundred Olsons in the Fargo-Moorhead phone book and five Marthas as well as three Olsons appearing with only the initial M. Pratt wrote down the addresses on a page from a Wellbutrin notepad that Jenson had scrounged from somewhere. Jenson himself was dozing in his chair, face down on a legal pad. He was a diabetic and prone to occasional narcolepsy. It was a slow day anyway. For a while they'd occupied themselves with straightening up the shop before surrendering to a couple hours of sloth in the office, watching the junkyard next door, where cars were being crushed in a portable machine trucked in from Canada. But even this diversion had grown old and Jenson had fagged out on Pratt, leaving him to browse the Merck index for untraceable ways to kill Bruce Carver should it ever come to that. When five o'clock finally rolled around, Pratt shook Jenson's shoulder. "I'm out of here," he said.

"Uhm-huh."

•   •   •

The first address was a north-side house, one of the thousands thrown up after World War II and now populated by elderly ladies and bikers. It didn't seem her style but he parked on the street and went to the door. A Rottweiler on the front porch turned Pratt around and he headed for the next address, still on the north end but closer to the river. He turned a corner and found himself entering a portal of lush elms and thick lawns. This is it, he decided, and at that moment he saw her, on her knees, stabbing at a flower bed with a hand trowel. She wore a loose summer dress and straw hat and could have been an old lady but for the way her rear end pressed against the fabric hard enough for Pratt to see that she wore no undies. It was the kind of thing that would normally bring him to arousal but now he just found it a fact, the way his chip shot from the rough the day before with Carver, forty feet and landing on the edge—*the edge*—of the hole had been a mere fact, the way Jenson's discovery of a dead cat preserved in an ancient paint can had been a mere fact, the way his father's worsening condition was a mere fact. His brother and sister were not speaking to him and this too was a mere fact. The only thing that seemed to move him lately was concern over his marriage, or more specifically, Patricia's possible infidelity if not with Carver then with someone, a someone probably younger and in better shape than Pratt, capable of pounding away for hours without getting winded from cigarettes or cramping in the legs or simply being too fatigued to get it up in the first place. He had thought of trying Viagra but heard on a radio show that once you used it, you needed to use it forever.

He pulled into her driveway and parked behind a Suburban with a heavy-duty trailer hitch jutting from under the bumper. Martha turned, shielded her eyes even though they were already shielded by the hat, recognized him, waved. He grabbed the painting and climbed out. She stood and wiped her hands together as if to clean them. "Dennis, correct?"

"Correct. Dennis Pratt."

"Well." Her eyes went to the painting under his arm. In broad daylight she looked even paler than before, as if light itself could travel through tissue, bone, emerge unshadowed, even unrefracted.

Pratt held up the painting. "What can you tell me about this?"

She reached out, grabbed his shoulders, turned him. The result of this clumsy minuet was that he was the one with sun in his eyes. She cocked her head this way and that. "Lots of eyes," she said.

"Fourteen," he said to show he was a close observer.

"Fourteen eyes. Yes."

"I think it's a pretty powerful piece. Er, painting."

"It is. You're right. Actually it's kind of disturbing."

"Yes."

"Actually very disturbing."

Pratt nodded. "But in a good way, I think."

"Do you mean that?"

"I think so."

"You think so."

"Yes?"

She laughed. "Dennis Pratt, would you care for a drink?"

"I think I would."

•   •   •

He had a hole in his sock, right by the toe, and tried to hide it by tucking his left foot under his right but the result made him look a bit fruity or worse, like a small boy in urgent need of a restroom. So he gave up and if she noticed the hole, she said nothing. She asked what he wanted and he said, "Anything," and she laughed again and suggested a gin and tonic, and he agreed that a gin and tonic sounded pretty good. It was a hot day. He closed his eyes and listened to her chopping a lime and for some reason this sound became very important, the emphasized words of a professor the day before an exam. She brought his drink to him in a heavy bar-grade rocks glass with a curl of lime hanging in the water like a fish hook. He gulped at it but slowed down when he saw how judiciously she was sipping, on her divan, legs crossed elegantly. The painting was propped against an end table and her gaze remained on it. It was as if she was seeing it for the first time and Pratt wondered if artists forgot paintings when they were finished, if whatever fire compelled them to create a given piece burned out with the last brushstroke.

"I didn't know you painted," she said.

"I don't."

She gave him a blank stare.

He gave her one in return.

Realization arrived with the power of a joint orgasm. They both laughed. Pratt lifted the painting and held it across his lap like a tray and studied the signature, a blob of green paint. He'd thought it looked like *Olson* but now he wasn't so sure. Martha came over and joined him on the sofa and stared at the name. "Omega?"

"Oswald."

"Orion?"

"Oreo."

"Oreo?"

"Like the cookie."

"Well," she said, running a long finger over the knot of paint. "I sign my work Holloway."

"Ah."

"You thought—"

"The eyes."

"My husband."

"The image stuck in my mind."

"I've never painted eyes."

"Never?"

"Look around."

He did. There was a painting on the wall just off the alcove. A figure was hunched over a table, arms hanging loosely, reading a magazine. The colors were dark. Shadows prevailed. The painting was reminiscent of something by one of the Italian masters but Pratt couldn't recall which one. He had taken an art history survey class in college but could only recall a visual cacophony of images played upon a white screen in a classroom, and the clicking, chunking sound of the slide projector behind him. Cézanne? No. He remembered. "Caravaggio," he said.

Her eyes brightened. "You know art?"

He wanted to lie and say yes, to pull from his memory whatever remained, but the steam for that kind of trick just wasn't there. "Not really."

"Well, Caravaggio is an influence. But we're all just products of our influences and I have many influences."

"I dig," Pratt said. He stared at her painting. There was something more disturbing and mournful about it, prosaic as it seemed on the surface, than the wild scattering of gloppy eyes on his lap. He tapped the canvas. "I bought this for my wife, for our anniversary."

"What anniversary?"

"Twenty."

"Twenty. That's a long time."

"It doesn't feel that long."

"It doesn't? I'd think it would."

"Well. Sometimes it does."

"Dennis Pratt, you crack me up."

"Why?"

"You talk like a politician but without the ambition."

He looked down at the painting, the eyeballs manically taking in the ceiling, his face, hers. They were unnerving so he stared at her bare knee just inches from his. He wondered if she knew her dress had ridden up midthigh. He looked over at the painting on the wall again. He didn't know much about art but he knew enough to know that it was well done. Well executed. She was no slouch. He realized that it was likely a bit insulting to have thought she'd painted something so amateurish.

"How much did you pay for it?"

"This? Seventy-five."

"Hundred?"

"Dollars."

She stood and walked over to the easy chair but she was only getting her drink. She came back and joined Pratt on the sofa. Again the bare knee. Her knee was pale but smooth. "Does your wife collect art?"

"She collects squirrels."

"Squirrels?"

"Squirrels. You know how it goes. Someone gave her a ceramic squirrel a few years ago, well maybe fifteen years ago, and she hung it up, and someone saw it and thought she was into squirrels, and the rest is history. We've got a goddamn squirrel clock with acorns for hands. That kind of thing. Squirrel wallpaper in the bathroom, believe it or not."

"Oh."

"She doesn't even *like* squirrels. We had one in the garage last year. It wouldn't leave so she gassed it."

"Gassed it?"

"Started the car and let it run for an hour. After the exhaust cleared she found it behind the woodpile and threw it in the garbage can like it was a gum wrapper. I mean, it wasn't hurting anyone, she just didn't want him there so she gassed the poor little bastard."

Martha was staring at him. He wondered if he sounded insane, if she was reconsidering allowing him into her house. But she patted his leg. "It's okay."

"What?"

"You're crying."

"What?"

She went out of focus. "I better be leaving," he said. He stood and his head felt like smoke. The painting flipped down from his lap and it was like being an open human jackknife and trying to walk. The painting cracked and Pratt fell over. His chin skipped along the white carpet. He tried to get up but he didn't have the strength. He saw a dust bunny clinging to the leg of the easy chair and found this reassuring for some reason. He heard Martha picking up a telephone. "Please," she was saying. Then something unintelligible. Then: "You'd better get over here right away."

25

THE DOCTOR didn't carry the black leather bag of yore, but he did have a sort of clear plastic tackle box in his hand. He smelled vaguely of horse manure and beat Pratt's speculation by explaining that he'd been out at "the stables" feeding Beowulf, whoever that was, when Martha had phoned his cell. Pratt had managed to get to the sofa and stretch out after she had assured him it wasn't the police she'd called, nor his wife. She'd fixed him a tall vanilla protein-powder shake in soy milk after he admitted he could not remember when he'd last eaten. After that she'd ignored his questions and busied herself picking up pieces of the splintered frame from the eyeball painting.

"How is Beowulf?" she asked Rayburn, who was pulling off his ostrich cowboy boots in the alcove. He was a big man and there was some huffing and puffing involved.

"I don't know. He misses you. The feel of your light ass, I think. When I ride him he gets fairly resistant. Well, downright recalcitrant. I'd sell him but I like hanging out at the stables."

"You like the accouterments."

"The tack, the aromas. The people. Horse people are the greatest. I could have him stuffed, I guess, and just go out there and brush him."

"Gary, you're terrible."

Pratt watched and listened like a child. Actually, he felt like a child under the afghan she had tucked in around him, sipping his drink through a bent straw. He knew this much: he did not want to leave and felt a bit annoyed at the arrival of the man Martha had introduced as Dr. Rayburn, who was interfering with the aromatherapy Martha had begun by lighting a coffee-scented candle, and the music therapy that consisted of Spanish guitar music played on a Bose system. In fact, Pratt thought that if he were going to die, this was as nice a place as any, with heavy Southwest-style beams dividing the ceiling, art on the walls, a pretty lady in a sundress doting over him.

Now Rayburn came in and stood over Pratt and stared at him. "Do you feel like killing yourself?"

Pratt paused.

"I have to ask."

"Well."

"If you answer a certain way I'm obligated to have you taken in for an evaluation."

"No."

"No what?"

"I wouldn't kill myself."

"Why not? Life sucks, doesn't it?"

"Not always."

"Lately?"

"I've got some issues, sure."

"Issues?"

"Sure."

Rayburn sank into the recliner. "I hate that word. *Issues.* When did 'problem' become 'issue'?"

Martha put her hands on her hips. "Probably around the time a nervous breakdown became . . . what did it become?"

"Psychotic break."

"No, Gary, it moved on from that too." She closed her eyes. "I heard a term on *Oprah* but I can't remember it now."

Rayburn held up his hand. "Top this. A kid came in, one of these pierced children with needles in his eyebrows, tattoos, the whole works. And when I asked him why he was there, he said, get this, 'I have issue problems.'"

Martha glanced at Pratt; he tried to look pitiful, replaying a moment thirty years earlier when he'd been afraid of a track meet at school and feigned illness. His mother had bought it and Martha seemed to as well; she came and sat on the edge of the cushion and pressed her palm against his forehead.

"'Issue problems,'" Rayburn repeated. "I mean, come on." He giggled. "Are you taking anything now? Drugs, prescription or otherwise?"

"Nope."

"Supplements?"

"Saw palmetto."

"For?"

"So I don't have to get up to pee in the middle of the night."

"Really."

"It works."

"Personally I like getting up three times a night. Makes me feel like I'm getting my money's worth out of my body. Are you a drinker?"

Pratt looked at Martha. For some reason he did not want to lower himself in her eyes any more than he already had. "Not often."

"What's not often?"

"I have a drink now and then."

"Every day?"

"Probably."

"Do you get drunk?"

"I haven't been drunk in years." Pratt closed his eyes. "Maybe since college. It's been a while."

"I can't remember what it feels like to be drunk," Martha said. "Tipsy maybe, but not shitfaced."

Rayburn didn't answer. He gazed at Pratt for so long that Pratt began to blush. "What are you preoccupied with?"

"Adultery."

"Yours?" He glanced at Martha. She glared back.

"My wife, Patricia."

"She's cheating on you."

"I hope not."

"You think she is."

"I doubt if she is."

"But you think about it."

"Yes."

"How frequently?"

"All the time."

"How many hours a day would you say?"

"Three or four. Six."

"Ah."

"You see?" Martha said. "Did I call it?"

"You called it."

"Called what?"

Rayburn unsnapped his tackle box. The plastic clasps sounded like gunshots. "You," he said, lifting a pill bottle and holding it up to the light, "have obsessive-compulsive disorder."

"OCD? I don't go around straightening towels and whatnot."

Rayburn shook his head. "Yours is primarily in the form of rumination."

"Rumination?"

"Obsessive thoughts. *Intrusive* thoughts. But I'll bet you've started some compulsive rituals too, without being aware of it. Quickly, what's the first thing you do when you get home?"

"Look in the garbage." He saw himself spreading the contents of the kitchen can on the counter like a fed looking for evidence of subversion or meth manufacturing. He'd recently spent an hour piecing together a widely scattered and variously stained greasy note that had turned out to be a phone number; heart pounding, head spinning, he'd gone to the computer and performed a reverse lookup only to discover that it was the phone number of Papa John's, a number Pratt himself had given his wife after he and Jenson had gotten a craving on a busy day and needed someone to pick up a large pepperoni for them.

"Ah. You see? What next?"

"I, well." He looked at Martha; she was nodding very slowly. "I count her panties." He glanced at Martha but instead of disgust her expression was exactly the same, the nodding continuing like his grandmother's plastic feeding hummingbird which had fascinated him so much as a toddler.

"You count her panties."

"Yes."

"How does that work?"

"How does it work?"

"Yeah."

"What do you mean?"

"Do you include the pair she's wearing?"

"Yes, then I add everything in the drawer to what's in the laundry room."

"You're looking for variation."

"A plus or minus, yes."

"Do you ever find a variation?"

"Not yet."

"Well, that's OCD. Plus you suffer from generalized anxiety disorder."

"Anxiety."

"And definitely some depression in the mix."

"Jesus. All that?"

Rayburn reached into his jeans pocket. Pratt heard change jingling. The doctor switched to the other side. Pulled out a pocket watch on a long fob.

"Are you going to hypnotize me?"

Rayburn laughed. "Believe me, I wish it was that easy."

"No you don't," Martha said. "You wouldn't be able to afford your hobbies."

"Heh," Rayburn said. He handed the watch to Pratt. "Look at the fob. My grandfather made that from strips of buckskin cut from my father's first deer."

Pratt rolled the fob between his fingers. The leather was black from age and use. "Very nice," Pratt said, though it wasn't, not in the aesthetic sense.

"Buckskin itself isn't very strong. That's why you can easily kill a deer with a .22 rifle. It isn't as tough as, say, rawhide or elk hide."

"Okay."

"But when it's braided, like this fob, it becomes very strong."

Pratt gave the braid a tug. "Strong."

"That fob is in your brain."

"My brain."

"These illnesses work in concert. It's called comorbidity. You should have come to see me twenty years ago before they braided themselves so tightly."

"It didn't occur to me."

"Of course not." He plucked the watch from Pratt and twisted the fob. "Depression. Anxiety. Obsessive-compulsive disorder."

"Wow."

"Score one for the artist," Martha said. She made a chalk mark on an imaginary blackboard.

Rayburn nodded. "Martha knows her mental illnesses."

She patted Pratt's thigh. "Gary will fix you right up."

26

JENSON said Pratt seemed to be moving slower and worried that he'd exposed himself to unknown fumes. He typed up a memo to Pratt insisting he wear his respirator or face "disciplinary action." Whitney thought he had hung up on her because one of his pauses oozed into silence. "Dad are you there? Dad?" His antidepressants were restructuring his brain somehow and according to Rayburn it would take some time before he saw improvement but the Klonopin given him for anxiety acted immediately and with a passion, like professional-grade drain cleaner. On Highway 10 in a driving rain he passed three wide-load tractor-trailers without giving it a second thought when normally he would trail a convoy like that until Patricia goaded him into finally hitting the gas and then his heart would pound and he'd floor it, hit ninety just to get it over with. This time he kept the cruise control on and spent no less than three minutes driving alongside the trucks, looking over at the freshly painted green combines squatting on flatbeds. He wondered what kind of farmer could afford a brand-new combine when farmers were all destitute according to John Mellencamp or Cougar and Willie Nelson. It was a little-known fact that in the Red River Valley between Wahpeton and the Canadian border, a relatively narrow strip of earth, you could find more millionaires per capita than anywhere else on the planet because of all the sugar-beet farmers with their subsidies begun in World War II and kept intact with strong lobbying. The fact that he could have these thoughts while hugging the left shoulder was remarkable.

He was driving in the driving rain to pick up his mercury from Cole. He was going to take the mercury and hand it over to Jenson and come clean about the whole situation and face the music. It was Pratt's intention to cleanse his mind of any negative ballast and the mercury had been nagging at him. He had told Rayburn about it at his follow-up session at Rayburn's tidy office on the sixth floor of MeritCare. Pratt had been a little disappointed by Rayburn's office, having seen shrink's quarters only in movies. He had expected exotic art and warm tones, Persian rugs, maybe the collected Jung on a mahogany shelf along with some African objets d'art. There wasn't even a couch in the office, just a desk and computer and an industrial wooden-armed waiting-room chair. Pratt had armed himself with a page of notes about his feelings but Rayburn had never given him a chance to discuss it. The doctor was dressed this time in a shaggy sweater vest over a plain shirt, wearing loafers instead of boots. The appointment had consisted primarily of Pratt looking at Rayburn's motorcycle magazines while Rayburn roamed the hallways hunting down free samples of Lexapro.

He pulled up at Cole's campsite. The lawn chairs were soaked, the fire pit a pond of gray water on which empty cigarette packages and chicken bones circled in a kind of lazy regatta. The trailer was there, padlocked again, and the truck was again gone. Pratt climbed from the car and picked his way over the muddy ground to the door. Knocked. Knocked harder. Knocked like the police. Nothing. He walked around to the other side of the trailer and cupped his hands around a curtainless porthole. Inside he could make out a vague mess of bedding and duct-taped cardboard boxes, a pyramid of beer cans. A one-eyed teddy bear stared back at him from the floor. He didn't see his mercury and he didn't see Candy. He lighted a cigarette and paced the campsite, looking around. He soon wished he hadn't. Under the trailer his pickle jars were lined up like army deserters about to be shot. Pratt crouched and examined them. The beaver skin was in one of the jars, pressing against the sides, floating in a murky brine. The other two jars held gopher feet, no doubt trapped by Cole for the fifty-cent government bounty. The fourth and fifth jars contained golf balls. Pratt peered deeper underneath but saw no sign of the silver liquid amid what looked like a garbage dump.

He retreated.

• • •

There was still the issue of the impending anniversary. During one of his paranoid evidence hunts, rummaging through Patricia's brassiere drawer, he'd found a receipt from Scheel's Sports in Moorhead for a five-hundred-dollar watch though no evidence of the watch itself. Paid for on one of their many credit cards. Patricia was deeply involved in a scheme, legal but somewhat shady, of continually getting zero-interest credit cards, transferring balances, canceling cards, ordering new ones. Occasionally she'd demand that he turn over a card and snap a new one down for him to sign. When push came to shove he had no idea how much money they had or didn't have. Pratt didn't spend much money; he had no "hobbies and interests" as they'd say. The golf he could take or leave though he was getting more into it. His only real hobby was smoking cigarettes, not a cheap hobby but nothing compared to, say, fly fishing, or amateur auto racing like his neighbor, who seemed to take delight in running the engine of his sprint car at all hours of the night, an engine louder than the trains going by two blocks away that rumbled Pratt's wooden floors and made the Princess House crystal in the china hutch sing. Patricia was always threatening to complain and so far Pratt had been successful in stopping her; he didn't want to make an enemy of the man, who Pratt had once watched pick up a live, stunned starling that had bumped into his window and hurl it against the concrete foundation of his house to kill it. That wasn't the kind of person Pratt wanted hating him. Even the man's name, Suggs, was a little intimidating.

Pratt had tried to buy one of Martha's paintings straight from her living room wall that day with her and Rayburn. She'd joked about his tastes being altered by his illness and Rayburn had said, rather too seriously to be completely joking, "Make no serious decisions for at least

six months." Then Martha had suggested that art was intensely personal and not an appropriate gift. This made complete sense to Pratt as
he remembered the broken eyeball painting. Now he couldn't imagine it hanging in the living room or even in the garage or garnering
him anything but shock from his wife. "Ideas?" he'd asked.

"Diamonds," Rayburn had said from the door. He'd handed Pratt
his business card. "Call me if you feel like killing yourself and make a
regular appointment for next week."

"Diamonds are so clichéd," Martha had said. "But they work."

"Do they?" Pratt had asked.

"Every time," she'd said.

· · ·

So Pratt opened an account at Zales at the mall. Within thirty seconds he was approved with a spending limit of five grand. The salesgirl, svelte and dressed entirely in black, looked at him with fresh
interest. He'd more or less sauntered in and banged his shoulder
against a decorative column hiding a metal rail for the steel gate they
unrolled every night at closing time. Pratt had seen the gate many
times before, when Patricia used to invite him to walk with her at the
mall early in the morning, before the stores opened, when it was
thirty below zero. There was always a clique of elderly people in colorful sweat suits moving briskly over the colorful tiles. If you got in
their way they weren't shy about snorting and sighing. Patricia had
stopped asking Pratt to come along when he'd complained about her
pace. He had tried bringing a book and cup of coffee but you
couldn't smoke in the mall and he'd felt odd reading in a commercial
space, reading literary novels, maybe the way an ardent churchgoer
might feel sneaking a peek at *Sports Illustrated* during a sermon. Or
something.

"Are you looking for anything specific?" the salesgirl asked.

"My anniversary is coming up."

"What year?"

Pratt had to think. "Oh. Twenty."

"That's so cool. Twenty years."

"Well."

By then Pratt had moved to the watches and was eyeballing a gold Movado that looked as if it had been smeared with a chunky peanut-butter-like crust of diamonds. But a warning bell rang in his mind: he foresaw a scene in which Patricia realized that each of them bearing a watch would be too much of a coincidence. Accusations might follow. He moved along the counter and fixed his gaze on bracelets. He was pretty sure the only bracelet she owned was a beaded string that some friend or other had brought home from Thailand or British Columbia. There were some pearls in her drawer as yellow as a hillbilly's teeth, pearls that her mother had owned and never worn. He stabbed his finger at a garish glittery strand of gold and diamonds. "That one."

"The tennis bracelet?"

"I guess so."

"That's a beautiful piece."

"Why do they call it a tennis bracelet?"

"Uh. I'd have to check on that."

She pulled it from the case and draped it over her own slim hand. Her skin was smooth, pale. Alabaster? Young, anyway. He lifted the bracelet from her hand and peered at the diamonds, small diamonds but plenty of them. The thing had some weight to it. Some heft. That mattered. "Yes, I'll take it," Pratt said.

"Excellent taste. Your wife is a very lucky woman."

"Can you put that in writing?"

27

IF PATRICIA noticed a difference in him over the next few weeks, perhaps out of a fear of jinxing it, she did not say anything. When she came home an hour later than normal Pratt said nothing because truth be told he wasn't fretting about it, had certainly noticed, but barely listened to the explanation she offered upon entering the room. He was at the dining room table studying Tiger Wood's *How I Play Golf,* which offered plenty of advice with excellent photography but failed to explain how to perform Tiger's magic; to Pratt it was like trying to learn how to write fiction by reading a book about it. He'd bought the book at Barnes and Noble after getting Patricia's bracelet. He was reading about Tiger's attitude toward inclement weather; that one had no control over it so rather than complain, you just adapted, which sounded awfully Zen-like but sensible and it struck him that might be the point of Zen. He was having more and more moments like this lately, not monolithic revelations but small bricks of clarity, and Patricia was rambling on about stopping to look for a baby-shower card for someone at work named Christine who was pregnant, they thought, by one of the married supervisors but why should that preclude her from having a baby shower, and Pratt nodded and studied the manner in which Tiger addressed the tee, they ate dinner, watched part of a movie, shared a bowl of popcorn, went to bed, didn't really talk but didn't pointedly *not* talk, fell asleep, feet touching.

• • •

Whitney nailed it within a minute of getting into Pratt's car. "You're on meds."

"What?" Pratt checked himself in the rearview to see if his pupils were wildly dilated. "What are you talking about?"

"Am I right?"

"That's a rather personal question, I'd say."

"You're my daddy. I have a right to know."

"Are you a lesbian?"

"Dad."

"Because if you are, that's fine with me. Really. I'm hip to that concept."

She crossed her arms.

Pratt smiled and pulled out from the lot and they drove down University. The trees along the English coulee were turning. "Fall is upon us," he said.

"Thanks, Einstein."

"You don't have to tell me," Pratt said. "That question was a bit out of line."

Silence.

"Yes, I am on meds," he said. "They're making me a tad more assertive. I yelled at someone today."

She laughed, feigned horror. "You *did?*"

"The clerk at Stop and Go? I go in there every day for cigarettes and one thing or another, gas and whatnot, and she never says thank you. Every fucking day I drop money in that place and never get a thank-you. I'm always the one to say thank you. I've been telling her thank you for three years. Hands me my receipt and I say thank you when it should be the other way around." He stopped to allow a herd of jostling young men to cross the road. In his day he'd been the lone coyote, crossing alone, but the memory didn't hurt; it was just a memory. "Well, today I just said, 'Enough!' Filled up on gas and bought a pack of smokes and some gum, filled my travel mug. I mean I dropped twenty bucks there and she does the same old routine, gives me a receipt and starts to walk away with this deadpan, no this fucking—pardon me—this *freaking* moronic look on her face, no, not even moronic but robotic, like that guy in *Star Wars*, not the one that looks like a vacuum cleaner—"

"C3PO?"

Pratt nodded. "The gold one. His expression never changes. That's what this clerk is like, like she has that disease, the one they did a Lifetime movie about, Bob Saget's sister has it, what am I thinking of?"

"I have no idea."

Pratt snapped his fingers. By then they were at Washington but instead of turning right to head down to Paradiso, he kept going straight. "Scleroderma. That's it. Are you familiar with scleroderma?"

"No, Dad, I'm not. Where are we going?"

"You'll see. Scleroderma is this awful disease, part of the arthritis family, related to lupus, actually, which is what your grandfather has. Scleroderma basically turns your body into concrete, you know, all your joints harden up and your face gets frozen. It's really awful. See that house there?"

"Which one?"

"The green one."

"What about it?"

"I lost my virginity in that house."

"Dad!"

Pratt stopped in the road, lighted a cigarette. "I was seventeen. She was twenty-one. Four years' age difference." He shook loose a cigarette and handed it to his daughter; she took it and lighted it and they stared at the house, a listing two-story with rotten steps. "Four years means less and less as you get older but to a seventeen-year-old it is a big deal. Well, it's almost a fourth of your life."

"Who was she?"

"That used to be a nice house. Her father was a carpenter and he kept it up. But he was a terrible drunk too. A mean drunk. Never said a word to me. Not a single word."

"Tell me about *her*."

"Well." Pratt stepped on the gas and they moved on. "Her name was Kim. She was in the same tae kwon do class as me. I didn't have a car. I had a bike. One night after class I came outside and my goddamn bike was gone so she gave me a ride home. She needed to talk to me, she said, and then she got on me about staring at her in class all the time. Which I was doing. I thought she was mad but she took me to her house and we went down into the basement and watched television for a while. Her father was upstairs drinking. We watched some MTV, this was when it was all videos and not all that reality nonsense, and we made love on the floor. I had fantasized about that kind of thing, you know, with her, with Kim, for months and then it came true."

"Did you keep seeing her?"

"What? Oh, for a while. She had a boyfriend, see. So we had to sneak and I fell in love and got too clingy and jealous. She'd pick me up at my house late at night after being with her boyfriend and it just broke my heart. Way too much stress for a teenager but at the time I felt this intensity, no, this purity, like a missionary or something. I believed we were destined to be together et cetera. Maybe we were, who knows? But she had this boyfriend, closer to her age, and he drove a Trans Am and I didn't even have a bike. You see?"

"Have you ever looked her up?"

"Nope."

"Why not?"

"Why?"

"For closure?"

"There is no closure. Life is not a book, Whitney, with neat chapters. Closure is a word like *normal*. It doesn't really exist."

His daughter drew hard on her cigarette. "Are you seeing someone?"

Pratt immediately thought of Martha, pictured her rear jiggling through her sheer dress as she bent over the flower beds. "No. I'm loyal to your mother."

"Not that kind of seeing someone. I meant are you seeing a therapist?"

"No. Well, I have a shrink, sort of."

"A psychiatrist or psychologist?"

"A shrink. You know, an MD."

"Is he a Freudian or a Jungian?"

"What do you know about that stuff?"

"I'm taking intro to psych."

"He's more or less a giant Pez dispenser."

"What are you on?"

"In the glove box."

Whitney rummaged for his pills, studied the labels. "What does Mom think?"

"Mom doesn't know and Mom isn't going to know. Not for a while."

"How come?"

"Daddy wants to surprise Mama by turning into a nice, normal daddy. It's part of my anniversary present."

"You should tell her."

"Take out that box. The black one. That's part of the present too."

She did. Opened it and looked at the tennis bracelet. "Holy Christ, Dad."

"Nice?"

"Are these real?"

"I've got the paperwork."

She shook her head, snapped the box shut.

"Think she'll like it?"

"How could she not?"

They rolled into the heart of downtown. The tae kwon do studio where he had met Kim was gone now, uprooted from the earth by the floodwaters of 1997. There was a metaphor floating about but before he could explore it, Whitney said, "Where are we going?"

"Just driving around. Are you in a hurry?"

"No. But you never just drive around."

Pratt spun his index finger around his ear. "I'm crazy."

"I've always known *that*."

"Really?"

"Well, not always. But remember when you had the floors redone?"

"Yes. Cost two thousand dollars."

"I came home from school one day and you were crawling around on all fours with socks on your hands."

"I was dusting."

"Do you remember asking me to invite my quote gal pals unquote over to dance in their socks in the living room?"

He tried to recall. But he could barely recall the floor now because it was just a floor, subject to normal wear and tear. He didn't even take his shoes off in the house anymore. "No, I don't."

"Well, you did. You kept pestering me to do it. Like I was really going to call a bunch of girls and say, 'Come on over, my dad wants us to dance on his new floor. He even bought special socks.'"

"Special socks."

"You really don't remember, do you?"

"What kind of socks?"

"You bought all these like heavy-duty basketball socks, you know, athletic socks. You had this plan for the girls to come over every week and dance on the floor to keep it new. Mom had to shut you down finally. You were awful about the floor. Well, obsessed."

"Sounds like it."

"You'd be sitting there and see a shadow or something and go wacko thinking it was a scratch or a stain." She started laughing.

"What?"

"I can't say. Mom would kill me."

"Come on."

"You won't tell her I told you?"

"You're not telling her about my meds, are you?"

"No."

"Well, it's a truce then." Pratt shook his daughter's hand. He noted her strong grip, a ring he'd never seen before gracing her middle finger.

"When you were at work one day Mom and I moved the couch out and carved our initials into the floor."

"No way."

"Didn't you wonder why we started laughing every time you sat on the couch?"

"I don't remember."

"You really don't? It lasted for weeks."

"No, I don't."

"I wish you did."

"Me too."

. . .

Driving home, on old 81 instead of the interstate, Pratt realized he'd forgotten to tell Whitney the rest of his store-clerk story. After lunch — not at Paradiso but across the Red River in East Grand Forks at Whitey's, one of his old college haunts, lunch which had included a beer for her even though she was underage but which she'd guzzled like an old pro — he had driven her back across the river and down Belmont, out of downtown and past grand old houses, showing her the tree he'd crashed into the night he'd turned twenty-one. He'd been working at Menard's Lumber and his cohorts in the plumbing and electrical department had taken him to the Southgate — Pratt retraced the entire route for his daughter, as much of it as he could recall — and plied him with exotic drinks, the only one of which he remembered was something called a "flaming jellybean," his last drink before pawing a married coworker, kissing her by the pay phone, the only woman besides Patricia he'd kissed in years — not counting Dr. Lambert with whom there'd been no actual *kissing* — and liking it, no, loving it, the feel of a strange tongue wrestling with his, the feel of different skin as he'd worked his hands under her shirt, the smell of her perfume—how could he remember all that but not his obsession with the hardwood floors three years ago?—before getting into his car and going home, taking a convoluted route—even Whitney noticed this—to avoid what he was sure was a police dragnet before hitting the tree, taking out his headlight and part of the grille, smacking his forehead on the steering wheel but somehow making it home and passing out in the car, door open, in the backyard, dreaming of fire before vomiting, waking at dawn still buzzed but with the thought, much like the flames rising from his last drink, that perhaps getting married so young was a mistake.

Of course he didn't tell Whitney all the details, didn't mention the hallway groping, or even his doubt. He rolled into Hillsboro, another dying farm town, and stopped at a bar. Ordered a Coors Light and asked for phone change and called his daughter.

"It's me," he said.

"Are you okay?"

"I'm fine. I forgot to tell you the rest of my clerk story."

"Where are you?"

"Hillsboro."

"Hillsboro? You couldn't wait until you got home?"

"Listen. When I was in the Stop and Go today, I said, I said, 'You know, I've been coming in here for three years and you've never once said thank you.' And she just stared at me like I was nuts. So I told her I figured she owed me about nine hundred and something goddamn thank-yous and she could start giving them to me right now or I was going to talk to the manager. I was hot. I mean, really fuming."

"Were you yelling?"

"My voice was raised. People were listening but I didn't care."

"Then what happened?"

"She said, 'Thank you.'"

"For real?"

"She said it but it sounded sarcastic."

"That doesn't matter. What matters is that you took a stand."

"I didn't feel guilty about it."

"Guilty?"

"The old me would have gone back in and apologized."

"The old you wouldn't have said anything."

"You're right, honey. That's a good point."

There was a pause. He could hear her music in the background, some new band with a hoarse-voiced lead. The bar he was in had a jukebox but it was, as his father-in-law might say, dark as Toby's ass. There were only a few people in the bar, Pratt and a decrepit alcoholic and two men who looked like salesmen, in suits and ties, drinking draft beer and numbly watching ESPN.

"Daddy?"

"What?"

"How come you gave me the grand tour today? What was that all about?"

"The Forks are part of my past. I thought it was about time I gave you a little history lesson. Were you bored?"

She laughed but it was a sniffly laugh.

"Are you crying, baby?"

"No. Yes."

"How come?"

"You're not going to kill yourself, are you?"

"Honey." The bartender was perceptive enough to recognize that something heavy was going on and brought over Pratt's beer and cigarettes. Pratt was genuinely touched by this small gesture of humanity. He mouthed a thank-you. A computer came on the line demanding more money and Pratt dropped the rest of his quarters into the phone. "I'd never do that," he whispered.

"Are you sure?"

"I wouldn't want to let your mother off the hook that easily."

"That's terrible."

"I know." Pratt cradled the phone against his shoulder and lighted a cigarette. "You don't need to worry about me."

"I do."

"You're young. You should be worrying about having fun. What to wear and all that. Not worrying about your crazy old man."

"You just scared me a little."

"I'm sorry."

"You were just acting a little, well, different."

Pratt winced at her use of that word, a colloquialism he absolutely detested. People in the northland weren't ever strange, they were *different*. Joseph's Technicolor dreamcoat would be politely called *different*. A flaming homosexual waiter was *different*. Pratt couldn't stand it any more than he could stand the local questions: Where is it *at*, where are you *at*, where is he *at*? Remnants of his English-major days. Ordinarily Whitney would have faced a lecture but he let it slide. "This is the new me, baby. Or the old me, the me you never knew."

"Then I like it."

28

JENSON had sorted through the storage room and found over a hundred cans of potentially reusable paint. They were a bit behind on this element of the job, providing the public with free items in the spirit of recycling. The facility operated a kind of free store where citizens of Fargo could load up on paint, stain, wallpaper paste, linseed oil, and the like. Checking the paint was Pratt's job and the one task he avoided mentioning when describing his duties. Hazardous waste disposal technician sounded if not glamorous than a little edgy, brought to mind well-trained people in special masks working slowly over smoking drums. It certainly did not call to mind opening dusty cans of paint and stirring them with a stick made heavy from thousands of layers of paint, dabbing the color on the lid, hammering the lid back on, organizing the paint on wire shelves. *Oil Acrylic Interior Exterior Enamel blah blah blah.*

"You've been busy," Pratt said, looking at the pallets Jenson had brought over.

"We've got a month to get everything done."

"What's the hurry?"

Jenson stroked his goatee, a feature Pratt noticed now for the first time. "Listen," Jenson said.

"When did you start growing the goatee?"

"Three months ago."

"It's not very thick for three months."

Jenson reddened. "Listen, I have to ask you something."

Pratt immediately thought of the mercury. His claim that he'd intended to bring it back would no doubt seem feeble if it came after he was caught. "Shoot."

"Are you on something, Dennis?"

Pratt laughed with relief. This opened a doorway to a memory of being in the third grade, how when interrogated for something he had not done—tripping a fat girl, Tammy Trigg—he had laughed and blushed and looked so guilty that he'd been sent to the principal's office and forced to sit in a plastic bucket chair looking at a long paddle with the words "Board of Education" burned into it. He had heard rumors of the paddlings and feared getting one but Tammy Trigg, after overcoming her hysterical weeping, pointed out the real culprit, that mean little redneck Terry Cooper, and although Pratt was not given an apology he was exchanged for Cooper and allowed to go back to the classroom.

Jenson watched him now, warily, until he regained his composure. "Are you?"

"What do you mean am I on something? My mother asked me that when I was fifteen."

"Were you?"

Pratt recalled smoking enormous doobies with some riffraff after school and walking into the house listening to Pink Floyd on headphones. "Yes."

"Then or now?"

"Both."

"Dennis."

"It's not what you think. I'm on some antianxiety pills." Pratt dug into his pocket for his emergency Klonopin, covered in lint and shreds of cigarette tobacco. "It's prescription."

Jenson took the pill, blew away the debris. "Anxiety?"

"Big time."

"You did seem a little tense there for a while."

"Can you see the difference?"

Jenson handed back the pill. "It really hit home the other day when you spent an hour out back holding a burning torch."

"You said to burn it off."

"Most people would light it and set it in a can or something. You just stood there holding it. For an hour."

"It didn't seem like that long."

"Well, it was. That kind of got me a little concerned."

"You could've said something."

"I'm a scientist," Jenson said. "First we observe." He reached into some recess of his blue coveralls and produced a small spiral notebook. He flipped it open one-handed in the manner of a private eye. "Incident one," he read. "This was last Monday. Subject—that's you—spent ten minutes weighing himself on the fifty-five-gallon-drum scale. Subject was evidently trying to determine if full or empty lungs caused any noticeable increase or decrease in body weight."

"It didn't seem to matter."

"I was rooting for you. Incident two. Subject made nine phone calls trying to determine which area florist had the freshest roses."

"I wanted more bang for the buck."

"I'll give you that one."

"I found out they all come from the same distributor."

"Really?"

"What else do you have?"

"Well, there's the torch thing."

"And?"

Jenson cleared his throat. "Incident four. Subject attempted to seal himself into a fifty-five-gallon steel drum."

"I can explain that."

"Okay."

Pratt wandered over to the open garage door and straddled the line between indoors and out. He lighted a cigarette. "One of my greatest fears has always been being buried alive."

"I thought it was water."

"Water, yes. Water is number one. But being sealed up, you know. Trapped?"

"I can relate."

"And lately I've had this urge to test myself. Go mano a mano with my fears."

"That's cool. But it's impossible to seal yourself into a barrel."

"I know that. I didn't want to actually do it, I just wanted to simulate the experience."

"So you weren't really trying to can yourself?"

"Of course not. That would totally defeat the purpose."

Jenson shut the notebook, returned it to its place in his clothing. "So what did it feel like?"

"Nothing. Because I knew I was only faking it."

Jenson's eyes took on a wickedly contemplative sheen. "Hmm," he said, glancing around. Again the goatee rub. Pratt caught on and a minute later he was lowering himself into a clean barrel, shiny black steel, bearing no particular odor. "When I tap, let me out."

"I'll let you out."

"There won't be much air in here."

"No there won't."

"Don't fuck with me, Jenson. I could die in here."

"You die and I'll have some explaining to do."

Pratt started to say more but Jenson put the lid on. He heard the squeaking of the ring bolt. Jenson was only supposed to finger tighten the bolt but Pratt heard the clank of the wrench and the awful sound of the ratchet clicking. As expected, he began to panic. There was the matter of available oxygen. Some time earlier Jenson had broken the news that oxygen and air were not synonymous, that oxygen made up only a percentage of air—how much was that percentage again? And what about displacement, how much space was Pratt's body taking up? How much volume did his gaunt frame represent? He was glad he wasn't overweight. The air in the barrel began to heat up. He banged on the wall. Nothing. Screamed and his voice sounded like a broken pull-string doll, Whitney's doll that had cried eerily when you yanked on the round plastic ring, even then dolls like that were being replaced with fancier versions that held more electronic sophistication than all of Pratt's toys growing up, was it possible that Jenson was in reality insane, maybe the guy responsible for several unsolved murders along Highway 2 between North Dakota and Montana no of course not but it was possible the excitement or intensity had put Jenson into a diabetic reaction and he was out of it or worse, slumped in his chair in the office for one of his hour-long comas. Pratt banged again, shouted. Logic kicked in and he realized his panic was wasting his oxygen. Then again, why die calm? Why go out peacefully like those guys on the submarines, breathing shallowly in their narrow bunks, waiting to fall asleep forever? He banged his head on the lid and it sprang open. A paint can was the only thing holding it on. The ratcheting had only been a spoof. Pratt climbed out and found Jenson in the office, reading a copy of *Waste Management Today*.

"You son of a bitch," Pratt said, but he was too relieved to be angry.

• • •

Jenson wasn't the only one watching him, evidently. After work Pratt changed quickly, drank a beer, popped a Klonopin, looked through the mail. Tried to call Patricia at work but her voice mail said she was "away from her desk," one of those phrases that drove him batty, though this time he simply said he loved her after the beep and hung up. He was vaguely aware that she could be as far away from her desk as Carver's bed but unlike other times, the idea was more like a hummingbird than a lumbering B-52 and flitted from his consciousness as he cracked another beer for the ride out to the Bonanza. He still had a chance to play in that window of time between the retirees and the after-work crowd since he'd left work at three. As he zipped down the highway listening to Kid Rock's *Cowboy*, pilfered from Whitney's room, evidently not in vogue enough to take to college, Pratt settled into a mode of positive visualization, seeing himself hitting a high straight one off the first tee, over the swamp, the ball landing with a nice thud a foot from the flag and not rolling anywhere at all.

But when he got to the course, as he was strapping his bag to the cart Tripp rolled up and blocked him in like a cop making a felony stop. The ranger gave Pratt his normal long stare which Pratt met with what he felt was a fair amount of ice. But he didn't have sunglasses to hide behind so there was no telling who was the fair winner; Tripp could have had his eyes closed for all Pratt knew. He was anxious to get onto the course. "What's up?"

"Your little girlfriend hasn't been selling balls lately."

"You ran her off?"

"You know I couldn't do that. She wasn't on our property."

"I figured you turned her in to the IRS." Truth be told, Pratt hadn't noticed Candy was missing because he hadn't played lately.

"I wouldn't turn in my worst enemy to those criminals."

"That's good."

"I saw you down at their camp the other day."

"Whose camp?"

"The girl. Her father. That camp."

"So?"

"Haven't seen her for a while, that's all. Then I see you down there."

"What are you getting at?" Over Tripp's shoulder Pratt saw a convoy of three cars coming.

"Not a thing, Pratt, not a thing. Just more or less wondering where she's at."

"I'd think you'd be happy she's not taking your balls."

Tripp started to say something but his clip-on radio squawked. The toilet in the men's room was clogged. He grimaced. "We'll talk later."

"Looking forward to it."

• • •

The positive visualization didn't produce the desired effect but there was a definite improvement in Pratt's game. His first tee shot did go high, did go over the swamp, but after hauling ass to the green he didn't find it a foot from the hole. In fact, he didn't find the ball for five minutes, was about to drop one on the green when he saw his ball on the gravel road. He hurried over to it. A pickup was coming but instead of kicking his ball or whacking it quickly, he took his time, made the truck wait, ignored what was possibly an insulting commentary coming from the cab. In fact he acted as if he had all the time in the world, which he did.

29

PRATT was in the driveway, whacking his golf shoes together to loosen dried mud from the cleats, when Patricia turned in. She feigned running him over. Gunned the engine. Then she sat in her car while something heavy on the bass thumped the windows. He watched her check her face in the mirror before climbing out. "Christ, I'm beat," she said.

"Sorry."

She reached down and took off her shoes. She had rather large feet, sometimes even wore Pratt's sneakers. She hated her feet. There was no surgery or exercise for making one's foot smaller. For some reason, Pratt found that comforting. Whatever she did to herself, her feet would always be ladies' nine wide. He noticed that she'd painted her toenails to match her fingernails, a bright summery orange that he found sexy, he'd told her, that orange against her tanned skin. But something was out of place and through the dust cloud generated by his cleats releasing their catch, he realized she wasn't wearing hose. He noticed this because he had always found pantyhose sexy. Even an old woman's foot looked pretty sexy when wrapped in sheer nylon. "What happened to your stockings?" he asked.

She didn't blink an eye. "Got a fucking run before my one o'clock meeting. And I mean *right* before. I literally took them off in the elevator and shoved them into that little box where they have the emergency phone."

"That's wild."

"Well, I wasn't about to wear them and I sure wasn't going into a meeting with my boss carrying some wadded-up pantyhose."

"Maybe he would have liked that. Give him a raise, then you'd get a raise."

"Simmons? Right. Good one." She leaned forward and looked down at her feet. "I'm getting sick of this color. I might go back to red."

"I hate the red. Everyone has red."

"Maybe there's a good reason for that. Maybe everyone has it because it looks good."

Pratt set his shoes down. "You know, that makes sense."

"What did you say?"

"I said it makes sense."

"God, I get sick of your sarcasm."

"I'm not being sarcastic. I mean it. You're right. Maybe the fact that everyone wears it isn't necessarily to conform but because it really is a good color."

She looked dumbstruck.

"What?"

"Are you high or something?"

"No, I'm not high or something."

"Well, you're acting like it."

"How so?"

"I don't know. You're acting, well, different."

"Different good or different bad?"

"Good. I think."

• • •

After dinner, which Pratt prepared—an Italian sausage and spinach calzone from scratch, something he hadn't made in years—Patricia announced that she was going shopping. Pratt hinted that he wanted to come along.

"You hate the mall."

"I wouldn't mind hanging out with you."

"Well, that's nice, but I might be getting some things I don't want you to know about."

"Ah."

"You know our anniversary is in a few days."

"I'm well aware of that," Pratt said, gathering up the dishes and carrying them into the kitchen. He started the hot water.

"But I was thinking we should put off celebrating until we get to Mexico," she said.

"How come?"

She joined him by the sink. "I don't know what you have planned but don't buy me anything expensive because the trip is expensive and that can be my present, you know. That should be our present."

"The trip has nothing to do with our anniversary. Those guys planned it and we're tagging along. They weren't thinking of our anniversary."

"I know." She scraped her plate into the garbage can. She'd only picked at her calzone, eating the cheese and spinach and leaving everything else. "But maybe it would be better to save our money and spend it in Mexico." She pronounced it "me-he-co," a new affectation that had begun to annoy him.

"You have a point. Fine, then. I'll cancel my reservation at Sarello's."

"Are you serious? You made reservations at Sarello's?"

He thought about fibbing but took the road less traveled. "No. But I was going to. Well, scratch that. I figured on dinner but that was as far as I got."

She leaned up and gave him a peck on the cheek. "I won't be gone too long."

"If I can't spend much then you shouldn't either."

"What the heck are you talking about?"

"You said you didn't want me to see what you're buying. Then in the next sentence you told me not to spend too much."

"You're right. I meant don't overdo it. Sometimes you overdo it, Dennis."

. . .

He finished the dishes, forgoing the dishwasher as always in favor of getting his hands into the hot water, in favor of grinding away at the plates with an abrasive pad. He wondered if this was another symptom of OCD or just a preference. From now on he'd have to wonder. Did his preference for sharp pencils, and he meant really sharp, to the point that one of his favorite appliances was an electric sharpener, did that signal obsessive behavior or just common sense, that a sharp pencil was, like a sharp knife, more efficient? Or what about his predilection for guessing the number of stairs in an unfamiliar building and then checking his results by counting them? On half impulse he picked up the phone and dialed Martha's house. She answered so coolly he almost hung up but when he identified himself she said that of late she'd been getting more or less stalked by someone she knew. She didn't elaborate. "But how are you doing?"

"I feel better."

She laughed. "I should hope so. I don't think you could have been feeling any worse than when you were on my floor, tangled up in badly rendered eyeballs."

"True." He decided to bypass his pencil question, which now seemed awfully narcissistic. "I think the meds are doing what they're supposed to be doing. I have all this extra energy. Not physical energy so much but mental energy. I feel kind of cooped up."

"You're not feeling cooped up."

"I'm not?"

"You're feeling the opposite of cooped up. You're feeling free. You just don't recognize it."

"Free."

"Free. You're used to being trapped by your mind. Ruminating."

"Well."

"Well what?"

"That makes sense."

"It doesn't even *need* to make sense. It's a fact."

"Wow."

"Get it?"

"Yes."

"The cage door is open."

"Open."

"Close your eyes and see it."

He did.

"Wide open," she said.

He could see it and he could hear opera playing in the background at her house though he did not know enough to name it or even ask about it.

"Do you see it?" she asked.

"I see it."

"Now," she said. "Fly."

30

PRATT stood in the water, up to his chest, in the cold
YMCA pool. He had signed up for the lessons under an assumed
name, "Dennis Frost," offering phony contact information on the off
chance a class would be canceled and they'd call the house and the
jig would be up. He realized that if he drowned Patricia wouldn't find
out until the mystery was cleared up and part of him wished for this
so that she might twist her hands with worry but then again, what if
his ghost saw instead his widow using his disappearance to cuckold
him? The notion of haunting her didn't hold much appeal. What
could a ghost really do? As a child Pratt had been so afraid of ghosts
that he'd undergone a nightly ritual of looking under the bed exactly
three times before allowing himself to fall asleep. The first time because the ghost might not be there, the second time because the
ghost might be expecting him to look, and the third because he could
vary the time and swing down, planting his hands on the carpet, and
surely catch the ghost off guard. His discipline had netted him only a
view of spider-like dust hanging from the old box spring and the odd
missing sock.

His instructor, Lucas, a lad who resembled a Nordic Greg Louga-
nis, watched him patiently. "You'll do fine. I have people who are
afraid to put their *face* in the water."

"It's just the deep I'm afraid of."

"That's all right. The deep is worthy of respect."

Pratt kicked off. He pumped his legs and flailed at the water until
his lungs were about to explode. When he surfaced he had made it
only a few feet away from Lucas. Pratt pushed his hair back and regained his composure.

"So," he said.

"So."

They both watched one of Pratt's classmates, a woman training for a triathlon, slip between them through the water like an eel Pratt had watched at the aquarium at the Mall of America, barely disturbing the surface. Pratt had assumed all the adult learners were like him, terrified, or at least embarrassed to be nonswimmers, but in reality he was the only one in the class of four who hit a sort of force field when he reached the border where the floor of the pool suddenly and sharply angled down into deadly nine-foot waters. The others simply wanted to improve what looked to Pratt like already damn fine abilities in the water.

"What do you think of my stroke?"

"It's got potential."

"Do I look like an eggbeater in here?"

"Well, eggbeaters are actually very efficient machines."

· · ·

He fell asleep with a copy of *Marlin* magazine on his chest. This and *Golf Digest* were the only two subscriptions he currently took. Whitney was well past the age of being part of the usual school extortion efforts involving candy-bar sales, magazine subscriptions, cheese-log catalogs; these two weren't subscriptions born of guilt or parental duty but of fear, basically, of looking like an idiot in Mexico. He did not expect to become an expert at golf any more than he thought he could, under pressure, distinguish a blue marlin from a black, but he wanted to be able to at least speak the language. *Marlin*, he'd discovered, was less about fishing than selling boats, but he still found the pictures intriguing and even allowed himself a fantasy about landing a record fish, getting his name in whatever pantheon was dedicated to such accomplishments. Then he'd read that if anyone else so much as touched the rod, a fish was ineligible for record status, even if it would dwarf the boat itself. This had prompted quite a bit of worry in Pratt's complicated head; he'd imagined scenarios in which the other members of the party insisted on taking turns holding the rod in order to gather scrapbook pictures, thus nullifying the record. He'd even brought it up to Patricia, suggesting that a rule be laid down that whoever hooked a fish had the option of doing it all him- or herself. He had drafted a simple contract on the home computer and wanted her to mail it around to her friends. "You're crazy," she'd said.

"I don't want to miss out on bagging a record marlin because Kelly wants to hold the rod for two minutes."

"Bagging?"

"I think we should get this stuff worked out in advance."

"What stuff? We're going fishing. *Fishing*, Dennis. It isn't a contest. It's an outing."

"You're proving my point. Maybe for you guys it'll be an ocean cruise but I'm going to take it seriously. And that means I want to do it right."

"You didn't even want to go. I had to twist your arm to get you to go."

"I know, but if I'm going, I want to do it right."

"Why do you have to take everything so freaking seriously? Why do you have to *read* about everything? Why can't you just go with the flow and have a good time?"

He'd not been able to summon an answer. Now he sat up on the sofa and tried to recall when he'd last let go and had a good time. Even during his wedding dance Pratt had been nervous, watching a fight brew between two of Patricia's uncles over a low flame all night. In college he'd spent most of his time holed up trying to conquer his degree in four years. And for what? He had had a friend, Ramiro, who'd taken seven years to get his degree in industrial technology. Seven years! For an IT degree. But Ramiro was never without a smile and had some interesting tales about the ΣAE house. He'd tried to get Pratt to join up but the notion had seemed as foreign to Pratt as joining the then-unheard-of Gay and Lesbian Club, or even the College Republicans.

He picked up the cordless phone from the coffee table and called Whitney. The phone rang and rang. He was afraid nobody would pick it up. He made a mental note to buy her a cell phone, something she'd been pushing for and he'd resisted because of concerns over brain tumors. Finally a girl answered. She sounded about as upbeat as Sylvia Plath turning on the oven. "Hello."

"Whitney Pratt around?"

"Um. I don't think so. Hang on." Pratt heard the phone bumping against the wall on its cord. Then murky silence, punctuated by an occasional echo. He hung on for so long he thought he'd been abandoned but then the girl came back. "Um. I can't find her. I think she was going out."

"Out?"

"She was going out to smoke with Carrie. Her roommate."

"Ah."

"Can I take a message?" She was almost whispering.

"Are you okay?" Pratt asked.

"Me?"

"You."

"Who is this?"

"Whitney's father."

"Oh."

More silence though he heard or thought he heard her heart beating, thumping slowly, and he pictured her, saw her, he wasn't sure if he was being psychic or just imaginative but he saw her, frail and almost transparent, dark-haired, big-eyed, in pajamas way too early in the day, looking out at University Avenue, maybe sneaking a cigarette, blowing smoke through the screen. Reading. "Are you an English major?"

"Yes."

"I was too."

"How did you know?"

"Know what?"

"That I'm an English major."

"I'm on medication."

A long pause this time. Pratt realized how crazy that sounded. "I'm on some meds and they're making my mind sharper. Well, not necessarily sharper but they're taking away a lot of junk that was getting in the way."

"What kind of junk?"

"Worries. Obsessions." He gazed down at the cover of *Marlin*, showing a beautiful fish with a gaff hook through its jaw being pulled aboard by a fat man in Bermuda shorts.

"You know what I'm talking about, don't you?"

"Yes. There's no room for anything else."

"It's like the tribbles on *Star Trek*."

"The what?"

"Or some kind of weed. Dandelions, maybe. Choking out the lawn."

"A computer virus?"

"Exactly."

"I don't even like to read anymore."

"You wonder what the point is."

"Like, who gives a fuck about fucking *Hamlet*, you know? About Shakespeare."

"Yes."

"I mean, I look at all these girls up here and they're happy and I'm wondering."

"You're wondering why they don't get it."

"Yes."

"Why they don't see how pointless everything is."

"Exactly." He heard her lighting a cigarette, heard someone make a comment.

"What did they say?"

"She said she doesn't appreciate the secondhand smoke."

"Tell her to fuck herself."

Laughter. "I'd like to."

"Do it."

"I can't."

"You'll feel better."

"Maybe later. Hang on. Your daughter is back. Whitney."

Pratt started to say something but then it was Whitney, her voice wet, perhaps with booze. He endured a brief terrible thought that he'd been paired with the wrong daughter. "Who was that girl I was talking to?"

"Mandy?"

"I guess."

"Why?"

"She sounded sad. Maybe you can talk to her."

"Sorry, not my job, Daddy-o."

"What does she look like?"

"Daddy, you sound like an old pervert."

"No. I mean, you talk to someone and you get a mental image and I'm wondering if I'm right on or way off."

"I do that with disc jockeys. They never look like you imagine. They're all fat and bald."

"True."

"Well," Whitney said, "Mandy is about five five and she weighs, I don't know, three hundred pounds?"

"No way."

"Way. She's got dyed red hair and someone fucked up because it's more orange than red. Not orange like she meant it to be orange either but fucked-up red."

"When did you start talking like that?"

"Hey, will you bring me some tequila from Mexico?"

"No."

"Come on."

"We'll see."

31

JENSON was apologetic but firm. "I have to write it up."

"I'm fine."

"If something happens, though, it's my butt."

Pratt was in the office with his head between his knees. His brain felt like an empty eggshell. "You didn't write it up when I almost blew my fingers off with that firecracker."

"Well, that wasn't a breach. That was new territory. You know?"

Pratt heard Jenson rummaging through the file cabinet. "Do you know where I put the incident reports?"

"It wasn't an incident."

"We're supposed to write up the close calls too."

"It wasn't even a close call."

"You stuck your nose in a container full of hydrochloric acid. That's a close call."

"I thought it was old motor oil."

"It said 'acid' right on the label."

"I was in a hurry." Pratt recalled the initial whiff, a lightning bolt zigzagging through his skull, his knees turning into hacky-sacks.

"You know you're supposed to waft. You had waft training." As if to punctuate, Jenson opened his perennial bottle of Diet Pepsi and waved his hand over the mouth, turned his head slightly, sniffed lightly.

"Fuck you, Jenson."

"I'm not going to write you up. I was just trying to use this as a teachable moment."

"Teachable moment?"

"Like in *The Karate Kid*. How do you feel?"

"Like crap. Better. Not too bad."

"You want to head home?"

"Are you being merciful or trying to cut costs?"

"Little of both. We're a tad over budget for the year."

. . .

Patricia worked in the tallest building in Fargo, the Radisson. Her years had earned her an office with a view of the western sky. She sometimes called Pratt to say she could see wall clouds moving in, potential tornadoes, the streets below her emptying as people took shelter and the sirens wailed. She was always calm about it. "If we get hit we get hit. Hasn't happened yet."

Pratt didn't like going up to her office. It wasn't just the height, which made him woozy even though it wasn't that high. Her building would have been dwarfed in Minneapolis or even Omaha. It was her office itself. Warm greens and mahogany woodwork couldn't hide the clinical scent of money; the canned music couldn't overwhelm the traffic of funds being transferred, the artificiality of it all. Patricia loved her job because by the time people came to see her, they'd been approved for loans, were closing on their first homes, moving into better neighborhoods, leaving the state for warmer places. They were almost always happy, she said, finding small joy in signing papers, and the free pens she gave them put them over the edge.

Now Pratt boarded the elevator and pressed the button. In his hand was a single rose. Spur of the moment. Spontaneity. Walk in like Valentino or Richard Gere and drop off a rose, leave just as quickly. Zorro. The Lone Ranger. He felt the odd pull of gravity and then the elevator stopped and the door opened. The receptionist was new and didn't recognize him. She rose from her seat when he headed for his wife's office. "Can I help you, sir?"

"Here to see my wife."

"Your wife?"

"Patricia Pratt."

"Oh." The receptionist looked more than a little confused. But then again, in this day and age one had, Pratt decided, to watch out for stalkers and terrorists. Even title companies weren't excluded.

Pratt smiled and kept going to Patricia's office, past a collection of duck prints, all the way down to the corner. Patricia was on the telephone with her back to the door, gazing out the window at a haze of postharvest dust looming on the horizon like smoke. "I don't know about *that*," she was saying. She laughed. It was a laugh he'd not heard before or one he'd forgotten could emanate from her lips. The word *lilting* came to mind. "Maybe," she said, "I'll need some kind of freaking pill to keep up with *you*."

He cleared his throat. She spun around. For a split second her face froze and then softened. She held up a finger. "I need to get going," she said. "My better half is here."

Pratt came in and stood before her desk like a customer. He had the rose behind his back. "Hi."

"Is everything okay?"

"Just dandy. Why?"

"You never come up here, that's why."

"I was in the neighborhood. Who were you talking to?"

She sighed. "Are you checking up on me? Because I thought we were through with that."

"Just curious. That pill talk and all."

She rolled her eyes and he felt the moment sliding into the pile of shards and ruins of their marriage, all the good intentions cracked by his comments or thoughts. He wanted to tell her then, explain, take his pills from his pocket and set the bottle on her clean smooth desk like a totem. See, I'm crazy and I can prove it. But he didn't. He brought the rose around and held it in front of his face so that her head appeared to be resting on the flower. "Brought you something."

"Dennis."

He handed her the rose; she reached across her desk and plucked it from his hand. A thorn scratched his thumb and it hurt. He watched his wife sniff the rose before setting it down neatly on her desk, parallel to a pen.

"You should get that into some water."

"I know." She glanced at her watch. "But I have an eleven-thirty closing."

"Oh."

"I'm sorry. It's these crazy interest rates. We've been hopping."

"No biggie. Just thought I'd drop in and say hello."

"Thanks honey. You're on your own for dinner, by the way. We've got closings up until eight tonight, believe it or not."

"I believe it."

She came around the desk and gave him a peck on the cheek. Then she literally pushed him toward the door. When he looked back she was behind her desk again, opening a manila file folder, her brow creased.

Out in the lobby an old farm couple was waiting. The husband was drinking coffee from a Styrofoam cup. He was missing two fingers from his left hand but it must have been an old injury because the skin over the stumps was as wrinkled and leathery as the rest of him. His wife was reading *Entertainment Weekly*. Pratt wondered if they were buying or selling, maybe dumping their house and moving to Florida. He wanted to ask but the receptionist gave him a stern look and he picked up his pace to the elevator. Riding down, he recalled Patricia's story about hiding her nylons in the call box. He reached for the handle. But he didn't open it.

Progress, he thought.

Up the street from the Radisson was a coffee shop and in the busyness of the morning Pratt had not taken in his usual quota. He left his car where it was and strolled past the library, around the corner where the telephone workers were gathered sullenly on the sidewalk, not on strike but to smoke cigarettes, sullen perhaps because in two months they'd be doing this in below-zero weather. It was hard in the north country to ever really forget about winter because you were either emerging from it or barreling toward it. Summers were compressed and frantic times. He wove his way through the employees, none of whom seemed willing to move for a pedestrian. He wanted to tell them they'd soon be replaced by robots but then he was past the negative cloud and at the coffee shop. He ordered a large Costa Rican and looked through some rather literary postcards on a rack by the door, wishing he knew the kind of people who might enjoy getting a photo of W. S. Merwin and Anne Sexton in the mail. Dr. Lambert might have, but she was dead. He sometimes wished he had gone on to get a graduate degree but not to the point that he ever seriously looked into it. He had also at times wanted to train for the careers of chef, paramedic, and highway patrolman but had never gotten beyond fantasy. He didn't think he had wasted his life but he had the nagging feeling that he could have actually done some of these things if he'd put his shoulder to it.

Something familiar moved past the window. His brain caught up with it a moment later: Patricia's car. He left the coffee shop and watched his wife haul ass toward Broadway, catch a yellow light, swing left, disappear. He looked at the bank clock. 11:30. *I have an 11:30 closing.* He knew they'd streamlined things with computers and whatnot but he didn't think they could do a closing in less than a minute. The notion that she'd been lying made his stomach fold into itself. He rushed back to his car, this time like a bowling ball, forcing the phone lackeys to jump out of his way, and tried to catch up to his wife. As if part of a conspiracy, all the lights were red when he reached them. At Broadway and Main he turned right and floated west, scanning the side streets for the Mazda. He tried to envision a situation in which she had to run after something but she had supposedly been promoted beyond that kind of thing. People came to her; that was the payoff for fifteen years with the same company. Far ahead at Twenty-fifth he thought he spotted her car making a left and when he reached the intersection he had nothing else to go by. He was driving too fast and so tunnel-visioned that he was unaware of his surroundings. This was how it felt to be a psycho, he thought, a killer. He needed a Klonopin or a beer or a Klonopin washed down with a beer. He took a right at Thirteenth and drove past West Acres Mall and cruised restaurant row, rotating his head like it was a machine and not a human head containing human thoughts, desires, fears, dreams, ideas, a head similar to Einstein's but also similar to Lee Harvey Oswald's if you believed in the lone-gunman theory, which Pratt didn't.

He saw her car at Red Lobster.

He drove by and made a U-turn and parked across the street and stared at the front door. Saw couples going in. Noted the fact that very few men held the door open for women. More barbarianism, like the baseball caps. In Pratt's mind there was no point in living in that kind of world. Not much earlier while taking a leak he'd noticed his neighbor's chain-link fence and the steel mesh had signified to Pratt the end of civilization, at least until he was done urinating and had gone on with his daily routine. Now he lighted a smoke and thought about driving his car across the street, picking up speed, crashing through the door. He'd climb out amid the chaos and screams and sit in the booth with Patricia and whomever she was with. Just sit calmly and flip through a menu.

He sipped his Costa Rican blend for the first time since paying for it. His hands were shaking. This wasn't supposed to be happening with medication and his newly rearranged brain. His heart was racing. He wanted to get to the truth. At that very moment Patricia could be sitting with one of her girlfriends. Perhaps her closing had been canceled. Things happened. But the coin flipped and he imagined her across the table from another man, giving him a gaze that should have been reserved for Pratt. Feet caressing calves under the table. He tried to see what other cars were in the lot but the lot was L-shaped and it was futile. Well, he had evidence. He had something. He put the car in gear and headed for Rayburn's office. Rayburn had said to come see him if Pratt was ever "in crisis." Pratt wasn't sure what he was in but *crisis* came pretty close.

32

"I WAS AFRAID this would happen," Rayburn said. "Your brain has adjusted pretty fast to the dosage. You're tolerant. I'm going to bump you up to fifteen milligrams."

"What if I adjust to that?"

"We'll go to twenty."

Pratt imagined a giant horse pill. "We just keep going forever?"

"No, no. We evaluate, try another medication, augment the Lexapro. Don't worry. This takes time. You golf, don't you?"

"I try."

"Look at all the work the pros do on their swing. They refine their swing, they hire coaches, you know. It can take years for them to get into the groove."

"I feel like I don't have years."

"Oh?"

"I guess I thought I'd start taking the pills and that would be it, I'd be cured."

"You'll never be cured. You'll just manage."

"Well, that sucks," Pratt said.

"But you knew that. You're an educated man. You were talking about Camus at Martha's house."

"I was?"

The doctor nodded. "This," he said, touching his stubby fingertip to Pratt's forehead, "is your Sisyphean boulder. Now, we can't make it go away but we can make it a little lighter and we can make you a little stronger."

"I felt back to square one at the Red Lobster. I felt totally insane."

"But how would you have handled it premedication?"

Pratt paused. "I would have gone in and freaked out."

Rayburn leaned back and laced his fingers across his belly. "But today you didn't."

"True. I wanted to."

"But you didn't. You recognized that you were having an episode."

"I didn't recognize anything. I was scared to go in. I thought I was going to have a stroke."

"You really should see a therapist, you know. Treatment is much more effective when it combines therapy and medication. Goddamn, I wish Martha was still practicing."

"Practicing?"

"She's a gifted therapist. We once talked about opening an office together. Then when Dale killed himself she quit."

"Really?"

"You didn't know this?"

"No. I mean, I knew he shot himself. In the eye, right?"

"Yes. He used a .25-caliber derringer. Martha didn't blame herself but she went through a period of, well, questioning. I mean, here she was helping all manner of fucked-up—no offense—fucked-up people with a suicide brewing in her own house that she didn't even see. I'm hoping she'll get back into it. The art has been good for her. People need diversions. Distractions. People like you especially. What do you do besides play golf?"

"I read."

"What else?'

"I worry."

Rayburn started writing a prescription. "Find something. Fly fishing, woodworking. Doesn't matter what. I have my horse and my motorcycle. On a good day I ride one of them and on a great day I ride them both."

"Will Blue Cross pay for a Harley?"

Rayburn laughed. "You have a sense of humor. That's a good sign."

"Gallows humor."

• • •

He didn't feel particularly like going home and going crazy there so after he filled his prescription and dropped a Klonopin, Pratt drove around and accidentally wound up at Martha's house. Her Suburban was in the driveway when he rolled past and he kept going, drove for another five minutes before accidentally winding up in her driveway. She was standing on the porch by the time he climbed out. Hands on her hips, she didn't look especially pleased to see him, and he wondered if he was turning into a pest. As he slunk to her door he tried to think up an excuse for being there. Maybe he could claim he was looking for something he'd forgotten. His credit card could have easily slipped into her sofa cushions. Or something. But when he drew closer the ruse wasn't necessary.

"I saw you drive by. I was hoping you'd stop."

"Well."

"I've been thinking about you and Rayburn has these strange relative ethics and won't say a word."

"There's not much to say. He lays drugs on me, I take them."

"You should be talking to someone as well."

"I'm planning to."

"Good."

He looked up at her. Again a dress and he wondered if she wore a dress every day. This one was a little more snug against the curves. Her hips were wide and jiggly. Well, it made his head swoon. He had no business being there but then again, who had any business being anywhere? We're not apes, after all, he thought.

"Are you coming in?"

"You want an honest answer?"

"It wasn't that kind of question."

"What kind of question?"

"*That* kind of question. Listen, would you like a drink?"

"Not really supposed to be drinking on this medication."

"Do you anyway?"

"A little."

"I'll make you a little one, then."

• • •

The way Rayburn had explained it, his obsessive thoughts, manifesting themselves in adultery concerns, had like cancer spread into all areas of his consciousness so that he was unable to smell, see, taste properly. Or something like that. He was, Rayburn said, "hypervigilant." In any event, a little calmer now and medicated, he was aware of the scent of jasmine in her house, the desert-like dry air, the absence of pet odor, the lack of traffic sounds by virtue of what looked like expensive double-paned, insulated windows. The temperature was cool. She came out from the kitchen and handed him a red concoction in a martini glass.

"What is this?"

"Taste it."

He did. "Good."

"Cosmopolitan. A lot of men won't drink something with a name like that."

"What's in a name?" He took another sip. "You can call it anything you want and I'll still take another after this one."

"I go in these phases," she said, joining him on the sofa. "For a while it was White Russians but they're pretty fattening. Us gals, as they say around here, are supposed to drink cranberry juice, so here we go."

"Down the hatch."

They drank and stared at each other. Pratt kept feeling like he should talk but nothing interesting came to mind. He didn't want to bring up the Red Lobster. He didn't feel the need to blow words into the space between them. He wasn't sure why. It was either the medication or something else, more progress. Or a relapse. He recalled a proverb, supposedly Vietnamese: *The strong man crosses his arms; the wise man closes his mouth.*

She had a grandfather clock, a real one, not a thousand-dollar furniture-store knockoff, and when it began to chime two o'clock he put his hand on her leg and pushed her dress up. He leaned down and kissed her knee. Licked her knee. She plucked his drink from his hand and held both martini glasses by the stems, up in the air, like she was bearing them for some invisible deity. He pushed the hem up farther with his nose and followed with his tongue. Her fleshy legs shuddered and he fell to his knees and went deeper The inside of her thigh was white as a bleached bone, soft as warm dough, a baby's butt, a newborn kitten, cashmere, his new calfskin golf glove, a million clichés in each square inch he traced and kissed, moving closer, moving in. He smelled the sea. He felt driven by a hunger that wasn't quite sexual. A hunger for something. A hunger. He went no further but instead licked a postage-stamp-sized square of her delicate territory and then stopped. Pulled away. Sat next to her again and took his cosmopolitan.

"I'm sorry," he said.

"For what?"

"Stopping. Starting. Stopping."

"Why did you stop?" She did not seem frustrated or upset. He wondered if his technique was off, if somehow Patricia's spine-tingling moans while he performed the same act were just a ruse, fakery, a big fat lie.

"What?"

"Why did you stop?"

"I'm not sure why. I kind of wanted to keep going but then what right would I have to complain if she—if my wife—was doing the same thing?"

"Ah. You wouldn't be the victim anymore."

"I might not only not be the victim but I might be the only guilty one."

"Because you aren't sure she's been fooling around."

"I still don't think she has. Physically. Yet."

"A couple weeks ago you were singing a different song."

"I feel more realistic now. Did I tell you about the snake?"

"The snake?"

"I was golfing the other day. My ball went into the trees." He recalled striding from the fairway with his nine iron, stepping on drying leaves, seeing in the corner of his eye something moving through the underbrush like a thread through a loom. "There was a snake. Just a little one but a snake is a snake. I've always been terrified of snakes. I used to have these nightmares where snakes were chasing me, I mean moving fast, getting closer to me no matter how fast I ran." He drained his cosmopolitan. Stared into the funnel of the glass. "Anyway, normally I would have said fuck the ball and gotten out of there. That would have been it."

He watched her slowly push her dress down again to cover her knee. "But instead I held the snake down with my golf club. And then I picked him up."

"Really?"

"Yes. I just reached down and picked him up by the tail."

"That's pretty amazing."

"Well, it wasn't that big a snake."

"Still."

"I picked him up and looked at him. Then he tried to curl up and bite me. And instead of panicking I gave him a little shake and set him down."

She took his glass and got up. "Another?"

"One more."

While she was gone he thought again of her thigh, the color of Vermeer's milk flowing from a pitcher. Almost against his will he got a hard-on. Regrets. He imagined her slipping out of the dress, imagined humping her on the huge sofa, her riding him on the beige carpet.

"So, a snake."

He took the new drink. "This is delicious."

"Thank you."

"Anyway, what I mean about the snake is that it wasn't that I was being brave because it was just a freaking garter snake, you know. Nothing heroic but I was realistic about it. Logical? I don't know."

She raised her glass. "To progress."

"Progress."

33

HE WAS a little buzzed when he left Martha's place. It was only four and here he was, semidrunk in broad daylight, with an indefinable energy. He would have preferred to still be at her place but she had to get ready for a meeting of a board of some sort for which she served as treasurer. There'd been a hint of regret when she'd mentioned it. He wasn't sure what was going on. The fact of licking her thigh now seemed less intimate than clinking glasses with her.

He drove to Long John Silver's and gorged on fish and chips in the parking lot, washing it down with iced tea until he felt less drunk than simply full. He watched two F-16s take off in unison from the air guard base, bank left, head west, disappear. They flew in circles all day and won national awards. He lighted a cigarette and wondered what to do with the rest of his day. He didn't particularly feel like golfing. His last score card had been an embarrassment, but his 64 for nine holes had been countered by picking up the snake. Until that point in his life he'd never touched a snake and he'd been amazed at how delicate it was, how perfectly suited for its tiny role on the earth, not like people with their gangly limbs and hanging balls and odd features. How two members of the same species could be so different was a mystery. Two people in the same family, even. His brother was blond. But he was pretty sure the snake's brother probably looked a great deal like the snake. Then again, he'd never really studied snakes and maybe a trained what—herpetologist—could point out a hundred subtle differences. Who knew? It struck him as a low-grade epiphany that there were a million things he knew absolutely nothing about.

• • •

At eight-thirty Patricia came home. Pratt had fully intended to not ask her about the Red Lobster. Rayburn's final comment had been that to fight off an impulse was to gather strength. But Pratt couldn't go all the way. The moment Patricia walked through the door he spat out a question: "How was work?"

"What?" She hung up her coat, flipped through the mail on the table. Held up the Target bill. "I just paid this last week."

"I said how was work?"

"Same as usual. Probably handled over three-quarters of a million bucks without seeing any actual money."

"How was your eleven-thirty?"

"What?"

"The one you blew me off for."

"I'm sorry about that. The rose was nice. But like I said, we've been really busy."

Pratt was at a crossroads here, he understood. His logical mind grappled with his emotions. He needed a distraction or he was going to blow a hole in the plane that was their marriage. He needed the phone to ring, lightning to kill the lights, he needed something because emotion and logic were beating the hell out of each other as his wife finished with the mail and came by his chair, pausing to kiss him on the forehead before heading for the bedroom to change, he needed a distraction, a Harley to ride or a horse to groom. Logic and emotion tied in their battle. "You know," he said, "I don't ask a lot of you but I hope you know I put a high value on truth."

"I know you do. And I give you truth."

"Always?"

"Dennis, what are you getting at? If you're getting at something I wish you'd do it and quit playing games."

"You don't like playing games?"

"I'm tired and I want to change and watch some television and go to bed."

"That's fine," he said. "I have an errand to run."

"This late?"

"Just to Wal-Mart."

"Will you get me some hairspray?"

"Whatever," he said because it seemed the only word that suited the moment. He could understand why she used it so often.

• • •

Just getting away seemed to help. He drove to Wal-Mart, grabbed a cart, went to sporting goods. There was nothing remotely related to deep-sea fishing though if he was interested in walleyes and northern pike it would have been like going to heaven. He bought some improbably large Strike King fishing glasses on an elastic cord. Picked up a package of Nike balls, a straw Topflite panama hat. Rolled down through the toys. On a whim he picked out a Barbie doll for Candy but then it struck him that she wasn't the doll type. What type was she? She'd probably appreciate a Zippo lighter or a carton of smokes more. He compromised and bought her a combination lantern and radio. Batteries. He almost forgot Patricia's hairspray but didn't. Went to the pet aisle and wished he owned a dog, not a Yorkshire terrier like Patricia's Fancy but something he could train and drive around with, a German shepherd or a Southern hound dog. He spent half an hour looking at two koi circling each other. He was joined by a small boy of about ten who rudely tapped on all the aquariums, sending all manner of tropical fish flitting around. "Koi are carp, did you know that?" he asked Pratt.

"I did not know that."

"Now you do," the boy said.

A million and one things he knew absolutely nothing about.

34

JENSON had some bad news. "Not entirely bad but potentially bad."

"What do you know about snakes?"

"I dropped herpetology and took ornithology instead."

"Oh."

"You can ask me about birds."

"Are their bones really hollow?"

"I think so. Anyway," Jenson said, lifting a paper from his desk, "I got this fax today. Scared the heck out of me since we never get a fax. Here."

Pratt took it. It was written in a shaky hand, the hand of an old man. Like his grandfather's poststroke hand, angular and uneven, as if life itself depended on getting the words out. How many times had he seen that handwriting in birthday cards, simply glanced at the message before pocketing the crisp dollar bill—always a dollar, even when he was seventeen—and tossing the card? A wave of sadness rolled through Pratt. His grandfather had been dead for twenty years.

In the middle of this reverie, Jenson plucked the fax from his hands. "So what do you know about this?"

"About what?"

"Mercury."

"Say again?"

"This guy he describes, well. It's you."

"Can I see that again?"

Jenson furrowed his brow. Stepped back a few feet. "I'll make a copy."

"Just let me see it. I didn't read it."

"You were staring at it for five minutes."

"I was looking at it, true. But I wasn't reading it."

"What were you doing, then, buddy?"

"I was looking at the handwriting."

"Okay. Well, I need to hang on to this. For your safety and for mine."

"Safety?" Pratt laughed. "What's with all the drama?"

"The drama? The drama? We get a fax from a guy saying he gave you five gallons of mercury *and* five hundred bucks and now he's worried about whether or not you handled it properly and you're asking me about *drama?*"

"Jesus."

"We're both going to be in some major deep kimchi if this guy faxed the same letter downtown. I keep waiting for the phone to ring."

"Jenson."

"They like to investigate this stuff. They'd love to rub me out because I'm this close to getting benefits and a 401K. They'll probably promote *you* and fire *me.*"

"Come on."

Jenson stared him down. Pratt shrugged, feigning indifference. Then he leaped forward to snatch the letter. Jenson had played football in college; moreover, he was adept at judo. Despite being a little doughy in the middle he stepped to the side and gave Pratt his hip; Pratt hit the desk and flew over the top. When he climbed to his feet Jenson was calmly taking a dip of Copenhagen. "When you lose control, you lose."

"Who said that?"

"Pembleton."

"Pembleton?"

"The black guy on *Homicide.*"

"That's right. I thought I'd heard it before."

"Let's get to work. We'll discuss this later."

"Let's."

· · ·

Pratt pounded on the trailer door. He could hear music coming from within, not hard Southern rock and roll or Merle Haggard like he would have thought but an eerie kind of New Age electrofunk. Not loud either. Pratt knocked again, harder, so hard his knuckles left slight dents in the cheap metal. This time the curtain came back and something hideous oozed against the glass and at once Pratt recalled seeing *Jaws* when he was a child, that particularly frightening scene when a severed head bounced against a porthole. He recoiled. It was Cole, or what had once been Cole. This was a different Cole—one whose mullet haircut had turned into a forest with wide clear-cuts of scalp showing. His face was bony and pale, covered with open sores. The effect was as if he'd been hit with a load of rock salt from a shotgun. His eyes registered no emotion.

"What?" he shouted.

"I need that mercury back now."

"It's gone."

Pratt held up a hundred-dollar bill, smoothed it like wallpaper against the rectangular glass. Held it there for dramatic effect and then pulled it back. Cole was gone. Pratt knocked and knocked. "Nobody home," Cole screamed.

"Where's Candy?"

"What?"

"Your daughter."

"Come back later."

"I need that mercury, Cole."

"Keep your money." The music went lower, then off completely.

"It's dangerous. You better not be fooling around with it. You can get sick."

"Lots of things can make you sick."

Pratt pounded on the door. "You want me to get the cops?"

"Do what you have to do."

"Because that mercury belongs to me."

"Progression is nine-tenths of the law."

35

DINNER at the Outback Steakhouse, which Patricia had been wanting to try ever since it had opened in Fargo. This was Pratt's idea. He intended to confess all to his wife, the mental illness, the mercury, Cole, the Lexapro and Klonopin, Dr. Rayburn, even his swimming lessons, though probably not Martha. Why complicate an already complicated situation?

He intended to confess all of this in the spirit of truth and new beginnings, also hoping it would prompt her own soul-baring, but then he made the grave error of ordering rack of lamb. When the waiter scurried off, Patricia glared at him.

"What?" he asked.

"You ordered lamb?"

"Yes."

The waiter came with their drinks, Patricia's margarita and Pratt's cosmopolitan, which he used as a stalling agent by sipping at it thoughtfully. It wasn't nearly as good as Martha's, tasted as if it had come from a plastic-bottled mix. When he glanced up Patricia was still glaring. "Whatever."

"What?"

"I can't believe you ordered lamb."

"It looks good. I'm tired of steak. Steak is lame."

"*Lame?* What are you, a ninth grader?"

"What's wrong with lamb? It's leaner than beef."

"You *fucker.*"

"Honey."

"You've forgotten about Baby?"

"Oh Jesus," Pratt said, and a thousand photographs flipped through his mind: Patricia at ten holding the newborn orphaned black lamb; Patricia feeding the lamb with a huge-nippled glass bottle, Patricia in bed with the lamb, et cetera. Even today Patricia kept a stuffed lamb on the windowsill at work in memoriam. At the Fargo Street Fair years earlier Pratt had bought two gyros from a booth owned by a Greek family and had realized only after paying for them that the meat inside was lamb; he'd decided not to mention it to his wife but after eating the gyro, and *enjoying it,* he'd later argue, she'd strolled by the booth and read the placard and vomited right there surrounded by thousands of attendees and hundreds of craft and food booths, power puked and he could still remember the arc of vomit, the crowd parting in panic as if she'd produced an AK-47 and begun spraying lead. He'd denied knowing it was lamb in the gyro and had made things worse by calmly finishing his own while she cleaned her mouth with a handful of napkins, too shocked at having eaten lamb to be embarrassed by the event.

"I'm sorry," Pratt said, now, "but I *like* lamb." He lighted a cigarette and held it away from the table, an old habit. "Lamb is delicious. When you see a lamb you see Baby, you see something to hold and take care of. When I see a lamb I think about lamb chops. I've had to avoid lamb for twenty years. It's your hang-up, not mine. I didn't have a pet lamb, you did."

Pratt's wife ran her finger along the rim of her glass and licked the salt. "You know what?"

"What?"

"You've been acting real different lately."

"Different?"

"Yes."

"Different how?"

"I don't know, Dennis. You've been like a pendulum, you know?" She made an elaborate gesture with her hand. "You're either out here or way out here."

"Where do you want me?"

"I want you in the middle is where I want you."

"The middle?"

"Yes."

"To be in the middle I'd have to be stopped."

She shrugged.

"I see," he said. He drew on his cigarette and one by one his planned confessions evaporated, popping around his head like defective balloons.

• • •

Because the eighth at the Bonanza was high on a hill, when you teed off the ball was already in the air and as a result Pratt, a low-baller, tended to do better on the hole. The eighth inspired confidence. You had a clear view of the flag. It was a good hole for a neophyte.

Pratt shoved in his tee and set a new ball, one of his gleaming Nikes, atop it. He was playing only the last three holes because it was getting dark. He'd been told in the office he had time for only three but he was allowed to pick which three. Three holes were better than none. Some old men were halfway to the green, taking their time, bent over like pretzels as they lined up their shots. Pratt doubted if his drive would even come close to hitting them, but he didn't want to jinx himself by not thinking he might make it that far. Besides, nobody was behind him. No pressure. He could still taste his lamb from dinner earlier. It hadn't been as good as he'd thought it would be and it didn't help that Patricia glared at him over her own bland chicken. If she'd had a chicken as a childhood pet then she'd be in real trouble, he decided. After dinner they'd gone home and parted company in silence. She'd gone for a bike ride, suiting up in what looked like a very expensive spandex outfit, while he shoved the new golf balls into his bag. A snapshot of suburbia and one that he wasn't all that happy to be frozen in. The only things missing, he realized, were a fucking cul-de-sac lapping at the edge of their lawn and a golden retriever. He was struck by yet another sort of epiphany: he wasn't at all sure that Patricia was the one he should be married to. All his worries over the last few months had revolved around the belief that she might be cheating; now, atop the hill, a faint evening breeze cooling the sweat that rose from the climb, he wondered why he was so concerned in the first place. If she wanted someone else it could be a blessing in disguise. He was trying to imagine how the dimensions of his life would change without her when a long shadow sliced through him. When he looked up he saw a silhouette in the brushy area behind the tee. Cole. He was loping away from the railroad tracks toward the trees in a manner that reminded Pratt of that 1970s shaky Bigfoot film, although unlike Bigfoot, Cole did not glance back. He was in an obvious hurry, moving with the highly focused purpose of the home- less who in Fargo always seemed on their way to something important in order to avoid loitering charges. Cole disappeared and Pratt wan- dered over to intersect his path. He wasn't entirely sure that Cole had not been an apparition but there were faint tracks in the dusty earth from hobnailed boots. Pratt followed them toward the railroad, trying like a child to match the long strides, then broke off and went back to the tee. The old men were gone, off to the ninth. Pratt hit one high and straight, one that traveled so far it might well have thumped one of the old men, at least until the wind carried it in a wide but unerr- ing arc into the rough.

36

ON THE border between the deep and shallow water, under the lifeguard chair, Pratt attempted to tread water. It was exhausting and Pratt had the distinct suspicion that it wasn't supposed to be. He recalled hearing of shipwreck survivors treading water for days. After thirty seconds of kicking he was clinging to the edge again, watching his skinny legs suspended like waterlogged branches. He looked for Lucas and spotted him massaging the triathlete's broad shoulders. Who could blame him, really? A man of almost forty afraid of water must seem like a total waste of time, Pratt decided. He looked up at the lifeguard's tanned legs, legs meant for a skirt but hiding what appeared, as she shifted in the chair, to be incredibly powerful muscles. Her name was Amber and she was Whitney's age if not younger. I want the last twenty years back, he thought. The last thirty. I want to pop a Klonopin at the Chicago pool and dive in with the rest of the boys. I want to laugh in the water. I want to be loose as a goose.

"Okay, you," Amber said.

"Me?"

"I want you to do something."

"What," Pratt asked, "do you want me to do?"

"I want you to stand up here and jump in."

"Not going to happen."

"You can do it. Go in like a pencil. Let most of your air out and touch bottom, and then push up."

"I don't know. I'm working in baby steps here."

"I've been watching you. You can do it."

"What if I don't come up?"

"There are three lifeguards here. We can carry your body pretty easily."

Pratt laughed. "What the hell," he said. He pulled himself along the wall until for the first time in his life as a swimmer there was no ground under his feet. Just getting to *this* point was an accomplishment that put holding a snake in the league of tying his shoes for the first time. Once in Maine on a trip with his father and brother Pratt had slipped a few inches into the deep end of a motel pool late at night and could still call forth the panic he'd felt, sliding down the slimy floor before lunging for the edge.

He pulled himself up and stood there getting cold. Tried to visualize the act but Amber wouldn't let him.

"Just do it. Don't think so much. Take a breath and do it."

He did it. Stepped off the edge and went down, blew bubbles. Felt his feet hit bottom. Made himself pause for a moment before launching up to prove he wasn't afraid. He was amazed at how quickly he rose. He broke through the water and breathed and grabbed the edge. Looked up at Amber like a hopeful child.

"See?" she said.

"That wasn't so bad," Pratt said. He sounded cool but what he wanted more than anything was to scream so that everyone in the crappy old building knew what he'd just done. Across the pool, small unworried children were floating like inflatable toys in the same depth. They had no idea what he had just done. It was like Camus and James Dean and Jackson Pollock and John Gardner slowing down at the appropriate time, getting out of the car, getting off the bike, drinking coffee, handing over the keys, going on to do more work, to grow old, to bear more children.

"Do it again."

He did. This time when he surfaced, he did not reach right away for the edge but instead tried to swim along the edge toward the shallow end. He almost made it, went under, felt nothing under his feet, panicked and thrashed his way to the edge, but regained his composure.

Amber had been walking alongside him. "Not bad. I think there's a swimmer in you dying to get out."

"A shark?"

"At least a tadpole."

. . .

"You smell funny," his wife said. She was astride him. He had come home from swimming so jubilant that even she couldn't resist him and walked by in her white nightie while he was changing into his pajamas, which meant only one thing. Pratt had been exhausted from the effort in the water but the victory had given him a new vitality and he was like a young man in bed, he thought. It helped that a side effect of the Lexapro was delayed ejaculation. Or, in this case, no ejaculation. He'd worn her out anyhow. Now she had stopped moving, looking down at him. In the dim light he realized he didn't quite recognize her anymore. Twenty years with one woman who then sheds the equivalent of a person, albeit a small person, and you wound up with a separate person. Breasts that had once pummeled his face like cartoon boxing gloves were hard to find in the darkness, sometimes requiring him to orient his tongue on a known landmark, her shoulder or throat, and navigate that way.

"Funny how?"

"Like bleach or something. Chlorine."

And he almost told her, largely because he wanted to tell *someone*. But he bit his tongue, imagining them all in Mexico, Patricia sipping a daiquiri and watching him dive into the pool, the shock and maybe pride on her face. "Chlorine?"

She leaned down and pressed her nose into his hair. "Yes."

"Work," he said. "We got some pool chemicals in and they were leaking all over the place. Jenson almost made me take a shower but they didn't burn or anything. You should have smelled me when it happened. About knock you out."

"Yuck."

"You weren't complaining a minute ago."

"I had other things going on in my body."

"Well, pretty soon we'll be in Mexico," Pratt said. "Next time we make love we'll be in a foreign country."

"Do you think it'll be different?"

"You'll have to say, 'Fuck me, fuck me,' in Spanish."

She climbed off him, reached around for her nightgown. "You're a pig."

"No hablo inglés, señora."

"I'm not nearly tan enough. I'm hitting the beds tomorrow."

"You're pretty tan."

"Compared to you. I wish you'd spent more time in the sun."

"Say that when you're fifty and wrinkled."

"I'll be dead by then, remember? Skin cancer?"

"That's right."

"What would you do?"

Pratt got up, pulled on his pajama pants and bathrobe.

"Did you hear me?"

"What?"

"If I died. What would you do?"

"How old would I be?"

"I don't know. Say, fifty-five. I'm dead. What would you do?"

"Eat more lamb?"

"Dennis, be serious."

"I don't know. I don't want to think about it."

"You always have a plan. You always have your plan and your backup plan."

"Not for this."

"I don't believe you."

"Do *you*? Have a plan?"

"Not really."

"Not *really?*"

She turned on the light, found her panties, slipped them on. "Not a specific plan."

"But a plan?"

"I've thought about it."

"You'd get remarried?"

"Well, I wouldn't rush out and get married but I wouldn't want to grow old alone, either."

"There are worse things."

"No, there aren't." She took off her earrings and dropped them into her top dresser drawer. He liked her to wear earrings when they made love and she always did. He liked some form of dress to be present, if only earrings or an ankle bracelet, sometimes a brassiere. He wasn't sure why. "I wouldn't want to be ninety years old just sitting around hoping to die."

"You'd have Whitney."

"Not every day. By then she'd have a family of her own."

"Knock on wood."

"What do you mean?"

"You know. Kids today."

"No, I don't know. Are you going to bed or staying up?"

"I'm getting up for a while. I'm hungry."

"Will you feed the cat?"

"Of course."

"That's another reason I'd have to get married again. I'd need someone to feed the cat."

"Funny. Do you have someone in mind?"

"No, I don't have someone in mind."

"What about Bruce?"

There was a pause so imperceptible Pratt wasn't sure if was a pause or just the time it took for his words to carry across the room, over the rumpled pile of clothes, to his wife, the time for her to process what he said and for the words to loop back toward him. She turned her back. "Bruce?"

"He's such a nice guy, maybe you could marry him."

"He doesn't seem like the marrying type."

"That wasn't the answer I was looking for."

"Dennis."

"Forget it."

"Why do you always do this? Why do you always turn something good into something else?"

"It was just a question."

"No it wasn't. And I'm getting tired of the fucking third degree all the time about Bruce. He's my friend. We ride bikes together. That's all."

"So there's no way you'd ever marry him."

"I'm not going to say it would never happen. I'm not going to make some promise to my husband beyond the grave, but you aren't dying anytime soon so it's a moot issue."

"You're the one who brought it up and what do you mean you won't say it would never happen?"

"I don't mean anything."

"You said it."

"I mean nobody can predict the future. Now can we please drop it?"

Pratt nodded and left the room. He grabbed a beer from the refrigerator and went downstairs. Pulled his copy of Zane Grey's *Tales of Fishing Virgin Seas* from the shelf and removed his bottle of Klonopin. Laid not a half tablet but a whole one on his tongue like a tiny yellow communion wafer, let it begin to dissolve before washing it down with Coors Light. The Silver Bullet. If he took all the pills and sat in his chair he'd simply fall asleep. In the morning she'd come down a few steps and bend down, see him sleeping there, a book on his lap. This had happened before and she always just let him be. She wouldn't worry until she got home and he was still there, stiff as a

board. She could call Carver and he'd arrive to save the day, comfort
her, handle the authorities. He put the pills back on the shelf and
paged through the Zane Grey. He was behind in his reading. He had
hoped to be able to throw out interesting facts as they trolled for marlin. *This is not far from where Zane Grey caught a two-hundred-pound
tuna.* Et cetera. He lighted a cigarette and stared at the small rectangular window near the ceiling, dusty and unblinded. He wondered if
anyone was ever out there looking back at him. He wouldn't know.
Someone could show up every night and get on hands and knees and
watch him reading and smoking. It wouldn't be much entertainment
but then again much of what he read just went into his head, swirled
around, and faded like smoke, sometimes not even leaving an odor or
stain. In that case he and the unseen stranger might be on even
ground. The stranger would go home when Pratt went to bed and
they'd both fall asleep none the better or worse for their evening. Pratt
raised his beer to the window. Then he gazed at his bookshelf but
nothing intrigued him very much. He'd barely cracked the *Saltwater
Gamefish* book beyond looking at the pictures, had not memorized
the Latin names of various species as he'd planned. He had not
learned much Spanish in spite of intending to for eight months. He
knew that *baño* meant bathroom. In a few days they'd be in Mexico.
He'd gone from excitement to dread to fear to ambivalence. He had a
feeling they wouldn't be seeing much of the "real" Mexico, the one
his own grandfather had seen as a fifteen-year-old runaway aboard a
gun-smuggling ship from Boston. Smuggling guns for Emiliano Zap-
ata. In his earlier years Pratt had imagined writing a novel based on
his grandfather's illustrious young life, during which, in addition to
being a smuggler, he'd been in the navy during World War I, on the
original USS *South Dakota*, and a professional gambler in Havana.
He had imagined going to Mexico for research, hanging out in small
cafés, making love to beautiful girls who were perhaps his illegitimate
cousins, and for some reason this prospect was titillating. Then the release of the novel and fame not only for him but for the family, the ul-

timate liturgy for a man Pratt had barely gotten to know but with whom he had always felt a kinship. His grandfather after all the adventures had been a respected artist and teacher in Arizona, painting abstracts that revealed a certain agony Pratt could understand. But he was an alcoholic and let himself die when Pratt was fourteen. Pratt had never begun work on the novel but had gone so far as to imagine the cover art, a detail of one of his grandfather's paintings. He wondered now, vaguely, if it would be possible for him to write a book. If he wasn't too old, but then again, there was that *A River Runs Through It* guy who'd pulled it off in his seventies. In any event Pratt had not tried in many years to write anything besides an occasional attempt at a journal, trying to turn his concerns and observations into something resembling art, something more interesting than a photograph or remark at dinner, the odd *I saw an eagle today* rendered quasi-poetic, but at some point he'd realized there was no point and shredded the entire collection without rereading a single word. Now he wished he still had it. Things didn't have to be either-or. He remembered being a Cub Scout, when the den mother had cheerfully announced they'd be going on a bike-hike at the next meeting. Pratt had not yet owned a bicycle; his father had been reluctant to buy one for fear he'd be run over by one of the college students in their neighborhood. So eight-year-old Pratt had helped plan the route, written down what he needed to bring, eaten his cookie and drunk his juice, and walked home crying, knowing it was his last meeting, the end of his career as a Cub Scout. He'd hung up his blue uniform shirt for the last time like a bitter war veteran. Now, thirty-some years later, it struck him that he could have simply told his den mother, a sweet lady, and she would surely have found a bicycle for him to use and nobody would have been the wiser. At the time, though, it had seemed a black-and-white proposition. He hadn't seen the color gray. If he had, he might have gone on to become an Eagle Scout and a pillar of the community instead of the guy who seemed to have an awful lot of extra time on his hands.

37

"I BOUGHT us some time," Jenson said.

"Why do we need time?"

"I told headquarters about the fax."

"Okay. Why?"

"The best defense is a good offense."

"Silence works pretty good."

Jenson seemed to consider this. "I said the mercury might be in the big room and it would take a day or so to find it."

"Maybe it *is* in there."

"I'd be pretty surprised. I think, and don't take this the wrong way. I think you have it."

"Is that right?"

Jenson was in his lab whites, standing behind a cart with a white cloth over it. Pratt wasn't sure but it looked as if he'd shaved more carefully than normal, and his usual grimy Minnesota Vikings hat had been replaced with a spotless Dale Earnhardt cap. "The evidence points to you," Jenson said. "I've conducted an investigation of sorts."

"An investigation?"

"It's my job."

Pratt laughed. "Does that come before or after mowing the grass on your job description?"

Jenson looked genuinely hurt.

"Well, go ahead," Pratt said.

"Exhibit one." Jenson reached under the cart and laid the thick book atop the white sheet.

"The Merck?"

"You've been studying mercury. You underlined the part that says, and I quote, 'Mercury has an affinity for brain cells.' Unquote."

"I don't recall doing that."

A "Hazardous Waste" magnet was serving as a bookmark. Jenson opened to the pages about mercury. "Notice the coffee stain."

"I see it."

"You're the only one here who drinks coffee."

"Guilty. I was reading about mercury. But flip through the book and you'll probably find coffee stains elsewhere. The other day I was researching DDT."

"Exhibit two. Your car."

"My car?"

"The suspension was under extreme duress."

"I told you. I had sand in there for our horseshoe pits."

"Ah. Exhibit three." Jenson produced a Polaroid photograph of Pratt's backyard, the horseshoe pits filled not with sand but with clay. It had been taken in darkness, with a flash. "You don't use sand. You use clay. Nice pits, by the way."

"Thanks. When did you take this?"

"The other night."

"You snuck into my yard and took a picture?"

"I didn't sneak. I walked."

"In the middle of the night."

"It wasn't that late. You were still up."

"How do you know?"

"I saw you reading and drinking beer in the basement."

· · ·

Jenson had given him a day to recover the mercury. Twenty-four hours, and for effect, he'd set the timer on his little digital folding travel clock and put it on the shelf. He wasn't clear what would happen otherwise but to Pratt it didn't matter one way or another. In fact he would just as soon forget about it and let the chips fall where they may, get fired or not, but he liked Jenson and felt obligated to return the mercury because of it. Things would have been easier if Jenson were an asshole. Jenson could occasionally be an asshole but that wasn't the same thing as *being* an asshole. Pratt's mind explored these notions as he drove home early. That is, he intended to go home but found himself pulling into Martha's driveway instead. This time he sat in the car and smoked a cigarette. Kissing her leg now seemed like a dream, déjà vu, or one of those strange presleep visions he'd been experiencing since starting on antidepressants. He closed his eyes and tried his damndest to remember if it had actually happened. He couldn't say for sure. The passenger door opened and Martha climbed in. "A gentleman would have opened the door for me."

"Sorry. I was trying to remember something."

"What?"

"I don't want to ask because you know the answer."

"Would knowing help?"

"No."

"Then don't ask."

They sat for a few minutes, not talking. She took one of his cigarettes from the package on the seat and lighted it. Rolled down the window a few inches. She was the first woman besides his wife and Whitney and Candy to be in his car in years. It felt oddly thrilling just to have her sitting there.

"So are we going anywhere?"

"Where do you want to go?"

"Where do you want to take me?"

"I have to go on a mission to retrieve some mercury or I'll lose my job."

"Let's go, then."

• • •

The trailer was gone. The truck was gone. The lawn chairs were gone except for one that looked as if it had been used to drag a river; the nylon was flaycd and the frame was bent. The fire pit was filled with garbage. Pratt found a stick and poked around in the pit while Martha sat on the edge of the damaged chair and watched him, her legs crossed elegantly. "I don't understand," Pratt said. "They were here a couple days ago."

"The hillbillies."

"Yes. Cole and his little girl. Cole for sure. I just saw him on the golf course, actually. I haven't seen the girl—Candy, I haven't seen Candy for a while."

"How long?"

"I don't know. I've gotten really bad about time. I think it's the meds." Under a bulging plastic bag he found a doll whose eyes opened when disturbed by the stick. He pushed on the doll until the eyes closed again. The doll looked fairly new, didn't have the sheen of grime that Whitney's dolls had always seemed to accumulate. Then again, Whitney's dolls had been subject to abuse, being nailed to makeshift crosses, tied to parachutes fashioned from garbage-bag plastic, their various limbs amputated and replaced with wire prostheses. There'd been a vague feeling that something in the picture was askew.

"So your mercury could be anywhere by now."

"I'm afraid so."

Martha got up and walked along the perimeter of the campsite, eyes on the ground. She picked up a handful of beer-bottle caps and brought them over to the fire pit and dropped them in. "Maybe they're coming back."

"No. He wouldn't take the trailer if he was coming back. And all this goddamn garbage. Well, it's my own fault. I feel bad for the girl, though. It's not much of a way to live."

"Did she appear to be abused?"

Pratt tried to picture her, picture Candy. It was hard. "She smoked. Acted more adult than she should have."

"Ooh."

"Not good?"

"Not very."

They got into the car and drove down into the park. The swimming hole was closed and there was only a single family in the picnic area, packing up. The father poured a jug of water on the coals and a giant white steam cloud rose, dissipated. "I'm going to Mexico in a couple days, did I mention that?"

"Mexico?" She sounded alarmed.

"Cabo San Lucas."

"I've been there. It's beautiful."

"Pretty touristy?"

"Yes, but you don't want to spend your whole vacation looking over your shoulder. There are still bandits. Don't drive at night, by the way."

"Got it. Don't drink the water, don't drive at night."

She nodded again. "Here's some advice people don't think about. Use bottled water on your toothbrush."

"Really?"

"It only takes a few drops of bad water to make you sick. People go out of their way to drink bottled water but think nothing of pouring tap water on a toothbrush."

"You're right. I wouldn't have thought of that."

"I had my honeymoon in Cabo. Well, not Cabo but San José, which is almost a part of Cabo. Just down the road."

"That's where we're staying. Halfway between Cabo and San José."

She laughed. "There's a particular tree along the road that may look more florid than the others. If so it's because I fertilized it on the way back from dinner. I ate some bad ceviche, I think, and couldn't make it back to the hotel and my husband was worried about damaging the rental car with my, well, my *offal*, as he called it, so he pulled over right on the highway. Gave a show to everyone on the road but I didn't give a damn because I was in agony and also angry at my husband. Did I mention it was my honeymoon?"

"Yes."

"Where did *you* go? On your honeymoon?"

"We didn't really have one. This is kind of going to be it."

"That's sweet."

"I guess so." He turned to face her. He wanted to put his head in her lap. "Can I put my head in your lap?"

"Like the other day?"

"Not like that."

She reached over and pulled him down. He pressed his ear against her fleshy thigh. She stroked his hair. "I just—" he said.

"Ssshh."

He nodded. He felt a pressure behind his eyes, something like crying but with no tears.

38

Pratt called work at six-fifty-five in the morning. Jenson, a farm boy at heart, was already there. "What's the timer say?"

"Seven hours fifty-three minutes nine seconds."

"Man."

"Seven hours fifty-three and seven."

"I got it."

This was the earliest he'd been up in years, he thought, or almost. He'd seen daybreak plenty of times but usually after a night of tossing and turning, endless treks to the bathroom or kitchen for water or down to the computer to check the weather satellite for blizzards. The rare times he'd been up at dawn he'd always thought it was truly magical but not magical enough to make a habit of it. Like anything else, he thought, less was more. He liked visiting his brother in Lincoln, Nebraska, because it seemed like a hopping and literary town. One time at the Mill Coffee Shop they'd spotted Sam Shepard in the corner drinking from a tall cup. Fargo's downtown with its decaying buildings and empty storefronts couldn't hold a candle to Lincoln's no matter how much talk was devoted to creating a "renaissance." But his brother had grown weary of Lincoln and liked coming to Fargo because it was smaller and he claimed the mall was better, so who knew? Husbands and wives grew bored with one another, slipped into affairs, divorced and remarried, found themselves staring into the same monotony wearing a different mask.

Patricia was off to Wal-Mart before work to buy more essentials before they headed down to Minneapolis in the morning to catch their flight. She was unhappy with her bathing suit because it revealed the loose skin around her thighs and wanted something that came with a "wrap," whatever that was. The bed was a sea of clothes, sandals, film, sunglasses, sunblock, crossword-puzzle books. It was like an art installation of tourism clichés. He wished he was a photographer because the scene had the makings of a great picture. While he sipped his coffee he tried to imagine the photograph hanging on a museum wall, beautiful people standing before it. *Deliciously tacky, don't you say?*

Pratt headed out to the Bonanza for one last round before playing with the big boys. He was the first one out and the grass was glistening with dew. Even Tripp had not yet been out in his patrol cart. The fairways were virginal. Pratt was under all kinds of mental pressure but played beautifully, bogeying every hole, a remarkable performance, until the eighth. As he topped the hill he recalled seeing Cole lurching through the trees and this made him uneasy enough that his tee shot cut forty-five degrees to the left and hit a tree so hard the sound was like a gunshot in the morning stillness. Pratt took a mulligan and set down another ball. Stretched his arms. He desperately wanted to par the next two holes and emerge with what for him would be a decent score, something to ride on down in Mexico. Momentum, as they said. *Pratt has momentum coming into the match.* He turned and looked again at the path where Cole had been, and again Pratt wandered over. This time he spotted something on the ground. He thought it was a quarter but when he reached down to pick it up it broke into dozens of fleeing balls. Mercury. His back prickled. He looked around but saw nobody. He followed the path Cole had been coming from the other day. This time he kept going into a narrow lane between the railroad tracks and the trees, and it was at the end of this lane that he saw the pool gleaming in the morning light. The mercury was running, no, it was *oozing* as a narrow river down the hill in a tight meander among the oaks. Pratt used his club as a staff to descend the hill, following the mercury.

At the bottom of the hill he heard something that made his hair stand on end. He heard *gurgling*. It was still early enough that the sun was not fully illuminating the dense stand of timber and for a moment he lost the mercury. He had to retrace his steps up the hill a few yards before finding it again. The sound of running water began to grow louder, it was Poe's telltale heart, and then he saw it, a nameless creek, one of a million little tributaries spiderwebbing across the earth carrying water to the next largest tributary and in turn to the next, in this case the Buffalo River. The mercury had created a little waterfall into this creek. Pratt felt as if he'd been hit with a stun gun. He could hear Jenson's monologue on the evils of mercury contamination, thousands of babies sick and dying in Peru or wherever from shamelessly unsafe gold-mining practices, the origin of the phrase "mad as a hatter" after felt-hat factory workers went insane from long-term vapor exposure, et cetera. Pratt turned in a circle looking for a bucket with which to contain the flow. It occurred to him that the proper thing would be to put his mouth to the waterfall since it was his fault the river would now be polluted. This would solve a number of problems, he thought. Why hadn't it occurred to him before? He thought he heard voices and panicked. He hurried up the hill and back toward his golf bag. He would play out the round and then make an anonymous call to the Department of Natural Resources. No. He'd call Tripp, let Tripp in his nosy way handle things. Pratt grabbed his driver and swung at the ball, hit it cleanly, hit it well, didn't even wait for it to land before half running down to the fairway, his clubs rattling, his heart pounding, his mind crackling like toxic fish in a frying pan.

39

JOHNNY DEPP was a pirate on the in-flight movie between Minncapolis and Phoenix but Pratt only knew this when he happened to open his eyes. He slept through most of the flight, urged deeper by the extra Klonopin he'd popped in the restroom. His usual flying attitude was a cocktail of panic and fatalism, his ears alert for every odd clunk and his eyes on the flight attendants for signs of distress. But a few weeks earlier while taking a smoke break at work, he'd watched a Northwest flight coming in from the south and been hit with the oddly—for him—rational thought that an airplane was nothing more than a vehicle and that while his cigarette burned down, thousands of such vehicles were in the air, operating smoothly, routinely. He had even almost—not quite but almost—begun to look forward to flying. And instead of gripping the armrests during takeoff as usual, Pratt had, in Minneapolis, allowed himself to lean across Patricia and look down at the city turning into fields turning into patterns. It wasn't so bad; it wasn't anything. It just *was*. Pratt had wondered if this was some sort of Buddhist-type awareness he was experiencing or just a drug-numbed response. He tried to summon panic but it was impossible. He added the image of the mercury but even that didn't work. He had called Tripp from a pay phone and in a voice that in retrospect sounded like a bad Clint Eastwood imitation said something weird was going on fifty yards northwest of the eighth tee. To his horror Tripp had said, "Pratt?" right before Pratt had hung up. He'd worried that perhaps Tripp had, in his utility room slash office, some sort of sophisticated voice-identification device. Then Pratt had called Patricia and used the same voice to ask about interest rates and she hadn't seemed to catch on. So who knew? Tripp couldn't prove anything.

He had made a final call, once at home, to Martha. Told her what he'd found. And she'd not sounded surprised but had only asked him how he felt.

"I want to feel very guilty but when I look at how fucked up I've been I can see how I could make mistakes, how I could be so obtuse. You could have run a locomotive through my living room and I wouldn't have seen it as anything out of the ordinary."

Pause.

"Are you there?"

"I'm there."

"I don't know what to do."

"You did it already. You reported it."

"Then why do I feel like shit?"

"Do you?"

"No. I don't. But I feel like I *should* feel like shit."

"That's because you've programmed yourself to feel that way. Now the program is changing."

"To what?"

"We'll have to see."

In the Phoenix airport Pratt found a hole-in-the-wall bar and grill where smoking was allowed. Patricia refused to go inside with him, citing the thick haze. "I'm going to find a magazine and a Diet Pepsi," she said, marching off. Pratt felt the old urge to follow her and catch her in the act of making an illicit telephone call but his lungs wept for nicotine and he went inside. Trouble was, the place was elbow to elbow with fellow tobacco fiends, lighting one cigarette from the butt of the first, chaining it between or before flights. An elderly gentleman with a sort of New England bearing saw Pratt searching the hazy air for a table and offered him a chair. Pratt sat down and lighted up. The old man was drinking what looked like a bourbon. Pratt didn't especially feel like talking but felt obligated. "Busy place."

"Utterly banal," the man said. He threw down a major league gulp.

"What?"

"I offer you a chair and the best you can do is 'busy place,' as if that's somehow original."

"Just making small talk," Pratt said. A harried waiter came by and stood before Pratt. "Bloody Mary," Pratt said. He looked at the old man. "Is that okay with you?"

"Now, that's better," the old man said. "I'll take sarcasm over banality." He held out his hand. "Stevenson Lake."

"Dennis Pratt."

"Dennis Pratt. I knew some Pratts from Oklahoma. Dirtiest people on the planet. I thought they were mulattoes until the first hard rain."

"I took a piss in a Stevenson Lake once."

"Ha!"

Pratt's Bloody Mary arrived, a tiny affair with an eight-dollar price tag. He gave the waiter a ten and lighted another cigarette. Lake ordered a Jim Beam. "Where are you off to, Mr. Pratt?"

"Mexico."

"Mexico? Going to take advantage of the terrible economy, are you? Stay at an all-inclusive resort and harass the staff? Steal the soap for souvenirs? Drink piña coladas and videotape the wife standing in front of the ocean?"

"Right after I buy a big fucking sombrero with my name embroidered on it."

"I'm having a hard time getting under your skin."

"I'm down to one thin layer so I have to keep it intact."

"Tale of woe?"

"Insanity and adultery."

"Yours or hers?"

"I'm the crazy one. Do the math."

"Sounds like my last novel."

Pratt stared at him. Something clicked. "You're the guy who wrote *Deus Ex Machina*. You're a novelist."

"I used to think so. Now I fly around squeezing every last drop of income from my reputation because I'm getting old and I have no 401K."

Pratt raised his glass. "Here's to planning ahead."

"Yes. What's your line, friend?"

"Until yesterday I handled hazardous waste but I think I'm fired."

"More woe. What's in Mexico?"

"Anniversary."

"What about the adultery?"

"It was never confirmed. That's where the insanity comes in."

"Trust your gut, sport. The gut *never* lies."

"That sounds like a line from a novel."

"Well, it is. And it isn't even mine. But it holds true. Nice to meet you." Lake pushed back his chair. "I'm off to some yogurt and basket-weaving college in California."

"Thanks for the space."

Lake raised his eyebrows.

"I know," Pratt said. "More banality. But I have to save the good stuff for the next guy."

"You sound like a writer yourself."

"I've tried."

"If you can write with that wit you'll be giving me a run for my money." Lake patted him on the back and disappeared, weaving a bit, through the veil of smoke.

Pratt downed his drink and smoked two more cigarettes in quick succession. Everyone in the place seemed to be part of a smoking contest. When his lungs hurt he left the restaurant to look for Patricia. She wasn't at the gate. He checked the newsstand but she wasn't there, either. He loitered outside the ladies' room for a while. He wasn't concerned about finding her so much as he didn't want her to nag him. In her mind he would be the one missing. Told to stay at the bar the way his mother used to plant him by the pattern cabinet at the fabric store while she ran her hands through reams of cloth. Even now he had an aversion to those places.

He went to the bank of pay phones along the wall and called Whitney with his Visa card. Her roommate answered. She sounded more crisp than usual when she heard his voice.

"Whitney's in class."

"That's okay. I was just throwing the dice," Pratt said. "How are you doing?"

A pause. Music in the background. Alanis Morissette or someone as intense and troubled as Alanis Morissette. "Listen, there was some kind of cop here asking Whitney about you."

"A cop?"

"He wanted to know where you were."

Tripp, Pratt thought. "Was this cop a short guy with a crew cut and mirrored sunglasses?"

"No, he was tall and looked kind of like Tom Selleck."

"Tom Selleck?"

"Pre-*Friends* Tom Selleck. Like, *Quigley* or whatever."

"Did he say what it was about?"

"No, but he was pretty serious."

"Jesus."

"She didn't tell him where you were. She said she thought you and her mother went to the Poconos."

"The Poconos?"

"I better go."

"Son of a bitch."

"I'll tell her you called."

"Yes," Pratt said.

He hung up and turned around expecting to see blue-suited feds threading among the travelers. But all he saw were the travelers. Patricia was among them, carrying a small shopping bag. When she joined him and saw the sheen of sweat on his face she accused him of being drunk.

"I'm not drunk. Just a little queasy. What's in the bag?"

"Something for Whitney."

"A souvenir from *Phoenix?*"

"Just a gift, okay? Do you have to know everything?"

Pratt held up his hands. "It was just a question."

"Well, you ask too many questions. I feel like I've been living under a goddamn microscope."

"Maybe you need a drink."

"Maybe I do but not in that lung-cancer factory."

They started walking. Pratt wanted to call *someone*. He felt parched for information. He tried to think of a good lie to get to an out-of-sight phone bank. But there weren't that many phone banks to begin with. He wished he had a cellular phone, wasn't paranoid about getting brain cancer, his old reason for refusing to own one. For one nanosecond he felt some empathy for his wife, having to probably or possibly come up with convincing lies. But just for a nanosecond. The moment reminded him of everything and he started to feel genuinely queasy. The edge of the blanket of obsessive thinking inched toward him as he watched her shopping bag rise and fall with her every step until they reached the gate. The medication was helping but not enough to keep him from peering into the bag once they'd sat down and she turned away for a moment to unzip her carry-on. Something silky and white inhabited the shopping bag. It didn't look much like a souvenir. She grabbed it and stuffed it into the carry-on and that was that. He started to say something but bit his tongue. New concerns were pushing away the old like snow covering unraked leaves in the yard. He tapped his foot. Picked up an abandoned newspaper and stared not at the words but at the blocks of text which appeared as wavy rectangles. He put it down. "I'm going to call Whit," he said.

"We're boarding in ten minutes."

"I'll be right back."

"Why call her now? You can call her from the villa."

"If the plane goes down I don't want my last thought being that I should have called her." He stood.

"You know, Dennis, you should really be on some kind of freaking medication."

"You're probably right."

He sat down again, recalling countless thrillers in which the police watched the clock while waiting for a trace to be completed. Of course it wouldn't take rocket scientists to check with the airlines. But that and even a phone trace seemed an unlikely effort over some stolen and spilled mercury. The Tom Selleck cop was probably reluctantly following up on a complaint from Tripp, who could hassle a Mormon into raising locusts. He probably wasn't even a real cop, maybe a health inspector, a low-level bureaucrat not even allowed to carry a gun.

An hour later, without a single word spoken between them, the Pratts were in California. The nature of the airport in Ontario was such that they had to hike to another terminal in obscene heat. Patricia still wore a sweatshirt. She trooped down the sidewalk like they were late for their flight, which they weren't. He trailed behind her, enjoying his cigarette. Cigarettes. He had never been in California before. He was disappointed they weren't at LAX, where you supposedly had a shot at seeing a movie star on the escalator, not Redford or Brad Pitt but maybe someone on the level of Harvey Keitel or Martin Landau. Ahead of him Patricia turned to glare. Things weren't improving much in that department. He had the distinct feeling that if he boarded the wrong plane, say, up to Anchorage, she would not lose much sleep. He wasn't sure where their marriage was headed but he was pretty sure they were in the process of coming up on an important turn. Rayburn had said not to make a serious decision for six months but what if a fork in the road came up sooner than that? Ask for an abeyance? Tell her that in a few months he'd be able to process events and information like a normal person, and, he would say, that could make all the difference? He tossed away his cigarette as they entered the terminal, feeling no more or less hopeful than he'd ever felt.

This time after dodging Patricia he bypassed calling Whitney and dialed Martha's number instead. She answered as if she'd been waiting for a call. "It's me," he said. "Your amigo, Dennis Pratt."

"My God, Dennis."

"What?"

"What? Oh, God, you don't know, do you?"

A knife blade scratched his spine. "Know what?"

"Cole is dead."

"Dead?" Pratt recalled Cole's features the last time he'd seen him, a face that had made someone conceived by Edvard Munch look fat and healthy. Mercury could do that if you breathed the vapors. Not long before, some rednecks in Oklahoma had melted dental plates on their kitchen stove trying to retrieve gold and had wound up in the hospital. Two of them had died what were described as "horrible deaths." Jenson had posted the article on Pratt's locker.

"They found him in the swamp at the Bonanza with his head bashed in."

"Thank God."

"Say again?"

"Never mind. His head bashed in? Who killed him?"

She paused. There was something palpable within the pause. "They're not saying much. I have a connection on the force from when I was counseling in the jail and Dennis, listen to me, Dennis, they're looking for you."

"Me?"

"That's not all."

"What's not all."

"The girl."

"Candy?"

"She's missing."

"Jesus."

"Dennis, do you have any idea where she is? Any idea at all?"

"No." The tone of her question caught up to him a moment later. "What do you mean do I have any idea? You don't think. . . . Why would I know where she is?"

Martha said nothing. Pratt leaned into the phone booth. "I have to go."

• • •

They flew south on Aeroméxico. Pratt had the window this time, a view of the endless Pacific. From so high up it looked as gentle as a backyard pond. A thousand miles from one end of the *baja* to the other. The flight attendants were tall beautiful Mexican women with perfectly manicured fingers and hair like fat ravens perched on their heads. Pratt fell in love with one of them who looked heartbreakingly just like the actress Maria Conchita Alonso. He imagined a new life. They'd live simply, in a beachfront townhouse. He wouldn't learn Spanish and she wouldn't learn English. They would enter their life together free of histories. They'd communicate in an unspoken way born of love. If you listened to all the daytime talk shows, lack of communication was a major problem in marriages, but maybe it was *too much* communication, husbands and wives forgoing civility in favor of being brutally and thoroughly honest. When the flight attendant came by with the drink cart—real bottles, fifths, not plastic miniatures—he ordered a gin and tonic and she asked in perfect English if he preferred Bombay or Tanqueray. "The latter," he said, and she knew what that meant, so his dream was scratched. Patricia was fast asleep, her head on his shoulder. He looked down at the sea, and closer, the jagged edge of the peninsula, and even closer, mountains. There seemed to be an awful lot of wild territory down there. Bandits. He remembered reading B. Traven's *Treasure of the Sierra Madre* as a teenager because his father had said it was as perfect a story as you could find. He sipped his gin and tonic. *Trust your gut.* He made a mental note to read more of Stevenson Lake's work now that he knew the author. He tilted his head so that his cheek was against his wife's head. If he could get inside it he could find out the truth. In his more paranoid moments that summer, he'd gone as far as to look into buying a voice-stress analysis machine to check out her stories. They weren't cheap, not something you could find on the shelf at Target. He'd also looked at a checklist on the Internet for determining if a spouse was having an affair. She'd scored a seven out of ten and he'd clung to the three innocent answers like a rock climber hanging from a cliff with a fraying rope.

He pulled the shade and tried to sleep but the conversation with Martha returned without the distraction of the view. Oddly, he wasn't terribly worried about Candy, at least not in the sense of harm coming to her. She was too wily and to be perfectly frank he had the feeling she'd been exposed to her share of horrors. It was likely that Cole had jumped out of the swamp to rob somebody and the somebody had killed him in self-defense and then hightailed it out of there. It could have been somebody important, but then again the very important men in the area held memberships at more prestigious clubs. It was also possible that a golfer fording the weeds for a lost ball had come across Cole trapping beaver or whatever and out of panic simply started pummeling him. Cole, after all, had looked a lot less like a Jehovah's Witness than a feral dog the last time Pratt had seen him. Possibly, too, some kind of a grifter scheme Cole had cooked up had gone haywire. Maybe he'd been trying to pimp Candy, "turn her out" as they said, and the whole thing had backfired into violence and she was hiding, maybe even pulling the trailer down to Orlando by herself. Pratt recalled her father's lascivious look when Pratt had asked if Cole wanted to earn a C-note for holding the mercury. He hadn't made the connection then but now it seemed pretty clear what Cole had been getting at.

He didn't like Martha's implication that he might be involved in the crime. He believed there was something between them, something viable like a fetus though not one that could survive outside the womb quite yet. Something he wasn't ready to think about yet or wasn't ready to *allow* himself to think about yet. But it was there and he was gaining some strength from it, building, however slowly, some immunity to impending heartbreak. There were moments when he could view his concern about Patricia's possible adultery as less a fear than a simple manifestation of his quote illness unquote. Or, if he were to believe Rayburn, illnesses, plural. Yet he was never quite sure because there were other moments when the notion of his wife changing her allegiance made his heart seize up like an engine suddenly deprived of oil. Much smoke and grinding and devastation. *Martha Martha Martha*, he chanted in his head. He knew this much: he had never felt as safe as he had in her living room. And too, in the shower, when "testing" the sexual side effects of the medication, it had been her lovely white thighs he'd pictured, not pale in an unhealthy sense but lush and rich like pearls. Well, he couldn't blame her for wondering about him and Cole. After all, he *was* crazy and had a doctor to prove it. Board-certified at that. *Rumination*, Rayburn called it. Obsessive thoughts. Dwelling on *anything* for three hours at a stretch wasn't healthy. Pratt had lost over fifteen pounds that summer. He needed a belt for more than cosmetic purposes now. His extra-large shirts hung as loosely on him as his father's old shirts which he'd taken to grade school to wear as smocks for art with a capital A. He wondered if they even allowed children to paint anymore or if the budget prohibited more than crayon work. He knew that Whitney had never needed one of his old shirts. It somehow seemed a shame. He remembered his father's shirts, smelling like pipe tobacco, sometimes with a few grains of Borkum Riff in the pocket.

He drained his glass and handed it to the pretty girl when she came back. There was no spark in her eyes. He was just another gringo on her flight. Patricia was awake now, chewing gum, staring blankly ahead. Pratt opened the shade again. Hoped that when they landed the *federales* weren't waiting for him. He was glad Martha was in his corner. Having old money on your side never hurt. The plane dropped. Pratt watched the ground coming up, felt no anxiety, heard the wheels screech, thought, *I am in Mexico.*

40

VILLA DEL SOL was in a guarded compound of opulent homes on a stepped hill above the highway midway between San José and Cabo San Lucas. When Pratt and Patricia—she drove, afraid his tendency to "gap out" behind the wheel would be fatal in Mexico— pulled up to the guardhouse, a bored-looking man slumped on a metal folding chair raised a wooden bar and let them in. Pratt waved and the man offered a sloppy salute. Nothing in his actions indicated that he'd been alerted to Pratt's arrival. They drove down a narrow lane while Pratt read aloud the e-mailed directions that Kelly had forwarded, and then they were there, parking under a canopy. Pratt jumped out and lighted a cigarette and inhaled the scent of manzanita and diesel fuel from the highway. They left the luggage in the car and went inside. It was fancier than even the photographs had suggested. The door opened to red tiled steps leading down to a huge living room, a giant smearless glass-topped dining table, and a kitchen straight from *House Beautiful*. Kelly had ordered food brought in and the fridge was stuffed, the liquor cabinet stocked, five-gallon jugs of water lined up against the wall. Pratt grabbed a can of Dos Equis and cracked it open. "Look at this," Patricia said, and he followed her voice to the master bedroom, easily as large as their living room back home. She was in the walk-in closet just off the bathroom. The luxury was a little overwhelming and Pratt went outside, lighted another cigarette, found himself standing on a covered patio under slowly rotating ceiling fans with the Sea of Cortez, quiet and boatless in the afternoon, in the background behind a line of hotels. He drank his beer and wondered where he'd gone wrong in not having amassed fortune enough to live this way all the time. Nobody in his family was very wealthy. His sister was an elementary school teacher in Idaho, which meant she was earning just a shade more than your average welfare recipient. His brother made more than he did, probably more than Pratt and Patricia combined, but still bounced checks feeding his three large sons and indulging their involvement in hockey. Their father had been a professor and although a good teacher who still received letters from students he'd had decades earlier would die having never owned a stick of brand-new furniture. But the villa was making Pratt feel a little resentful, childishly, maybe, but resentful nonetheless that his father hadn't "gotten on" as a manager with Weyerhaeuser Lumber when he'd had the chance.

Patricia came out in her bathing suit. "Join me by the pool?"

"Maybe later," Pratt said.

From above he watched his wife go to the pool, test the water with her toe, and jump in. Kelly and the others weren't due until the next day; they'd gotten some kind of great deal on airfare that meant giving up a day at the villa. So Pratt and his wife had the place to themselves and Patricia had said she thought it was a deliberate move on Kelly's part to allow them a private honeymoon period. Kelly was like that. It was she who'd insisted the Pratts get the master suite in celebration of their twentieth anniversary, for example, ignoring Patricia's protests. Now Patricia stood up, running her hands through her wet hair. "Why bother with the swimsuit?" Pratt asked.

"I don't know. Habit."

Pratt pulled off his shirt, kicked off his pants. He was a little buzzed from the single beer, maybe a result of being tired or in different air. Or a potential fugitive. He dropped his boxers and went to the edge of the pool. Stood there letting the breeze tickle his privates. "Is it cold?"

"Warm," his wife said. She was floating with her eyes closed. "And don't worry, there is no deep end."

Pratt nodded and stepped in. He was actually annoyed when his feet met the bottom and the water only came up to his waist. Another first. He had never swum naked before. Once at the YMCA he'd jumped into his nine-foot heaven and air had collected in his baggy trunks and prevented him from sinking. He'd had to climb out and release the air, an embarrassing sight, so he could see why competitive swimmers wore those tight little Speedos. Now he could understand why swimming naked was so appealing to generations of teenagers. It felt, well, it felt *right*. He thought he recalled something about the early Olympics being played in the nude. He could see the swimming part but would feel a bit self-conscious running a relay with his manhood flopping around. He dunked himself, stayed under until he felt adjusted to the water, much warmer than at the Y, then rose. He wanted to float on his back and look at the Mexican sky but stopped himself. The time wasn't right to demonstrate his new ability. He needed deeper water, an audience. Patricia drifted over to him. "What do you think?"

"Perfect," he said.

"I can't wait for Kelly and them to get here."

"That'll be fun."

"Dennis are you *naked?*"

"No, I'm in my birthday suit."

"Whatever."

"You like what you see?"

"Kind of hard to see."

"Ha ha."

• • •

They didn't make love in the master bedroom as Pratt had not so much hoped as halfway expected given Patricia's intoxication with the suite and the lingerie she'd purchased in Phoenix. After the swim they snacked on tortilla chips and mango salsa and explored the rest of the villa. There was a lower-level game room with a sauna and pool table and a small library on the second floor, stocked primarily with junk left behind by other renters—romance novels, *Shogun*-type literature, the odd Michener—but also what looked like twenty years of *Marlin* magazine as well as a television and video collection, which they both ignored. "Who would come to Mexico and watch television?" Patricia remarked.

"People who can afford to come every year."

"Well, if I turn it on, shoot me."

"Is there a house shotgun?"

"I wouldn't doubt it. They have everything else."

Pratt tried to embrace his wife at that moment but her frame was stiff and it was like trying to love a bony stray cat. She returned his hug but announced that if he had any notion of "getting some" he should jump in the pool. "I'm not in the mood and I'm not going to be."

"Today or ever again?"

"Today for sure. I'm beat. I was up all night trying to think if we forgot anything. And that goddamn flight from Phoenix to Ontario, my God, I thought the wings were going to shake off."

"I didn't notice."

"I know you didn't. You were in la-la land."

So Pratt watched her go off to nap and then sat at the glass table with the book he'd brought along, McGuane's *The Sporting Club*, which he had not read since college. Among Kelly's liquor supply was a bottle of high-grade tequila, one hundred percent agave, and the shot Pratt sipped was to Cuervo what McGuane was to one of the slim bodice-rippers on the shelf upstairs. It went down way too easily and he had another and another. He got a little too drunk to read and went outside, swam again, climbed out and sat on the retaining wall. The highway was a good hundred feet below, down a steep hill on the verge of being a cliff. Pratt wasn't a racist by any means but he was glad for the guardhouse at one end of the compound and the wall at the other, capable of repelling all but the most dedicated burglars. He'd heard all his life that Mexicans were lazy and, though he didn't believe it, giggled for some reason at the idea of thieves being too unmotivated to scale the wall and cut the throats of two Minnesota gringos. Just for thinking it he deserved to have his throat cut, he decided. He went back for a beer and sat on the wall with a towel around his back watching the Sea of Cortez darken and then disappear. The night was warm and he smoked half a package of cigarettes, throwing the butts down to the highway, watching them arc like tiny comets. He had the sense, living in the villa, of being immune to the law. There would be the assumption by those moving back and forth below that he was a rich gringo, someone to be deferred to. Although drunk, Pratt found the notion a little disquieting, antithetical to his upbringing. He recalled the way his father had always addressed gas station attendants and motel clerks as "sir." His father would have fit in south of the border but then again he wouldn't have been caught dead in anything called a *villa*, just out of principle. When he'd told his father about the trip, Pratt had avoided mentioning the cost, the luxury, almost making it sound like they were staying in a youth hostel. His father had been lucid and feeling better. The crisis of a few weeks earlier had been a result of his prednisone giving him diabetes and causing his blood sugar to skyrocket. That was under control now and he'd even been able to go for a short hike. Steven and Marcia were furious at Pratt for aborting his trip to see the old man, but his father had claimed to be glad Pratt hadn't come. "Too much like a goddamn wake," he'd said. "I love your brother and sister but I felt a little like I was under a deathwatch. Don't drink the water," were his last words before hanging up.

The sea disappeared. The stars came out. Pratt drained his beer, drew his arm back to throw the can over the wall, thought better of it and went inside. He made sure Patricia was sleeping and went to the telephone in the kitchen. The instructions for placing a call, posted on the wall, were maddeningly complex. He figured them out with the help of another tequila and a few false starts. This time when he got Whitney's voice mail he did more than grunt. "Listen," he said, "I'll call soon about this business. Please don't call here. I don't want your mother to get upset."

41

FOR BREAKFAST they ate fresh pineapple and scrambled eggs on the patio. A good night's sleep and the sun, the presence of palm trees, the lack of *federales* storming the wall had lightened Pratt's burden a bit. Every hour that passed meant the authorities were closer to unearthing the truth about Cole, whatever that truth might be. And that funky truck and trailer couldn't get far without being noticed by some responsible citizen.

Nine o'clock and already it was hot enough for a swim. Out on the sea, five small boats moved in a neat convoy along the coast. Pratt went in for a refill of coffee and rejoined his wife. She was reading one of the romance novels from upstairs but put it down and rested her chin in her palm. She looked thoroughly unhappy. "What's wrong?" he asked.

"Nothing's wrong."

"What should we do today, then?"

"Well, I don't really want to shop until the others get here. You guys are supposed to be playing golf the day after tomorrow so I thought us girls could shop then. What do *you* want to do?"

"Makes no difference. I'm happy just being here in Mexico. We've been talking about it for almost a year."

"You didn't want to go."

"Say again?"

"You didn't want to go from day one. You were negative about the whole thing."

"I changed my mind."

"Well, it kind of pisses me off."

"Why?"

"Because I've been pro-Mexico from the start and I feel like I had to drag you kicking and screaming into the trip. Now you're here and you're acting like you were gung ho the whole time. Even with the golf. I bought you the golf clubs and they just sat in our bedroom for months and now you're all into golf."

"I changed my mind. Is that a crime?"

"No, it's not a crime but it makes me wonder if you have something up your sleeve. If you're faking it to make some kind of point."

Pratt eyeballed the outdoor fridge just a few feet away. He knew it was crowded with beer. Normal time protocols should not apply on a Mexican vacation, he decided. Back home they had friends who'd pace around at ten to five waiting to have a drink. They were religious about it. But Pratt sensed that to go over and pluck a beer from the icebox during this particular conversation would be seen as a statement in itself. So he sipped what remained of his coffee and said nothing.

"And that bugs me," his wife went on. "You don't know what it's like to want to feel excited about something but to have this part of your mind, this *percentage*, telling you it might not work out. I mean, up until we were on Aeroméxico yesterday I was still waiting for you to find some reason to bail."

"That's ridiculous. I told you I'd go. I do what I say."

"Really? Let's see." She closed her eyes. "Oh," she said, "you were going to get your real estate appraisal certificate. We even found an accelerated course for you in Minneapolis. I told you the local appraisers were backed up for months. You could have made a boatload of money and you could have worked out of the house. It would have been perfect."

"For you," Pratt said. "You wanted me to do that. I can't think of anything more like death than nosing around in houses and crunching numbers."

"You said you'd do it. I had to pull some strings to get you into the program. I had to shuffle a bunch of closings."

"My heart wasn't in it."

"But your heart is in opening old paint cans all day."

There was a time when such a comment would have sent Pratt's heart sinking or turned him into a knife thrower. Now he just smiled, Buddha-serene. Lighted a cigarette and looked at the ocean. "Here we are on the tip of the Baja Peninsula, having a rerun argument." He tapped the book on the table. It's like these novels where the plots are all the same. Only the scenery changes."

"Whatever."

"But without the romance."

"Don't start." Patricia lifted her plate and set it over Pratt's.

"Start what?"

"I know you're horny but you know what? I'm not promising anything. I'm here to have fun and get a tan and forget about goddamn titles and closings."

"Where did that come from?"

"What, Dennis?"

"You're acting pretty hostile."

She aimed her finger at him. "And that's another thing. Lately you've gotten this, I don't know, this holier-than-thou attitude. You're acting all calm and reasonable and you know what?"

"What?"

"I think you're doing it to annoy me. Or, like I said before, you have something up your sleeve." She pushed back her chair and stood up. "I'm taking a shower."

"I'm going for a walk, then. I want to touch the sea."

She stopped and turned around. "Do you think that's a good idea? Walking around here alone?"

"This place will be in sight the whole time. I'm just going across the street behind those hotels."

"Well, be careful."

He looked for some sincerity in her face but saw only a blur with the sun in his eyes. "Do you really mean that?"

She ignored him and went off for her shower. Pratt stuffed a twenty-dollar bill into his pocket and left through the front door, walked down the narrow lane. Said, *"Buenos días"* to the guard, who looked like the same guard from the night before, and Pratt wondered if the poor sap worked all the time. It was possible because the guard was sleeping and woke only enough to give a nod before leaning back in his chair again. Pratt wondered where he lived, what he thought of the grand homes he was protecting, at least symbolically. From the guardhouse it was a steep grade to the highway, with a switchback halfway down. Pratt paused there to light a cigarette. He had a bad taste in his mouth, either from last night's booze or the argument or both. He kept on going, down to the highway. Looked left and right and it was like the Daytona 500 seen through an LSD haze. He could not calculate the right timing to run across the highway. People were driving at various speeds. He couldn't see a traffic light anywhere. He almost went back, then, to the villa. He had a wicker chair waiting for him, an ashtray and coffee, the McGuane which he was starting to get into. But it seemed insane to be so close to the ocean and sit around the house like it was any Sunday back home, killing time until the next day. He watched the cars for a while. He was able to identify quite a few rental cars, some with surfboards strapped to their roofs, some stuffed with pale faces. He saw some odd-looking rigs, what you'd imagine when you thought of Mexico, ancient VWs, old Ford Fairlanes, station wagons converted into pickups. The occasional dump truck but no police cars. Pratt got tired of waiting. He felt like he'd been waiting all his life for his life to start and here he was on the edge of forty, waiting to cross the fucking street like a child. He stepped from the curb and started walking, his eyes on the red façade of the hotel across the road. He felt something brush his back or maybe it was just the slipstream of a fast-moving car but either way, he did not look back. He heard engines gunning, the sound of brakes being applied but not screeching. Horns varying from electric Japanese beeps to deep 1970s honks. He never wavered and then he was at the curb and walking by a crew of three bewildered-looking hotel men in starched white shirts. He waited for one of them to say something like *"Loco gringo,"* but nobody did.

• • •

His shoes were off, laces tied together and over his shoulder, pants rolled up, and he was standing in the Sea of Cortez. Every few moments another wave came in against his calves and almost toppled him. He'd had no idea the sea was so strong, or so warm. He was struck with the urge to disrobe and try his hand at swimming but there were limits to how far even he would go, regardless of medication. There were people on the beach, couples walking, vendors setting up tables along a clothesline fence strung behind the hotel property. There was a sort of festival atmosphere cooking, but a tawdry one. He was glad the villa was up on the hill even if these folks had better access to the water. The seclusion was worth the distance. He knelt down and grabbed a handful of sand and opened his hand and watched it swirl away. How could someone not want to live by the sea? he wondered. He thought of North Dakota and western Minnesota, all the dour faces, the wind-burned noses and puffy coats, every parking lot in winter under an exhaust fume haze because people allowed their cars to run all the time. God's country, the locals called it. Keeps the riffraff out, they'd say. Back home the closest things to oceans were the endless farm fields but in drought years they turned into dust that permeated everything in the perennial wind. Everyone was overweight and cynical or overweight and clueless. Well, not everyone. But they by and large met those specs. He heard giggling and turned to see several Mexican schoolgirls in navy-blue skirts and white blouses walking by. They looked like a painting of innocence though it was entirely possible none of them were innocent. But they looked that way and Pratt thought about Candy, doing a pretty good Tatum O'Neal, or Jodie Foster in *Taxi Driver,* without knowing it. He hoped she was okay.

Pratt walked in the water, kind of following the schoolgirls. Their voices in the lulls between waves made for an orchestra that broke his heart until they outdistanced him. He trudged from the water and stood on a flat stone and let the sun dry the wet sand on his feet before putting his shoes on again. He walked along the beach in the general direction of San José. There were more vendors now, waiting for hotel guests to come over from the pool area. Evidently there were rules about how close they could get to hotel property. The vendors stood before their card tables patiently. Pratt wandered over to see what they were offering. It was a mistake. It was like a gauntlet of carnival barkers. It was hard to be rude to someone mano a mano with two feet between you, he realized. He feigned deafness or stupidity and walked quickly, glancing down at keychains, t-shirts, painted maracas. Junk. Patricia still had, in her dresser, a coconut carved like a monkey that her parents had brought her from somewhere, Hawaii maybe, the kind of passive-aggressive detritus that remained move after move, purge after purge. He did not want to burden their home or his daughter with that kind of thing. They'd had the usual demands from family and friends—one of Patricia's sisters wanted a poncho; another had requested a bottle of Kahlúa. Jenson wanted a switchblade. Pratt's brother was hoping for Cuban cigars, not because he smoked them but to offer casually to his boss the way one would offer a monkey a banana, albeit a monkey capable of giving you a raise. Although he was walking fast, something caught his eye. Tiny skulls on a bracelet. He picked up the bracelet and examined the skulls. There were eleven of them, carved of wood, each the size of a marble. Pratt slipped it onto his wrist. "How much?"

"Oh, for you, maybe twenty."

"Twenty dollars?"

The vendor looked off at the sea.

"I don't know," Pratt said. "What can you tell me about it?'

The vendor peered at him. He looked vaguely Indian, with sharp features and a hawk nose. "The skulls show us that we're all the same inside."

"That's good."

The vendor took a deep breath. "They became popular in the Victorian era, when people were consumed by overwrought fashion. An artistic movement grew out of that banality and skeletons, skulls, became a popular motif for protesting the material excess and false class distinction. There was a slightly how would you say it *subversive* quality to the work?"

"Heavy. You have very good English, by the way."

"I was a guest of your country's penal system as a young man."

Pratt handed over his twenty with no attempt at haggling. "I've never viewed skulls as bad."

"They're not bad. This bracelet will bring you good luck, my friend."

"I could use some good luck right now."

The vendor handed back a crisp ten.

"I thought it was twenty."

"Ten if you get it. Do you dig it, man?"

"I do."

"I know you do."

"Well, *gracias*, then," Pratt said.

"Peel away our rotting flesh and we're brothers, *amigo*," the vendor called after him, very seriously.

"I dig," Pratt said.

The bracelet had Whitney all over it but Pratt kept it on his wrist. He continued walking along the beach. He picked up a tiny shell and then ten yards later dropped it, realizing he had no need or even desire to own a shell. To his left was a virtual wall of hotels and when he saw a gap he cut through it toward the highway. There was a dirty-windowed store and he went inside. Bought a can of Tecate and a package of Boots cigarettes. He did not get much change back and was probably being ripped off but he didn't care. Out on the sidewalk he opened the beer and took a long drink. He scanned the hillside across the highway until he thought he could identify the villa. The wall, anyway, looked like the same wall. He stood in front of the store and drank and smoked and admired the bracelet. Some effort had gone into carving the individual skulls. Not that much effort—they were rough cut, painted white with black eye sockets, separated by black beads. He wondered if the vendor had made it or perhaps his wife or child. Maybe they sat in a hovel all night carving skulls together, talking, listening to music. Loving each other. It sounded like a pretty good life.

42

KELLY and Tim had arrived, and Bryce and Jenna, whom they'd flown with. Kate and Bill were due in on a later flight. They were all tan, Jenna and Kelly lean and smooth, the men showing signs of middle age in hairline and gut, not overly so but more so than Pratt. By the time Pratt climbed the hill, huffing and puffing, and entered the villa, everyone was in the pool in various stages of drunkenness and bliss. Pratt said his hellos to Tim and Kelly, introduced himself to Bryce and Jenna, and went inside to fix himself a drink. He surveyed the bottles lined up on the bar. Considered Absolut, considered Tanqueray. In the end he mixed himself a whopper of a White Russian and went back outside, down to the pool, and sat on a rattan chair next to a table. Kelly swam to him and draped her arms over the ledge. "Dennis, Patty looks awesome. I couldn't believe it."

"She worked hard."

"Tim's eyes just bugged out when he saw her. Well, we haven't seen her in a year and it was like, holy shit."

"I know."

"You look like you've lost weight too."

Pratt nodded. "I wouldn't want her to be thinner than me."

Kelly slapped his leg. "Get in the pool, you goof."

It was only noon but Pratt was already buzzed and wobbled back into the house for another White Russian. Lifestyles of the rich and famous, he thought. When he stirred his drink the bracelet rattled like actual bones and he thought of Whitney. Picked up the telephone and after some drunken button navigation got through to her dorm. "Hey, baby," he said. "I'm in old Mexico and I bought you something."

"Daddy, are you drunk?"

"Moderately. Or as they say up north, fair to middling."

"Daddy, listen."

"I hear you, sweetheart. Loud and clear."

"Daddy, I said listen. Be quiet and listen."

"Okay. Hey, I bought you something. This really cool bracelet—"

"Daddy!"

"What?"

"I wish you'd tell me what's going on. The cops are looking for you. There's a guy they found dead at the golf course and they're looking for you."

"I am innocent. I am guilty only of crimes against nature. Don't eat fish from the Red River, by the way, for about twenty years."

"What are you talking about?"

"Nothing, baby. Seriously, when it comes to murder, like Billy Joel would say, *I am an innocent ma-a-an.*"

"What are you going to do about it, then?"

Pratt looked through the window at the frolicking happy bodies, letting the water wash away travel fatigue, monotonous careers, dubious marriages, difficult children, hectic commutes, thinning hair, drooping tits, complicated tax brackets, widening asses, budding cancers, closing arteries. "What I'm going to do," Pratt told his daughter, "is go for a swim and then sit in the hot tub for a little while. And then tomorrow I'll deal with this, whatever this is. It's just a misunderstanding. But I don't want you to worry about it."

"Like *that's* going to happen."

"You have to trust me."

"I'm not stupid, Dad. I'm not the same little girl you told you had God's phone number. I still remember the number. Seven seven seven seven seven three four."

Pratt laughed. "Did you ever figure out what that meant?"

"No. Only that it wasn't real because I tried calling him once."

"Write it down."

"Now?"

"Why not?"

There was silence and then she came back on. "Okay."

"Now turn it upside down."

"Oh, now I get it. *Hell*."

"With some extra ells thrown in."

"Funny."

"Did I tell you I bought you this really nifty skull bracelet?"

"That's nice."

"I'm wearing it right now, do you mind?"

"That's okay."

"I'm a little buzzed."

"I know. Are you supposed to be mixing booze and meds?"

"Not really."

"Be careful, Daddy."

"Always."

• • •

Kate and Bill showed up at three. Everyone got sunburned and drunk and tired and fell asleep or at least retired to their rooms for siestas by five, except Pratt. He brewed a pot of Sumatra coffee. In his new bright-yellow swim trunks he tried to practice chipping in the lush grass but couldn't stay focused. He thought of those drunks who managed to remain perennially drunk while maintaining the ability to function. But for Pratt it was always a wolf or a rabbit, never a beast in between. Sober or walking into walls. He went down to the pool and jumped in, no testing the water or chilling himself with a cold shower like at the YMCA, where the water was cool and the shower made it seem warm by comparison. It seemed to him, sitting in the shallow end, looking up at the sky, the Mexican sky as opposed to the Minnesota sky or, in the case of the Y, a moldy-looking stucco, that much of life was an examination of relativity. Back home a common saying was, "Things could be worse," and this banal maxim was just as easily applied to the weather as cancer. The neighbor who'd lost his left arm was happy it wasn't his right. Your wife might have cheated on you but at least she wasn't the town pump, making a fool of you every time you drove your big rig out to Seattle and back. Life shouldn't be that way, Pratt thought. Life should stand on its own merits without comparison. Even art couldn't escape the comparative eye. *This book is reminiscent of McGuane and maybe Jim Harrison with perhaps a little Raymond Carver thrown in.* Why couldn't things just *be?*

"Howdy, neighbor."

Pratt looked over. It has to be a hallucination, he thought, fueled by Lexapro and Klonopin and two shots of one-hundred-percent agave tequila atop a foundation of White Russians. Pratt did what they did in the movies. He stood up in the water, rubbed his eyes, ground at his eyes in a manner that would have shamed Oedipus. Opened his eyes and Bruce Carver was standing there, at the edge of the pool, in khaki shorts and a t-shirt depicting a man clubbing a marlin with what looked like a fat baseball bat. Next to Carver was a pretty woman at least twenty years his junior, a blond in a baseball cap with a ponytail riding out the rear. She was in a loose dress with sandals and rings on nearly every toe.

"Hello?" Pratt said.

"We let ourselves in. We knocked and nobody showed up but the cars were here and we thought you'd all be down at the pool."

"Everyone crashed. We started partying a bit early."

Carver grinned. "It's the law down here." He put his arm around the girl. "This is Serrina. Serrina, this is Dennis."

She smiled. Pratt waved. "Nice to meet you." Then to Carver: "What brings you down here?" As if they'd run into each other at the Fleet Farm store instead of a thousand miles south of Tijuana.

"The billfish tourney. I keep a time-share down here. It was Dad's. I've been offered mondo bucks for it because my week usually coincides with the tournament but I'll never sell. I love the tourney."

"Are you in it?"

"No. But it's one big party down here this time of year."

"Like Mardi Gras with *fish*," Serrina said. "That's what he says."

"I had no idea," Pratt said. He waded to the edge and climbed out. Wrapped up in his towel.

"Well, I'm not here to intrude. But I thought maybe we could have dinner tonight. A welcome-to-Mexico dinner. My treat."

Pratt drew a smile across his face and gave Carver what he hoped was an evil eye. "I wouldn't stand for that."

Carver's eyes more or less gleamed. "I'd insist."

The sliding door opened. Patricia came out. She'd somehow found time to puff up her pool-damaged hair and change from her suit into her own summer dress, slinky enough to make her look taller and even thinner than she already was. She flowed down the steps like a pageant winner ready to be crowned. "Bruce, you showed up after all."

Carver kept his eyes on Pratt. "I haven't missed Cabo in October for years."

Patricia laughed. Pratt looked down at his pale feet. He wished he'd spent more time tanning before coming down.

"I was just telling Denny I want to take you and your *amigos* out to dinner."

"That sounds fun. I'm starved. But it'll be our treat."

"I consider myself a kind of Baja ambassador. Besides, I write all this shit off. Anyway, I made enough money on your daughter's teeth to pay for my boat."

"You have a boat?" Pratt asked.

"Well, there are boats, and then there are boats. I have the usual runabout, my Lund at Pelican Lake like everyone else, but my pride and joy is the *Root Canal*."

"*Root Canal?*"

"Thirty feet of mean machine just down the road."

"I'm hungry," Serrina said. She seemed numb to both the familiarity and the tension.

"I'll check with Tim and Kelly and the others," Patricia said. She flitted away. Pratt thought he detected a little more jiggle in her wiggle but he was at the moment overwhelmed with chaos. Where were the transcendent effects of his new prescriptions when he needed them? He wanted to go back into the water and submerge himself, reemerge, and have the patio dry and clear of Carver and Serrina.

Carver slapped him on the shoulder. "So have you adjusted?"

"To what?"

"The lifestyle, *amigo*, the lifestyle."

Pratt paused, looked around. "I'm getting there."

43

DOLCE, in San José, open-air, strung with white lights, featuring a live tree in the middle of the floor, was not crowded at dusk. A maître-d' resembling a military interrogator, with darting, concerned eyes, seated them at a long table. Carver sat at the head. Of course. Pratt wasn't surprised, nor was he surprised when Carver demanded to choose the wine, going so far as to taste it for them, theatrically sniffing and letting his tongue loll out like a helmeted retard at the zoo. Patricia and Serrina flanked him; Pratt sat next to his wife, outside the point of this triangle. They all watched as Carver chose a pinot grigio and leaned back in turn as the waiter, a short, thick Mexican with a nervous bearing, poured their glasses. When Pratt took a sip he nudged Patricia and did a quick imitation of Carver, snorting as he stuck his nose into the glass, that gathered him only a dirty look. Under the table he tried to squeeze her hand but it evaded him like a slick bar of soap on the shower floor. He tried to feel something like rage but the steam wasn't there.

Carver raised his glass high. "To being in Mexico but having the ability to return to the good old Estados Unidos," he said.

Glasses came up, a few clinked sloppily. Pratt waited a moment and raised his own. He recalled a line from a Jerry Jeff Walker album. "Here's to duck who swum a lake and never lost a feather," Pratt said. "May this time another year we'll all be together." He delivered the toast so deadpan that everyone nodded reverently.

All lifted their menus. Husbands conferred with wives. Pratt zoomed in on the seafood linguine. He felt the need to eat something from the sea. It didn't matter what sea, whether it was local or flown in from a California broker. It didn't matter. He was starving.

His belly was a swill of booze. He elbowed Patricia. "What are you having?"

"I don't know. Everything is so expensive," she whispered.

"I'm having the seafood linguine."

"That's four hundred pesos."

"So?"

She shook her head. Pratt glanced around the table. His eyes met Serrina's. She looked bored. She was chewing gum. "So where are you from?" he asked.

"LA."

"How did you and Bruce, uh, meet?"

She looked at Carver. He stroked his chin. "I've known Serrina forever."

"Ah."

They placed their orders with the jittery waiter. Small talk set in, the consumption of tiny loaves of bread and plates of appetizer calamari. Pratt felt ill suddenly, felt that he was floating upward, above the table, into the starry night. Only disconnected words reached him: *new drain tile took a hit on my investments don't think the Yankees can do it again without a Hemi engine I don't plan on doing much of anything except laying in the sun and drop a few fucking tactical nukes over there and show them what happens when the big dog bites back in Wisconsin it was thirty degrees the last time I went surfing was in Hawaii on our honeymoon in Vegas I lost my wallet with everything that's going on in the world today I got my period can you believe it?* Pratt closed his eyes and felt the gentle breeze, smelled the Mexican night, which didn't really smell like anything in particular but the food being carried around the restaurant. But he thought, I am here and it feels good regardless of everything else. He found it impossible to believe that the largest body of water he'd seen in forty years was Lake Superior, nothing to scoff at for sure but certainly not an ocean, and he'd not dipped his foot in the lake because it had been April and cold. Despite the lack of a ceiling he suddenly felt awfully constrained. He wanted to be out doing something, anything, beyond sitting at a table. He felt that he had wasted the last twenty years, like a man locked in a cell, and it was time to make up for it. He regarded his wife, her bare, smooth, pretty shoulder inches from his, so close that it occasionally bobbed against him like a boat against a dock bumper yet the distance between them was palpable. It struck him that a single word, *distance,* was what defined the last several months, maybe the last year. There was a wall between them, as clichéd as that sounded. And yet something was different, Pratt realized, in that he did not feel helpless and hopeless as before, as if Patricia were an anchor keeping him from shooting off into a constellation of desperation. Well, she had been, but that was when he'd been as crippled as any paraplegic, maybe like that poor sap in the Kenny Rogers song. *Ruby, don't take your love to town.* Not too long ago Patricia had brought home the Richard Gere film *Unfaithful* on DVD, and Pratt had vomited midway through, claiming a "bug" he'd caught from Jenson but in reality finding it too close to home. This was right before his collapse at Martha's. The mind was a terrible thing, he thought, capable of turning on itself the way his father's lupus was tricking his body into attacking its own organs.

The waiter began bringing out their food. Much to Pratt's surprise, his seafood linguine came wrapped as a foil swan. Everyone paused to admire it. Someone took a photo. The presentation almost brought Pratt to tears. He wasn't sure why. The waiter paused a few moments for everyone to get a chance to admire the work and then approached the swan from Pratt's left with a knife in his hand. The maître-d' was nearby, arms crossed, glaring intently. There was obviously some kind of testing going on. Perhaps the waiter had screwed this up before and was getting only one more chance. It was likely jobs in high-grade restaurants were rare and sought after. The blade of the knife vibrated as it drew closer to the swan. The waiter lowered his head. Pratt wished he knew how to say something encouraging in Spanish but all he could muster was a whispered, *"Bueno, bueno."* The words seemed to calm the waiter. The knife pressed against the swan's neck and with his free hand the waiter gripped the tail and with one deft motion the head came off and the linguine spilled not unlike stringy guts over the white plate, spreading perfectly to the edges. The foil disappeared, crumpling in the waiter's hand. Pratt heard the waiter breathe with relief; the maître-d' nodded and turned away. Pratt began to applaud and embarrassed the others into joining him. The nervous waiter smiled and disappeared with the foil carcass as Pratt began to devour the clams, the squid, the pasta. Something bright hit him in the eyes. It was the reflection from Carver's watchband, which he was making a great show of studying. He caught Pratt watching. "I'm not meaning to appear rude. I couldn't care less what time it is. I'm not in any hurry. But I just got this and I can't keep from playing with it."

"Quite a watch," Pratt said.

Carver stretched his arm out. A myriad of complicated dials and knobs appeared under Pratt's nose. "A very special friend gave it to me."

Pratt looked at Serrina. She held up her hands. "Don't look at me. He's so anal already why would I buy him a fucking watch?"

Pratt laughed with the others and resumed eating, letting the act of twirling pasta around his fork dissipate some of the odd emotions bubbling in his heart. He glanced at Carver, who was now holding forth about NAFTA with Tim and Bryce. He remembered the watch receipt in Patricia's brassiere drawer. He sipped his wine, laughed at the punch line to a Viagra joke he hadn't heard the beginning of, and polished off his linguine. He caught his wife's eye but her return gaze was, as Yeats would say, as blank and pitiless as the sun. He grabbed his cigarettes and lighter and excused himself. He'd been told that Bill's wife, Kate, was allergic to smoke and had been encouraged to practice his habit away from her to the point that he'd been asked not to smoke in the villa. Pratt had pointed out to Patricia that he was paying for one-fourth of the villa and could fill one-fourth with smoke if he wanted to. But of course he'd deferred. He wasn't a barbarian, after all. On his way past Carver their eyes met and Carver winked. Pratt ignored it and wandered over to the doorway. He lighted his cigarette and watched his table. It did not seem any less lively for his absence.

Their waiter came over. He seemed like a man who'd had his sentence commuted. "Good dinner," Pratt said. "Excellent."

The waiter nodded. "Visiting San José?"

"Yes. From America. You guys down here all seem to know a lot more English than we know Spanish. Doesn't that ever piss you off?"

The waiter smiled. "Where in America?"

"Minnesota. Are you familiar with Minnesota?"

"No."

"Far north," Pratt said.

"Ah. *Norte.*"

"*Sí.* Way way *norte. Mucho norte.*"

The waiter nodded gravely. He was so ugly he was fascinating, like certain dogs or burn victims. He had a thick scar that ran from the corner of his mouth to his ear. Pratt wanted to ask how he'd gotten it but wasn't sure what the local etiquette was. Were such questions universally taboo? He realized he'd fallen into what he'd always viewed as the worst thing about locals anywhere and that was the cataract quality of their worldview. He indicated his wife with the tip of his cigarette. "See the *señora* there, *amigo?*"

"Uh."

"In the black dress. *Negro dresso.*"

They both regarded Patricia, glittering at the table like she was born to it.

"*Mi esposa.*"

"*Sí.*"

"See the *hombre* with the big watch?" He tapped his wrist. "*Mucho grande watcho?*"

"*Sí.*"

"That *hombre* has been making hoochy-coochy with *mi esposa.*"

The waiter nodded.

"*Comprende?*"

"No."

Pratt turned his back on the table and ran his forefinger through his closed left fist. "*Hombre* and *mi esposa*. Fucky-fucky."

The waiter stared at Pratt for a few moments. Then he pulled up his sleeve to reveal a tattoo, very crude and faded, of a heart around a name. Much fresher was a dagger through the name, dripping three drops of blood. He slapped the tattoo. "*Comprendo.*"

"They think *I* don't *comprendo*." He spun his finger around his ear. "They think I'm *loco*."

"No."

"What would you do, *amigo?*"

The waiter's face went blank.

Pratt pantomimed shooting a pistol. "Should I shoot him? Bang bang?"

"No."

"Cut off his balls?" Pratt turned his fingers into scissors "Cut off his *cojones?*"

"Maybe, *señor,* or maybe, how do you say, feed him to *los tiburones?* Sharkes? *Entiende?*"

"Sharks?"

"*Sí.*"

Pratt offered his hand. They shook warmly. They talked some more. The waiter's name was Antonio. His brother captained a fishing charter, he explained. *El Pelicano*. The Pelican. "Can he find me some sharks?" Pratt asked. They laughed together. Pratt felt closer to this man than he'd ever felt to his own brother. He was aware that his wife and the others were now watching and this made him feel very good.

44

TOO EARLY in the morning, someone was pounding on their bedroom door. Pratt's eyes flew open. The cops. He wished he had taken that ocean swim after all. He sat up and looked for an escape route.

But it was only Kelly, her voice bright and cheery. "It's shopping and golf time, people." Pratt was still numb from going, after Dolce, to a crowded Cabo dive called El Squid Roe. He had surprised everyone including himself by dancing, first on the table and then jumping like Spiderman to a windowsill serving as an ad hoc stage to do the bump with two Mexican gals whose husbands, just a few feet away, did not seem concerned by the sloppy affections of this thin *gringo* in a violent yellow golf shirt with huge half-moon sweat stains and two left feet. Pratt had tried in vain with some tequila-fueled gestures to get the others to join him but they had ignored him; only Serrina, perhaps suffering from terminal boredom, had finally stepped her long slim legs up to the window ledge, plucked Pratt's glasses from his head, put them on, and begun to perform a kind of lambada-like routine so risqué that even Pratt felt himself reddening a bit. They wrapped their arms around each other's shoulders and bumped to Rick James. "You're too good for him," he shouted.

"For who?"

"Carver."

"It's not what you think. But thanks for the compliment."

"I think he's been balling my wife."

"I wouldn't put it past him."

"Say what?"

"Never mind. It's just the alcohol talking. I better sit down."

Then one of the Mexican girls had grabbed him around the waist and hoisted him high in the air while her partner grabbed Pratt's shorts and yanked them over his hips. He'd fallen in a heap of laughter and watched as his shorts flew over the heads of drunken fishermen and college students and honeymooning *gringos*, pale northerners, underworld sharpies. Then the shorts had been thrown like a hot potato around the bar while Pratt continued dancing in his underwear until finally Patricia came over and demanded that he come back to the table right now. "I'm having fun, baby," he'd protested.

"Bruce said I better reel you in before you get into trouble."

"I'm not getting into trouble."

"He's been watching those husbands and they're getting ready to beat you up."

"Nonsense."

"Bruce knows the territory."

"He should stay in his own fucking territory."

"What's that supposed to mean?"

"Come up here and dance with me."

"You're making a fool out of yourself."

Now in the morning light Pratt studied the shorts. They were only slightly the worse for wear although by the time he'd found them at Squid Roe, hanging from the sail of a giant blue marlin, the pesos and dollars he'd been collecting as change all night were gone. Still, he determined them lucky and pulled them on. He went to the walk-in and squeezed past his wife, found a loose Hawaiian shirt. Buttoned it slowly, watching Patricia, fresh from the shower, select an outfit with as much care as if she were going to a board meeting instead of shopping. He moved past her again to the sink and splashed cold water on his face. Put on his golf shoes. Looped his Strike King fishing shades over his neck, pulled on his Topflite hat. "The maid is coming today," Patricia said.

"So?"

"So I think we should take all our cash with us."

"The maid is not going to steal our money."

"I'd feel better if we took it."

"We can just hide it."

"They always know where to look."

"They?"

"Maids."

"Fine. Take it in your purse."

"You take half and I'll take half."

"Fine." Pratt wandered out to the bedroom, lifted the television, unused except as a stash, and slid their cash out. He counted eleven hundred dollars. Put five hundred into his pocket. Shoved the rest into Patricia's purse. The old impulse to dig around came but went. Memories of the night before started to clarify like buildings and trees in a waning Alberta clipper. "Did you have fun last night?"

"Not as much as you did." She had decided on orange shorts and a t-shirt over her swimsuit.

"I had a blast. Best time I've had in years."

"I could tell," she said. Her face looked like a dried apple.

"You don't approve?"

"Not to that extreme, Dennis. Like I said before, you're either out here or out here. You acted pretty stupid if you ask me."

"I don't get it. You didn't like me uptight and you don't like me cutting loose. What do you want?"

"I want to go shopping and have lunch with my friends and have a good time and not worry that you're going to act like a fucking idiot. Okay?"

Pratt saluted. "Yes'm."

• • •

Hungover, red-eyed, reeking of stale smoke and booze, still wobbly, they loaded their golf bags into the trunk of the rental Mazda and climbed in. Pratt was dismayed to see that the guys all owned real clubs, Pings and Nikes and Callaways in good bags. When he shoved his no-names into the mix it was like letting a randy mongrel into the kennel club. And did that mean he himself in this situation was a mongrel among purebreds? His goal was simply to keep up even though he'd begun the morning by announcing while they chugged juice and coffee that he sucked at golf and should perhaps just caddie for the group. Immediately after saying it he'd been angry at himself for it was exactly the kind of utterance he'd expect from the old Pratt, not the new Pratt.

On the way to the course—recommended by Carver, with the tee time subsequently set up by Carver and with Carver invited along, something he'd seen coming like a locomotive at night—Pratt threw out a worm and hook. These were reasonable gentlemen who would no doubt have seen through Carver's veneer. "Good thing we have *the dentist* down here to lead us around."

"Like having our own private tour guide."

"The guy knows Mexico, that's for sure."

"And what about that chick Serrina? Man, what I wouldn't give."

"Tell me again why I got married?"

"He might take us surfing on Friday. Knows where to catch some good waves."

"I'm in."

"Me too. Do you surf, Dennis?"

"No."

"That's right, Patty said you're not a swimmer."

"Not much of one."

It wasn't the piling-on he had hoped for. Pratt rode the rest of the way with his face pressed against the window, feigning great interest in the local vegetation while the others talked about boogie-boarding, scuba diving. Not soon enough they were at the course, Cabo Real. Several Mexicans emerged from under a thatched-roof hut to take their bags to the carts. They went inside the clubhouse and found Carver already there, negotiating in Spanish over the price. He looked at their group and waved. "They're trying to shaft us. The greens are brown but they want full price. No way." He continued berating the man behind the counter in fluent Spanish until the man held up his hands and agreed to chop the price by twenty-five dollars apiece. Pratt found the whole thing unseemly. He paid his way and went outside to smoke a cigarette. He was already sweating. It seemed anathema, being so hot so close to the water, but he realized he was thinking like a Minnesotan. The others came out, orbiting Carver. They loaded into the carts. Pratt teamed up with Bryce. On the first tee Pratt's shot went sharply left and disappeared into the rough, like a sinner among saints. The other guys tore off like demolition-derby drivers to get their balls while Pratt thrashed around in the *ocotillo* or at least what he thought was *ocotillo*. Bryce offered to wait for him but Pratt waved him on. Pratt stepped carefully with rattlesnakes on his mind. He saw a blur of gray and raised his iron in reflex. Either a big dog or a wolf was sprinting away from him. One quick glimpse and it was slipping through the brush silently, like an apparition. He hoped it had been a wolf. He looked down and found his ball in a terrible lie but he resisted the urge to kick it to better ground. He would not cheat. He gave it a whack and laid it up on the green, which was rather brown as Carver had said.

The second hole was better; at least Pratt was able to keep the ball on the fairway. Raw and absolute fear ruled his game, not an appreciation for the sport or anything resembling enjoyment. Each putt attempt had staked to it a Faustian deal. At the ninth he was able to not only make par but come in ahead of Carver and Bryce. He celebrated by buying everyone an ice-cold Corona at the stand by the pro shop before they went back out. In fact he would have been happy to quit after nine, having redeemed himself. But soon they were racing the carts again. Pratt provided a humorous moment when his ball went over a fence and into the yard of a condominium; he scaled the fence and tore a hank from a well-groomed lawn getting his ball back to the fairway. The others seemed to take the second nine less seriously and

Pratt was able to carry his momentum, as it were, to the seventeenth, which rolled down to the Sea of Cortez. The view at the seventeenth was so spectacular that he boffed his second shot because he was intoxicated by proximity to the water. Playing along the sea, finishing their game, they were watched by a crowd of people at the outdoor restaurant patio attached to a hotel, imbibing afternoon cocktails and not shy with their comments. When Bryce was on his backswing someone shouted to screw him up and succeeded. Bryce swore, dropped a ball and sent it like a mortar round over the black iron fence. As if on cue, Tim did the same, then Carver and Bill. Pratt slid his nine iron from the bag like a long, elegant pistol and sent one high; he heard a definite cry of pain when it landed and received high fives for his effort before they jumped into their carts and drove like hell back to the clubhouse. The Mexicans cleaned their clubs while Carver brought out Coronas with limes and they compared their scorecards with the abandoned eighteenth left off. Pratt had, amazingly, come in ahead of Carver by two strokes. He could have been no happier at that moment than if he were slipping on the fabled green jacket at the Masters. Carver grinned around a Cuban cigar. "Had the old foot wedge out again, did you?"

The others laughed.

"No," Pratt said. "Just my Wal-Mart specials."

The Mexicans emerged with the clubs. Pratt dropped a dollar in the hand of the man toting his bag and started for the car. He was admiring the way the men had gotten the grass stains out when he noticed a club was missing. His three iron? He stopped, began to turn, but changed his mind and kept going. He didn't use it much anyway. It could have been on the garage floor or in the lost and found at the Bonanza for all he knew. He wasn't about to cause a scene. In the car after they parted company with Carver, Pratt conceived of a fantasy in which one of the Mexicans was slowly putting together a set of clubs for his son by lifting them from wealthy gringos. If that were the case, Pratt decided, he could live with it.

. . .

They cleaned up and changed at the villa and hooked up with the women in San José, which Carver had said was a better shopping destination than Cabo itself. There seemed to be quite a few police about, in blue jumpsuits and combat boots. There was something military about their presence that served as a reminder that they weren't in Kansas anymore. Pratt was happy to be wearing tourist garb with a group of others in tourist garb, some of whom had cameras looped around their necks. Their outfits were like armor against abuse, Pratt thought, and he was relieved, against his sense of dignity, to look like a geek. In a bottle shop they tasted almond tequila poured lovingly by the proprietor, and Pratt bought a Cuban cigar for ten dollars. Next door Patricia picked up a t-shirt for Whitney and one for herself. While she haggled with the clerk, trying to save a dollar, Pratt left the store to smoke a cigarette. A dog wandered by and looked up at him with a practiced yearning. Pratt had nothing to offer but a pat on the head, which the dog did not seem to need or want; it hurried down the sidewalk. Patricia came out and headed for a boutique with the other women. Tim and Bryce and Bill camped out on a bench to talk about the NFL. Pratt went into a gift shop and looked at souvenirs, more as a sociologist than as a tourist, he wanted to believe. He admired a giant mug shaped like a brown breast with an enormous red nipple bulging from it. Under glass he saw three switchblades, the old-fashioned Italian type with mother-of-pearl handles. He remembered Jenson's request. Fired or not, he liked Jenson and it would make a nice peace offering. He asked to see one and closed the blade, hit the button, watched the blade spring open. It was not as junky a knife as he would have thought. He couldn't carry it on the plane but he didn't see why putting it his suitcase would cause a problem. He could always plead *gringo* ignorance. He bought it for forty dollars and stuck it in his pocket.

Outside, the others were nowhere to be seen. He was abandoned in San José, Mexico, and he was not completely unhappy about it.

Then he saw them up the street, filing into an ice-cream shop. Pratt found a pay phone and called Martha.

"It's me," he said.

"Dennis?"

"*Qué pasa?*"

"*Qué pasa* is you are in big trouble. I've got a call in to a friend. Bob is about the best defense attorney in the valley."

"I didn't kill Cole. You have to believe that. The only thing I'm guilty of is polluting the creek."

"They found the girl. Candy."

"They found her?"

"She's okay. But they found her in your garden shed."

"What?"

"She was blindfolded and taped to your lawn mower. With duct tape. The police had a search warrant for your property and they found her."

"My *lawn mower?*" He pictured the mower, until then a benign, almost friendly lime-green tool whose smell was comforting. Pratt's head felt like a can in the crusher at work, being flattened by the hydraulic arm, paint squirting through the fissures into a drum filled with a hundred different colors congealing into one ugly shade of gray.

"Dennis, they've probably figured out where you are by now. I'm waiting for Bob to call."

"Bob?"

"The lawyer. I think he's pheasant hunting. He owes me a favor."

"My God."

45

PRATT felt as alert now as a Rottweiler on meth. Everyone on the sidewalk was a potential detective tracking him down. He went back to the gift shop and bought a sombrero, a simple straw one, and pulled it low over his eyes. He bought some outdated aviator sunglasses. He sat on a bench and lighted his Cuban and puffed very hard to let the smoke obscure his face. Again he tried to meditate on the events, let the memory of a repressed crime reveal itself, but nothing came forth but general terror. Still, reality for Pratt, and he understood this, had become like the wolf at the golf course, there but hard to see, constantly moving and certainly nothing he could grab by the tail and hang on to. For example, he wasn't sure whether his conversation with Whitney the night before had actually taken place or whether he'd dreamed it. His dreams had gotten strange with the medication and when he added some booze his dreams were like something cooked up by Tim Burton and Oliver Stone after they'd shared a peyote button. He needed to get a grip, he knew that much. No, he hadn't killed Cole. He hadn't kidnapped Candy. Everything was upside down; the earth was spinning backward. His *garden shed?* It was an obvious frame-up but who would frame him? Carver? Impossible. Carver seemed to be getting what he wanted without trying very hard. Pratt had no enemies that he knew of. It was further testament to the bland human he'd allowed himself to become that people tended to either like or be indifferent to Dennis Pratt. No, he thought, it had to be a different kind of setup. Cole himself had to have been involved. Some extortion plan that had gone awry. And he didn't like to think about it but Candy herself could have been a full partner, her eye on that house next door to Disney World.

He watched his wife, with the others trailing behind, coming up the sidewalk bearing huge sugar cones. "Where were you?" Patricia asked. "You were with us and then you weren't."

"Buying a hat."

"Buying a *stupid* hat. How can you wear that thing in public?"

"You missed the ice cream," Kelly said.

"I was happy just sitting on the bench and people-watching," Pratt said.

"Well, you'll have to watch us. We're sick of shopping and we want to go home and eat something and relax."

Bryce slapped him on the back. "You wore us out last night, buddy."

Pratt forced a smile. "You haven't seen anything yet."

•   •   •

Pratt kept one hand on the door handle of the rental car as they approached the villa. He was ready to bolt. Take his chances jumping over the wall. But the guard looked as lethargic as ever and when they grew closer to the driveway there was no phalanx of patrol cars waiting for them. Inside, the villa was not torn apart as in homicide movies; no drawers were dumped on the floor, toothpaste tubes emptied, books splayed open. In actuality the place was spotless and bore the strong scent of Pine-Sol. The maid had even arranged their bottles in a neat row on the bar shelves after cleaning the glass.

Pratt poured himself a drink, thought better of it, thinking he needed his wits about him, and when nobody was looking started to dump it down the drain. But then it struck him that it could easily be his last drink for a while so he replenished it and stood in the kitchen watching Kelly and Jenna and Patricia and Kate set to work on dinner. They were having grilled tuna and a smorgasbord of appetizers. Pratt picked up the phone, heard a dial tone, and hung up.

"Expecting a call?" Kelly asked.

"It's just so weird to have a phone that never rings."

"I'm glad it doesn't ring," Kelly said. "I only gave the number to my parents and they're only supposed to call if it's an absolute emergency."

"They wanted my number at work," Patricia said. "I told them we were staying on an island with no electricity or phone."

"Did you give it to Whitney?" Pratt asked.

"I e-mailed it to her."

Pratt had an image of the police combing through their computer. They would discover that he occasionally looked at soft-core porn though no kiddie porn, and that he'd been reading up on clinical depression and golf tips. They'd find all of Kelly's e-mails about the villa including links that offered photographs. The villa itself had served as their screensaver for months. The police were doing it at that very moment. He could see them searching through his files, nodding and making calls. He started to panic. "I'm bored. I think I'll go for a ride."

"A ride?"

"A ride. I know how to drive."

"Dennis, you'll get lost driving in Mexico."

"I won't get lost."

Kelly held up her hands. "Should I make Tim go with him?"

"No," Pratt said. "I'm just going down the road and back."

"Oh," Patricia said. She smiled apologetically at Kelly. "You need cigarettes? Is that it?"

"Maybe."

"I told you to buy them at home and bring them along."

"They're cheaper down here."

· · ·

He changed shirts in the bedroom. Slipped on the skull bracelet. Patricia met him at the bedroom door and pushed him back in. "Why are you being like this?" she hissed.

"Like what? I need smokes."

"You could have picked them up when we were downtown."

"I forgot."

"You never forget cigarettes. In twenty years you've never been without cigarettes. You've forgotten Whitney's birthday and you've forgotten where you parked the car and you forgot to pick me up at the doctor when I was loopy from medication after getting my mole cut out but you've never forgotten cigarettes."

"What are you driving at?"

"You're being rude to my friends, that's what I'm driving at. You should be hanging out with the guys. You're acting like you're above them."

"I just have a lot on my mind."

"Like?"

"Like why you were at the Red Lobster when you were supposedly at a closing last week."

She slapped him. Pratt didn't see it coming. It sounded like a gunshot. He saw stars, just like in the cartoons.

"How dare you spy on me."

"How dare you lie to me."

"When we get back," she said.

"What?"

She took a deep breath. "I will be civil to you in Mexico. You will not ruin my vacation. I'm not like you, Dennis. I can separate things in my brain. But when we get back, well."

"Well what?"

"I'm sick and tired of your crazy jealousy and the third degree and the spying. You don't have any idea what it's like to feel like you're living under a microscope or something. I'm through."

"Maybe *I'm* through."

"Good."

He went to his shaving bag and removed the slim box containing her tennis bracelet. He handed it to her. "Happy goddamn anniversary."

She barely glanced at the box. "We're not married anymore."

He had never seen her look not so angry but so *cool*. He was in an odd way admiring of her resolve. Or jealous of her resolve. Something, anyway. He suddenly wanted to embrace her and make everything all right but when he moved closer she crossed her arms and looked not at him but through him. He took the bracelet and fled.

46

HE INTENDED to get to the bottom of things, at least those things he could get to the bottom of thousands of miles from home. What he needed first of all was clarification from Carver about Patricia. Something straight from the horse's mouth. Yes, no, it didn't really matter. He wanted the truth, like the Warren Commission. After that it was anyone's guess but it struck him that if he was already facing hard time he might as well have pummeling Carver to reflect on while scratching tally marks into a cell wall. At the thought of jail he started to "wig out" as Whitney would say. He felt the same tunnel vision he'd felt while following Patricia to Red Lobster. The streets of Fargo that day could have been lined with nude swimsuit models and armed Nazis and he wouldn't have noticed. He popped a full Klonopin and stopped at a *cantina* for a six-pack of Tecate and cracked one open. He drove toward Cabo, drinking and chain-smoking, surrendering himself to the insanity of the local traffic pattern or lack thereof. He passed Cabo Real. The notion of whacking a little white ball on desert ground broken and tilled and chemically rendered green by California real estate developers seemed absolutely trivial if not sacrilegious and he realized he would never play golf again, never even *want* to play golf again. His strongest memories of playing golf involved picking up the garter snake at one end of the spectrum and finding the missing mercury at the other. Even his victory over Carver was hollow.

Carver's condo wasn't hard to find because Carver had pointed it out when they'd been hanging out in town, invited them all to stop over for a drink before they left Mexico, though even Carver had had to admit that the villa was hard to match for amenities. Except for the view from 1111, he'd said, which was of the marina and peerless at night from the balcony with a drink in your hand.

Pratt rode up in the elevator, eyes closed to avoid his reflection in the mirrored tiles. He knocked on Carver's door, saw a shadow darken the peephole. The door opened and he was face to face with the dentist, shirtless, muscles rippling, wearing rather minimalist leopard-print trunks that revealed much more than Pratt wanted to see. Carver poked his head into the hallway. "Where are the others?"

"At the villa. I was bored so I went for a drive. Thought I'd see how the other half lives."

Carver laughed. "Slumming it, huh?" He stepped aside. "Come on in."

Pratt followed him into the living room, which lacked the Mexican styling of the villa and looked like any apartment back home but with a little more wicker than you'd find up north.

"You want a beer?"

"That's fine," Pratt said. "Where is Serrina?"

"She went home."

"Already?"

"When you live in LA, Mexico doesn't have the same charm as it does for us Midwesterners."

"That makes sense." Pratt took the offered beer and guzzled half of it. "Did I interrupt you?"

"Actually I was going down for a swim but that can wait. You really should learn to swim. You're missing out on a great total-body workout."

"Probably," Pratt said. He aimed his beer can at the dentist. "Have you been fucking my wife?"

Carver didn't blink an eye.

"Patricia and I are through, so you might as well tell me."

"You were through a long time ago."

"So have you been?"

"I won't answer that."

"Why not?"

"Because if I say no you won't believe me, and if I say yes you'll try something crazy like kicking my ass and just be further humiliated."

"Don't count on it."

"I was in the marines for four years. I killed two Panamanians by cutting their throats while they slept. I hold a double black belt in aikido. I have walked on fire and glass and back again."

"Well."

"Just so you know, Denny."

"I appreciate it."

Carver opened his own beer and sat on the arm of his sofa in a posture that would have looked menacing if he hadn't been almost naked. "Was that all you wanted?"

"I want my watch."

"What?"

"The watch my wife gave you. I want it."

"This watch?"

"That watch."

"This watch is good down to two hundred meters. This hand shows the depth of your last dive. This watch would be wasted in your fucking *bathtub*, Denny. This is a *man's* watch. Patty told me that when she gave it to me."

Pratt remembered Jenson's switchblade. It was still in his pocket, right next to his pill bottle. There was some irony there, in his khaki shorts. A choice to be made. *Let's Make a Deal* but with heavier ramifications. He looked at Carver's mouth, his world-class smirk. Pratt pulled out the knife. This was rational irrationality, he realized. He understood he was being insane, acting on an impulse, when he pressed the button and the blade emerged, in slow motion, to point directly at Carver. He understood the implications but didn't care. This was, he decided, oddly another sign of progress. Maybe.

Carver laughed. "A *switchblade?* What are you, going native?"

"Give me my watch."

"Or what?"

"I'll cut your balls off and feed them to one of the stray dogs hanging around the marina."

Carver regarded him with a gaze that held more pity in it than Pratt cared to see. He wanted to fold the knife and put it back into his pocket but there was no graceful way to do this without looking like a complete fool. He had already been made a fool of and wanted to make a U-turn on that particular avenue. He understood with great clarity the reasoning behind so many violent events among the less prosperous of society, those shirtless angry men on *Cops* flailing about like overturned beetles under the weight of a dozen officers. Without your dignity you were truly impoverished. He didn't intend to hurt Carver but he suddenly needed the diving watch as much as he'd ever needed anything in his life. He jumped up on the sofa with the intent of using it as an ad hoc trampoline to gain altitude and land on Carver but something went wrong and his feet sank deeply into the high-grade leather cushion. He was stuck and tried to leap free and onto Carver. There was a blind scuffle; the knife clattered against the tiled floor and then Pratt was on the balcony, his throat against the rail, his arm locked behind his back, the same thing Terry Cooper had done to him, what, thirty years ago, only with more precision. Carver had him in a boa-like hold and squeezed until Pratt almost passed out from lack of oxygen. He was blacking out when Carver released the pressure, just a bit. Pratt gasped for air. He was acutely aware of Carver's muscular, hairy body pressed against him. This was almost more disturbing than being helplessly pinned in the dentist's arms.

"Now what do you have to say?"

Pratt looked at the sea, the boats coming into the marina. "Nice view," he wheezed.

"It's perfect. I like the movement. You have a nice view at the villa but the flat sea gets old after a while."

"We won't get tired of it in a week."

"You'll wish for that view when you're in Stillwater."

"Stillwater?"

"Prison."

"Ah."

"It was like chum fishing. You know what that is?"

"Where you throw out bloody meat?"

"Exactly. To attract game fish. I just tossed out the pieces and you gathered them up. Splash, there's the mercury. You know I've got my pick of deadbeats willing to do a little acting in exchange for having a rotten tooth pulled."

"Nice."

"I thought you would have gotten in more trouble for that one. Especially after I faxed your boss. I forgot how you city guys cover up for each other. The goddamn corruption never ends."

"Can't argue with that one."

"Splash, there's a little waif selling golf balls. I knew you couldn't leave her alone when I buried her in dust that day. You're way too nice a guy. Then all I had to do was float a suspicion by Tripp and he was all over it. He *lives* for that shit."

"Seems to."

"I didn't know you'd lay that mercury on Cole, though. That was a gimme. It's like you *wanted* to self-destruct. Actually it was just like aikido. Just like when you tried to take me down a few minutes ago. I just took your own energy and redirected it. You made it easy."

"You really put some time into this project."

"Ninety-nine percent of dentistry is as dull as a butter knife. I can do a fucking root canal in my sleep. You get a lot of time to think. Plus it's your own fault to some extent for being so obtuse. You didn't even notice when I took your three iron last week. You were too busy destroying the fairway with your inept play."

"Three iron."

"My advice to you," Carver said, "is to go back to the villa and enjoy what little free time you have. Your lovely view of the Sea of Cortez.

Your lovely boring friends. Drink some tequila and try to breathe in enough fresh air to last fifty years. You might want to work on your tan. And don't worry about Patty. I'll be glad to keep her company."

Pratt tried to struggle free but the metal was against his throat again. He could hear people laughing and splashing around in the pool below. What would they think if they looked up? *What happens in Mexico stays in Mexico? Party on, dudes?*

Carver let up a bit. "Hey, it's the least I can do for my old college pal Denny."

"Can I ask a question?"

"Shoot."

"Why?"

"Why? You have to ask why?"

"I do."

"You are such a retard, Denny. I can see why Patricia is tired of dealing with your shit. She's a saint for putting up with you. My god, I'm going to get a madonna complex. I'll have trouble getting it up." He laughed. "No, I won't, by the way."

Pratt felt lost. "You're losing me."

"Kathleen Lambert."

"Dr. Lambert?"

"Do you know I started smoking because of her? Do you know I checked out French-language tapes at the library? *Où est la toilette? Le café, s'il vous plaît.* Do you know how hard I tried?"

"A lot of people had a crush on her."

"It wasn't a crush. It was real. I took every course she offered including literature of feminism, where I was the only straight guy in class. I stood up and denounced straight white males. I was a traitor to my entire fucking race *and* gender, that's how much I loved her."

"You were young, for Christ's sake."

"I finally got enough nerve to make my move and she laughed at me and then she fucked *you*."

Carver had backed off a little and Pratt was breathing easier. He wanted to make a move but had no move to make. "I didn't ask for that. I was pretty high on the merlot."

"You really think that helps?"

"I never talked to her afterward. That should make you happy."

Pratt felt Carver's mouth against his ear. His breath was hot and moist. "*I* talked to her. I went to see her, you know. In Manhattan. I wore my uniform. The sidewalk was crowded but the crowd parted like the fucking Red Sea for *this* marine, motherfucker. That's what it's like to be a Leatherneck in dress but you'll never know that feeling. Look at you, forty years old and you're crushing paint cans for a living. No wonder your wife doesn't respect you."

"I do more than crush paint cans."

"Shut up. I went up to her apartment and I was going to carry her downstairs like Richard Gere in fucking *Officer and a Gentleman*. I hadn't seen her in five years. I was even more buff than I am now. Knocked on the door and she looked foxier than before. She was wearing a black cocktail dress. She had those faint lines in the corners of her mouth. I loved those lines. Man, I get hard just thinking about those lines."

"I can tell. I was thinking for a second here that you really liked *me*."

Carver grunted and turned on the pressure, much harder this time. Pratt felt his Adam's apple begin to cave like a stepped-on Ping-Pong ball. "I should fucking *kill* you for that," Carver said. As his head went light Pratt thought Carver might do just that and felt ambivalent about it, much to his own surprise. But Carver abruptly loosened his grip again and Pratt coughed life into his body. Then Carver's lips were against his ear again, even closer this time. "You know what she said to me?"

Pratt tried to shrug and couldn't.

"She said, 'Who are you again?'"

"Ouch."

"I'm standing there like a fucking *hero* and she doesn't remember me. So I try to take her back in time and you know what she says? She says, 'Oh, weren't you Dennis Pratt's friend?'"

"Really?" Pratt's chest puffed a bit. He'd always assumed he was simply one of many forgettable diversions.

"Well, you know what?"

"What?"

Carver's words came out as a wet, hoarse whisper. "I'm the only one on the *planet* who knows that those were her last words, *amigo*."

The comment made Pratt's skin break out in goosebumps despite being blanketed in the hot Mexican air and Carver's warm body. Carver had never entered his mind when he'd read about Lambert's New York City death. To him it was just another good argument for living in "flyover country."

Carver released him then and leaped back like a cat into a Bruce Lee–type fighting stance while Pratt stood and unkinked himself. "It all goes back to that night in Grand Forks. I almost drove my Benz into the Red knowing you were up there with her. I heard you guys going at it. Well, I heard *her*. It was like looking at a car wreck. I couldn't leave. *I* was supposed to be up there with her, not a pencil-neck bookworm like you. I couldn't go back to the English department after that. Why do you think I dropped out of college and joined the marines? Why do you think I went to dental school?" He threw a couple punches into the air and scowled. "You think I like being a dentist?"

"You're a success. You're rich. You have a handmade copper door on your house."

"I've spent the last fifteen years with my hands inside thousands of mouths pretending to care about oral health. I pull down well over a hundred and fifty grand a year but I feel like a fucking *child molester* whenever I leave the house in the morning. Nobody likes dentists. We have the second-highest suicide rate in the country. You know what it's like to spend ten hours a day smelling rancid breath and drilling into rotten teeth? Do you know what it's like to have people perform lines from *The Marathon Man* whenever they find out what you do for a living? I swear if one more person makes a drill sound and goes, 'Is it safe? Is it safe?' at a cocktail party I'm going to snap." Carver put his hands on his hips. He looked a bit ridiculous, raging in his Speedos. He pointed his finger at Pratt. "You did a number on me. You and Lambert. Mostly you, Denny, because you knew how I felt about her."

"You said you'd give your left ball to sleep with her. That isn't exactly professing your love."

"Why did you stick around her place that night when you could see I was trying to achieve a specific objective?"

"You've got some issues."

"You gave them to me."

"You can take a pill for them, you know."

"Pills are for weaklings."

"Why didn't you just kill me too? Why frame me up?"

"I want you to *suffer*. In jail. In hell."

Pratt made his way to the doorway, opened the door, stood with one foot in the corridor, one foot in Carver's living room, and considered this. He wanted to leave yet he found himself oddly comforted by the familiarity of a person he knew compared to the great unknown of what remained of his life as a free man. His options seemed pretty limited. He wished he'd stuck with the martial arts and could backflip across the carpeted room and neatly kick Carver over the balcony. But he had no lemons to make lemonade with. At the most a little twist of pulp in his hand. "I'll always have whipping your ass at Cabo Real."

"Sorry. Patty asked me to go easy on you so you wouldn't embarrass her. You really do suck."

"Well, then," Pratt said, "I guess that's that."

"*Semper fi*, man." Carver snapped to attention and threw him a salute.

"And I thought *I* was crazy," Pratt said.

"You'll know crazy when you're in your cell getting butt-fucked by a Chippewa."

• • •

He made one more phone call. Two, if you counted information.

"Tripp here, what you got?"

"This is Dennis Pratt."

He heard a chair creaking, a match being struck. Then some fairly obvious clicking sounds. "You know something, Pratt?"

"What?"

"I knew from the first time I looked in your eyes that you were riding one hell of a runaway engine. I just wasn't sure where all it was going to end up. But I knew it wouldn't be pretty. I'd be dead a dozen times over if I didn't know how to read a man's eyes. There was a night in nineteen and seventy-four when I cornered two bums in the Dilworth yards and they were sweet as pie yes sir no sir but one of them had *the eyes* and by the time I drew my piece he was swinging at me with a rusty spike on a rope—"

"I don't have much time," Pratt said.

"You have plenty more time than that fellow you killed."

"What makes you think I killed him?"

"I'm the one who found him. Found your bloody club right there next to him. Piece of junk was bent like a pretzel. A good club wouldn't bend like that. Always buy the most expensive clubs you can afford."

"I'm giving up golf."

"You should. Golf is a mental game and you aren't even smart enough to wipe off your fingerprints."

"Crimes of passion, you know? People don't think."

"Speaking of passion, I don't know what you did to that girl before you taped her up but perverts like you don't last long in the joint."

"I have no intention of being taken alive."

"Well," Tripp said, "that's a good decision. Wise play for a change."

47

HE DROVE down under the bridge, passed what looked like a drug deal taking place, waved at the participants, and bulldozed the rental as close to the sea as he could before the front wheels became mired in sand and spun uselessly. An old man was surfcasting, listening to what sounded like a soccer game on an antique leather-cased radio atop a plastic bucket. He turned, regarded Pratt, and went back to his fishing. Pratt climbed from the car and sat on a beached log and watched the sea, the dimming light on the surface. He wondered if everyone was crazy when you got right down to it, if it was just a matter of the laminations being more brittle and prone to splitting apart in some more than others. He was crazy but then so was Carver and maybe Patricia, and Martha at some point had probably been crazy, and Tripp certainly wasn't wrapped too tightly. Cole for sure. Now Candy would likely be.

He kicked off his sneakers and set them on the log. The five hundred was in there and he rolled all but a hundred and pushed the roll into his plastic pill bottle and screwed down the lid. Took out his wallet and set it next to his shoes. Fastened the tennis bracelet over his left wrist. The diamonds glittered even at dusk. He heard a phone ringing and the fisherman lifted a cell and started talking cheerfully into it, destroying the *Old Man and the Sea* imagery he'd been part of moments earlier. Santiago's story would have been quite a bit different if he'd owned a Samsung flip-phone. *Hey, I've caught this fucking record fish on a ball of string, can you guys come out and help me?* Maybe a camera phone so he could send the evidence to *Marlin* magazine. Pratt lighted a cigarette and dug his toes into the hot sand. He almost never went shoeless and didn't think anything had ever felt so fucking good. He realized that just a month ago he would not have been aware of how good it felt, nor would he have been aware of the subtleties of the breeze, the music of waves lapping nearby, the tai-chi-like movements of an old man making long two-handed casts with an antique rod. And he realized that regardless of what his wife had done or not done, she had helped trigger something that had led him to Martha and Rayburn and what were most definitely the moments of greatest clarity and even joy he'd known in his life. So he owed her for that. Irony yet again. But then again, maybe irony was the natural state and the opposite of irony was the aberration. He looked back at the bridge. The drug deal was over, the cars gone. He walked down to the old man. "*Amigo*, how would you like to make a hundred dollars?"

The old man held up his hands. "Sorry, no drogs."

"Not drugs. One hundred dollars to make a phone call."

The old man handed him the phone. "*No dinero*. I have many free minutes."

"No, no. I'm going to start swimming." Pratt pantomimed the act. "I want you to wait an hour, *un hora*, and call the police—*policía*."

"*Policía?*"

"*Sí.* And tell them a *gringo*, an Americano, went into the water and didn't come out."

The old man screwed a long finger into his ear and twisted it. He looked skeptical.

"Please. I've been dishonored."

"Dishonored."

"Yes. Dishonored in the worst way, *señor*."

The man raised his gnarled fist. "You should get a lawyer and fight those who dishonored you."

"This is beyond lawyers."

The two regarded each other for a long moment. The old man seemed to be reading Pratt's face, his dark eyes roving around until he'd covered every inch.

"*Comprendo.*"

Pratt handed over a hundred-dollar bill. "*Gracias.* Don't tell them I asked you to call."

"*Sí.*"

Pratt shook his hand, surprised at how strong it was. He waded into the water. Stood there in his shorts, bedecked in a diamond bracelet and cheap skull trinket. Looked back and the old man was fishing again, head slightly askance so as not to watch him directly. Pratt kept going until he was up to his chest. The force of the water worked against him. He had never been so deep in a natural body of water. It was very hard to keep his balance. It was hard to keep his balance on his legs but he had other options now. It wasn't just one thing or another anymore. It wasn't either-or. He took a deep breath and went under. Lucas had said the human body was more buoyant in saltwater than fresh and he had been right, although the stillness of the YMCA pool seemed to counter whatever benefit there was to being in the sea. Various lessons rang in his head: *Don't take such big breaths, arch your back, turn your head, spread your fingers,* but it was, oddly, Bruce Carver's enigmatic golf course words, *Slow down,* that were most helpful. *Slow down.* Pratt stopped his energy-draining thrashing and swam slowly, trying to stay more or less parallel to the beach line. He thought he saw the dark-green oasis of Cabo Real's final holes hugging the water. He pretended he was a fish as Lucas had suggested, even suggesting Pratt go to Pet World and actually look at fish, which he'd done not wanting to question the wisdom of a teacher no matter how young and cocky the teacher was, young enough to be his son. Slow, even strokes, loose feet. *I am a fish,* he thought, *not a marlin or a shark or cobia but a simple trout making my way not in the sea but in a friendly little Minnesota farm pond, the kind of prairie pothole you drive by every day on your way to work without giving a second thought to, without knowing there are fish living in there, living and dying and living.*

48

ONE year later a young woman waded along the brim of the Sea of Cortez, the rolled-up cuffs of her jeans black with water. Her eyes were on the sand as if looking for something but occasionally she lifted her head to stare at the horizon.

"Whitney."

She turned. Martha was behind her, holding her straw hat to her head against the stiff breeze. "Are you ready?"

"You couldn't tell anything bad ever happened in the ocean."

"What do you mean?"

"Like if there's a car wreck on the highway. You'll drive by later and see the skid marks or broken glass or a piece of the bumper or whatever. Even a year later. But if something happens in the sea you'll never know. I mean, people drown, ships sink, and it looks exactly the same as before." She looked down. "Even my footsteps are covered up already. The sand is all smooth again where I was walking."

"She keeps her secrets, they say."

"Yes."

Together they watched the water until the shimmering was too much to bear. They started walking again, their tracks forming a crescent on the sand as they curved back toward the area where Pratt's shoes and rental car had been found. "What did your mother say?" Martha asked.

"Whenever I bring him up she cuts me off. The last time, she put her hands over her ears and started singing Patsy Cline."

"Which song? 'Crazy'?"

"No, it was 'I Fall to Pieces.'"

"Hmm."

"Anyway I'm like, whatever. I won't bring it up again until she does."

"Good."

• • •

Miles away a tan, lean man with a shaved head and arms wiry from working on *The Pelican,* a gig he'd gotten through his friendship with the waiter Antonio of Dolce, walked into the visitors' room at the largest prison in the Baja. The room was a William Blake illumination of crying women and bewildered children, obsidian-eyed guards and chipped walls, the echoes of decades of anguished wailing still snaking around the ceilings. The man was directed to wait his turn behind a woman talking to a teenager who was likely her son. The boy was trying to remain stoic but he was crumbling around the edges and the man had to look away. He watched the smaller children instead, some of them running around oblivious to the horrors they were in proximity to.

When it was his turn he sat and waited and before too long another man, a former dentist, a man named Carver, appeared. He looked ten years older than he was; there was a fresh welt above his eye and he sported a haircut that looked like it had been given to him by a blind barber. When Carver saw his visitor the welt and everything around it turned white. He seated himself.

"You're alive," he said. His two front teeth were missing.

"Can't you do better than that?"

"Than what?"

"Than a B-movie cliché?"

"Denny."

"There is no Denny anymore."

"You've got to help me. Help me get out of here, Denny."

"Denny died, remember? And you don't look so hot yourself."

"I need money. Serrina cleaned me out. I gave her power of attorney so she could get me some cash and she fucking wiped me out.

She even sold my Torino. You can't get a fucking lightbulb changed in here without bribing somebody."

"You're in the dark."

"I never balled your wife. I was just playing her. She's hooked up with an over-the-road truck driver now. I asked her for money and she sent me a postcard from Alabama. They told me I had mail and I had to trade a filling to get it but it was just a goddamn postcard. She's getting a commercial driver's license so they can team drive, did you know that?"

Pratt didn't. The news meant little to him beyond bewilderment at why someone would choose to yank a trailer around freeways for the rest of their life. The notion made him want to yawn. He thought of an incident a few days earlier when a client had almost been pulled overboard by a marlin after the leader wire had gotten wrapped around his hand. If Pratt hadn't been Johnny-on-the-spot with his wire cutters the man would now be a human kite tail, bones rattling in the deep. "So how did it feel?"

"How did what feel?"

"When they opened your carry-on and found that revolver and coke?"

"How do you think it felt? It felt like a kick in the nuts. Listen, Denny. I've been praying for a miracle and you're it. I won't make it in here much longer."

Pratt leaned close until his face was almost touching the mesh. He caught a whiff of the dentist and recoiled. "What's my motivation?"

"I'll tell the truth about Cole and everything else. The girl. I'll tell them how I pumped nitrous oxide into the trailer and taped her to your Lawnboy. I'll tell them everything if you help me get out of here. Stillwater would be like Disney World compared to this fucking hole."

"Sorry. I spent the last of my vacation money on that Colt and the drugs, *amigo*. Remember that drunken Mexican who bumped you in the bathroom at the airport? The one you shoved and called a quote spic unquote? That was a new friend of mine. One of the best pick-pockets in Cabo. You're lucky he was my friend or he would have cut your throat for the insult."

Pratt pushed back his plastic chair. He felt imprisoned himself, suddenly. From the moment he'd arrived wet and exhausted and shoeless at Dolce, hiding in the alley until Antonio spotted him and took him home, treated him like blood, like a *hermano*, to his days out on the sea, rigging lures on the *Pelican*, scanning the water for floating logs that might be harboring fish, watching yellow butterflies during the dead hours, pouring cold Evian over the red bald heads of chubby clients fighting fish as if they were fighting for something much more important, something that could sustain them once back in Des Moines behind a desk, the image of facing the caged dentist had been in the back of Pratt's mind and now he realized it had been more like a tumor, all along, than a jewel. He had looked forward to this moment and now he just wanted it to end. He got up to leave.

Carver grabbed the screen and shook it wildly. Two guards approached him and they didn't seem very friendly. Carver began to howl.

Pratt didn't look back.

· · ·

Martha was waiting for him behind the wheel of the air-conditioned Suburban, listening to a Jack Johnson CD Whitney had brought down. She leaned across the seat and kissed him.

"Where's Whit?"

"I dropped her off at the beach. She wanted to get in as much surfing as possible. Last day here and all."

"That's the old Minnesota attitude. Get your money's worth."

"She said she's getting you on a board today or she'll drop out of college."

"Funny."

They pulled from the lot and roared down the highway.

"So."

"So."

"How was it?"

"It was pretty ugly. I'll let him cook in his juices and then we'll see."

"How long?"

"I don't know. I'm not in any particular hurry."

"I wouldn't be either."

He opened his notebook, a beautiful leather-bound French *cahier* she had ordered from an art-supply store in New York. He had in mind starting a novel, of all things. She was urging him on. She'd also brought his prescriptions and, for his birthday, a satisfyingly heavy Mont Blanc Hemingway fountain pen. He was trying to get her to stay, at least for the winter. She was considering it, selling the Holloway and getting a place by the sea. Jim had finally finished his boat. When she'd said that with Pratt gone Fargo really held no appeal he'd felt like a teenager again.

"I think I have my first line," he said as they topped a dune in four-wheel drive and saw the sparkling Pacific, saw his daughter standing in thigh-deep water holding the rented surfboard under one arm like a scene from a pulp paperback cover.

"Terrific."

While Martha gathered her easel and paints, he wrote, in very bold strokes, black ink heavy on the stiff white paper:

Jesus, he didn't want to go to Mexico.